PERESTROIKA IN PARTYGRAD

ALEXANDER ZINOVIEV

Perestroika in Partygrad

Translated from the Russian
by
CHARLES JANSON

PETER OWEN · LONDON

PETER OWEN PUBLISHERS
73 Kenway Road London SW5 0RE

Translated from the Russian *Katastroika*

First published in Great Britain 1992

A Catalogue record for this book is available from the British Library

ISBN 0–7206–0847–3

Printed in Great Britain by Billings of Worcester

I should like to thank Martin and Marina Dewhirst for their help.

Charles Janson

PERESTROIKA IN PARTYGRAD

PROLOGUE

In the old days Partygrad was closed to foreigners. For two reasons. First, because there was nothing to show them. True, there were a few churches, but without any historical or architectural interest. And all were shut except the most wretched one of all. There was indeed an old monastery, but they'd put an anti-religious museum in it. In Partygrad one couldn't even find painted spoons, saucers or *matryoshka* dolls (which the West regards as the highest achievements of Russian national culture, though they've been made in Finland for a long time now). In the whole of Partygrad there was only one samovar, and that was in the museum of folklore.

The second reason why Partygrad was closed to foreigners was that it had a lot that foreigners *shouldn't* see: many military factories and schools, a chemical complex which turned out not so much washing-powder as – more to the point – a secret weapon, a microbiological centre for ultra-secret research and a psychiatric hospital with the most lurid reputation in dissident circles. Corrective labour camps were sited round the town, also well known to dissidents; and an atomic factory which, though devoted to peaceful ends, had still managed to turn the whole region into a highly radioactive zone. But what foreigners above all must not see were the monstrous dwellings of the people, the empty shops, the long queues and all the other attributes of Russian provincial life. But when Gorbachev began his perestroika there a fundamental change came about. Not in the sense that the country or the life got better – sometimes they became worse. What did happen was that the government's view of the country and its life worsened. Thus the first period of Soviet history ended: the fault-hiding period; and a new epoch began when deficiencies were laid bare and officially acknowledged. Moreover, the authorities laid the faults bare not so much to their own citizens, who'd been quite aware of them without official guidance, but also to the West. It is not too much to say that the Soviet authorities initiated an orgy of admiration of their own ulcers and of boasting about them to the West.

This breakthrough coincided with the breakthrough in Soviet-Western relations. The West became interested not in the defects of the Soviet way of life but in the fact that Soviet officials recognized the presence of the defects; so that the recognition itself became the greatest virtue of the Soviet way of life. The confession by the Soviet authorities that things were done badly in the Soviet Union and that its inhabitants lived badly was interpreted by Westerners as meaning that things in the Soviet Union were *not* going so badly, and that its people did not live all that badly. In sum, the West forgave the Soviet Union all its evil, domestic and foreign, because it had confessed to an insignificant part of that evil.

Next, hordes of Soviet people rushed into the Western countries praising 'perestroika' to the skies, at the same time laying hold of everything there that was in short supply in the Soviet Union. The West began to compare Gorbachev with Peter the Great, ascribing to him the same intention to open a door into the West.

Then the Gorbachevite leadership decided to reinforce this breakthrough in Western public opinion by organizing a flood of Westerners into the Soviet Union. It was with this in view that the Central Committee of the CPSU decided to turn Partygrad into a model indicator of the progress of perestroika, in fact to make the city perestroika's 'lighthouse' and lay the place wide open to foreigners.

As we shall see, the implementation of this momentous strategic plan was to be in the hands of a native of Partygrad, none other than Pyotr Suslikov. But first we must turn our attention to an even more exalted personage.

AT THE HIGHEST LEVEL

When the General Secretary of the Central Committee of the Communist Party of the Soviet Union grew weary of carrying out reforms, he would leave his office in the Kremlin earlier than usual and make his way to his dacha outside Moscow. This time he was not in a good mood, and for that there was reason enough. The workers were not obeying him. Instead of drinking the mineral water that Mikhail Sergeyevich was advising them to drink instead of vodka, they were drinking home-made hooch and indeed any old liquid that would render them unconscious. It was harder to supply them with mineral water than with vodka. Of course the workers *could* enjoy tap-water. (In Russia it tastes no worse than the mineral water.) But they didn't cotton on to this either. Evidently there was a gap in their ideological education which had to be filled in. There must be an acceleration in ideological training. Of course in communist education the Soviet Union had outstripped the West. Now was the time to accelerate the outstripping of the West in this matter of education. It made good sense to start to switch over the workers to a system of self-education, in the same way as in economic life there was to be a switch-over to a self-financing system.

This idea did something to raise Mikhail Sergeyevich's spirits. But not for very long. He remembered that Soviet productivity had begun to grow at a quarter per cent less than had been intended, and that the Western press was beginning to hint that 'Gorbachev's great reforms are threatened with breakdown'. Why the devil were these data published in Soviet newspapers? Where did they get them from? If, as the saying goes, you force a fool to pray to God, he will be only too delighted to bash his forehead in. Glasnost is a fine thing but for heaven's sake let's cork up the bottle sometimes. . . .

At home another unpleasantness awaited Mikhail Sergeyevich. His beloved spouse, Raisa Maksimovna, whom adoring workers called 'Gorbachushka', announced categorically that she wished to go to Paris. She longed to see the Eiffel Tower. She wanted to wander around the Louvre. But there was something more important still: her beauty, which had stirred the entire world, was fading. In a year or two Nancy, the aged wife of former President Reagan, would again be calling herself 'Miss World'. The Americans had gone a long way in cosmetics; they could make an Egyptian mummy into Miss America. On no account must Raisa lose the beauty race to Nancy. That would be a crass ideological, political and even military mistake. But to keep ahead in the beauty contest Raisa Maksimovna had to have a new wardrobe from the first fashion houses of Paris.

Mikhail Sergeyevich would indeed have been glad to visit Paris himself in order to reinforce his reputation of being the planet's sexiest man and its most bewitching smiler. (In the field of smiles, at least we have caught up with and surpassed the United States.) But he couldn't manage to get away for a couple of days. Each day he had to introduce a reform, if not two or three. And he had to keep a beady eye on his colleagues. If he stood still for a moment and dithered, they would accuse him of going too far or not far enough or of deviation. Then they would chuck him out and change the reforms. And then he wouldn't be buried in the wall of the Kremlin but in the Novodevichy cemetery, somewhere near Khrushchev.

So that's why Mikhail Sergeyevich would take full power into his own hands. Then he would show them all where they got off.

With such thoughts as these, Mikhail Sergeyevich decided to invite round his dacha neighbour, Pyotr Stepanovich Suslikov. Suslikov had recently been elected a Central Committee secretary. As such he was the head-of-operations of all the Soviet institutions that watched the West, educated it in a pro-Soviet spirit and used it for the good of the Soviet people. Pyotr Stepanovich was not only of Mikhail Sergeyevich's way of political thinking and his close colleague, but also his personal friend. So Mikhail Sergeyevich asked Pyotr Stepanovich to look in for a moment for a heart-to-heart talk.

He invited him to tea, not to a bottle of vodka. Naturally, for a friendly talk vodka was preferable, but the Party had declared its implacable war on drunkenness. And so these outstanding Party leaders had to content themselves with a thoroughly boring non-alcoholic drink. If their fathers and grandfathers had lived to learn about the new custom, they would have regarded it as a betrayal of Russian national traditions owing to the machinations of Zionists and freemasons.

As we have already noted, the dachas of Mikhail Sergeyevich and Pyotr Stepanovich stood side by side. There was a special gate in the fence that separated them and this was guarded on both sides. The guard on Suslikov's territory saluted Gorbachev and breathed vodka fumes at him. Pyotr Stepanovich took note of the fact that the sentry drank 'Stolichnaya'. The guard on Gorbachev's territory also saluted Suslikov and wafted him a spirituous air that reminded the General Secretary of 'Zubrovka'. Pyotr Stepanovich was suddenly seized with nostalgia for the old times when they, the Party leaders, also lived together in fellowship. But he pulled himself together and followed Mikhail Sergeyevich into his study.

A HEART-TO-HEART TALK

A domestic servant who was the exact copy of Suslikov's (presumably the KGB puts its stamp on them all) served tea. To the very last moment Pyotr Stepanovich had hoped the word 'tea' was merely a euphemism for something more substantial, so he was a bit depressed. But he didn't show it (good Party training) and greeted the tea with all the enthusiasm of a champion of the Party's general sobriety line. Actually the conversation was about the internal difficulties of implementing the said line. The two men complained of the way in which drunkards and bureaucrats were casting spanners in the works from within. Then they talked about the external difficulties and how the Western imperialists were casting spanners from without. They spoke about deficiencies, and about successes.

Then they passed on to the question of Pyotr Stepanovich himself. Mikhail Sergeyevich said that an especially important task was about to fall upon his shoulders. Western public opinion was a great force. What counted there was the mass media. They must be made to serve the Soviet Union. But for this purpose great suppleness was needed. Nowadays hardly anybody believed in communist fairy-tales. Westerners must be led to believe that we don't believe in them much either and that we are now ready to approach everything in a practical, one could say pragmatic spirit. They love that. They think we are like themselves. This is something we must make use of.

Pyotr Stepanovich listened attentively to Mikhail Sergeyevich's flow of words, fiddling with his spoon in the cold tea left in the cup. Mikhail Sergeyevich had got into his stride now and was enjoying the flow of his thoughts and the intimate sincerity of his own voice. They spoke about glasnost.

'It's a funny thing, Pyotr Stepanovich, in the old days they used to blur our failures and blow up our successes. Now it's the other way round. Now we are ashamed to speak about our successes and we blow up our failures to the skies. But what Lenin understood by glasnost means that the people should be told the whole truth, not hiding either failures or successes.'

'A very true and original thought, Mikhail Sergeyevich,' Pyotr Stepanovich agreed enthusiastically, taking a little gulp of tea and choking because of his unfamiliarity with non-alcoholic drinks. 'That's very, very important.'

'That's what I think. The thing is to let more foreigners come more often to see how we live and how we struggle with our shortcomings, and what successes we achieve. They'll see it all with their own eyes. They'll go home and tell everyone what they've seen. That will bring us substantial support in the world arena.'

'A very true and original thought, Mikhail Sergeyevich! For a long time now I've had the notion of organizing more delegations to represent the different social strata in the West and to show them not churches, museums and ballet but our actual everyday life. Let them take a look at our Soviet way of life! Of course there are things to criticize. But we have much that Westerners could envy. For example, we've no unemployment. We've no terrorists.'

Pyotr Stepanovich failed to notice that in speaking of 'what we have', he included in it 'what we *don't* have'. Mikhail Sergeyevich, accustomed from childhood to the pearls of Party rhetoric, missed the point too.

'We must choose an *oblast** where perestroika is going well and turn it into a demonstration model, one might say into a leading light of democratization,' continued Pyotr Stepanovich. 'We should use such beacons as weapons of revolutionary transformation, of all that is being achieved under your leadership. In the West, Mikhail Sergeyevich, they compare you with Peter the Great who cut a window through to the West. But I think they diminish your role. It's not a window you're cutting through but a door. Not even a door, but a gate. Or, to speak still more precisely, you're

* The Soviet administrative unit which is larger than the region and smaller than the republic.

breaking through a wall. One could say you're pulling down a Wall of China that separates . . .'

'I fully approve your notion, Pyotr Stepanovich,' Mikhail Sergeyevich cut into Suslikov's dithyrambs, as if he were not a vain person. 'But to speak of a Chinese Wall is to put it too strongly. Well, all right, a door into Europe. And then we'll break down the whole wall. What we need now is to turn lighthouses of democracy into doors into the West by calling them free zones. Let the foreigners come through these doors to us and see our revolution with their own eyes. Which oblast should we start with? What do you think?'

COMMENTARY

Having read these pages, the reader will exclaim: 'It's all an evil fabrication!' But it's not an evil fabrication, it's a good one. I knew Suslikov personally. I knew him, I can say, from his cradle. I noted above just two inaccuracies in his description. But they don't make him worse, they idealize him: Pyotr Stepanovich did not drink tea instead of vodka. Far from it. He always drank vodka instead of tea. Nor did the Epoch of Total Sobriety free him from the habit. The second inaccuracy: in the whole of his conscious life Suslikov did not speak one single grammatically correct sentence. This wasn't a matter of his being uneducated. Suslikov underwent the very highest education: in fact not one education but two, if one can count the Higher Party School run by the Central Committee of the CPSU. The fact is that to speak ungrammatically is a quality inherent in the professional Party worker.

THE CHOICE OF THE LIGHTHOUSE OF PERESTROIKA

As perestroika's lighthouse Suslikov chose the oblast of Partygrad; the very place in which he had made the grade from spermatozoid to First Secretary/Obkom.* In his exposé he omitted to mention the fact that quite a short time ago the Partygrad oblast was mentioned in a leading article in *Pravda* which said that the oblast was one which had not yet seriously tackled the question of perestroika. Of course instead of the Partygrad oblast, *Pravda* could just as well have cited any other oblast. Partygrad was chosen in order to discredit, and dismiss, the obkom First Secretary, Zhidkov, who was a Brezhnevite; and to put in his place the Gorbachevite Krutov. Mikhail Sergeyevich didn't mention the matter either, as he had got his man into Partygrad.

In his Partygrad-for-Lighthouse proposal, Pyotr Stepanovich advanced the following arguments. The oblast was situated in the very depths of Russia and the West considered it the very symbol of the Russian backwoods and provincialism. So when the foreigners came to Partygrad and saw all the features of contemporary urban life, they would be stupefied. Besides, until very recently Partygrad had been closed to foreigners. Now the interdiction would be publicly removed. Floods of foreigners would sweep into this former top secret Soviet town in which rumour had it they made the very latest atomic, chemical, biological and genetic weaponry. This declassification would itself have an additional propagandist effect.

But the main reason why Pyotr Stepanovich had put forward Partygrad was that he hoped to receive a second gold star as Hero of Socialist Labour and that his bust in bronze would be placed on a granite pedestal in Partygrad, his home town. That would add quite a bit to his world fame. Foreigners for sure would point out Suslikov's monument and talk about his career. And, who knows, one day they might change the name of Partygrad to Suslikovgrad?

'We won't put this project on the back-burner,' said Mikhail Sergeyevich, 'otherwise our conservatives and bureaucrats will ruin our auspicious beginning. If you run into difficulty, come directly to me. To put our seal on this you and I should really celebrate with something more significant than tea. But you know how it is . . .'

'Of course I do, Mikhail Sergeyevich. We are conquering drunkenness and we shall break down a wall into the West. When all

* Party HQ for the oblast.

that's done, we'll celebrate our historic victory not with tea but something stronger!'

Then the two great historic operators took leave of one another. What they subsequently drank by themselves will remain for ever one of history's riddles. But the consequences of this sober meeting of theirs became quite plain to every historian.

THE PROPHETIC DREAM

Suslikov had a prophetic dream. He had a vision of his native Partygrad. At first he didn't recognize the town. He saw blocks and blocks of skyscrapers made of glass and steel and all the luxurious shop windows. In the sky gigantic electric letters announced SUSLIK-YORK. In the distance where the Statue of Liberty used to stand he could see the monument to Suslikov himself. It was only by the dug-up streets, by the long queues and the drunks lying about the pavements, that Suslikov could recognize the old Partygrad. In the town centre a great hole yawned.

'What's that hole?' asked Suslikov.

'The Big Hole into Europe,' answered an inner voice. 'It's through there that the workers go to the West to get foreign goods.'

'But why go to the West to get foreign goods if they've got all they want in Suslik-York?'

'There the goods were indeed in the windows, but not in the shops. After all, it wasn't capitalism they had in Suslik-York but socialism. Besides, our people go West after foreign goods so that none of these goods should be left in the West. Then the Westerners can come to us to ask us to allow them to get their foreign goods in our country.'

'But then the West will close its own frontiers to us and won't give us visas. They haven't gone quite mad there yet!'

'The West will try to limit the entry of our nationals. But in reply we can then ask them point-blank: what's happened to your famous democracy? And what about human rights? And then they would become frightened for their reputation and open the frontiers to us again.'

'But why aren't there any portraits of Gorbachev?'

'They chucked him out.'

'Why was that?'

'Because he opened too narrow a door to the West. Tanks couldn't go through it. The rockets got stuck in it. And then Gorbachushka put a guard on the door who wouldn't allow the wives of other members of the Politburo through. She wanted to keep all the loot for herself. So they all set on their husbands to give Gorbachev the push.'

'But whom did they put in his place?'

'Why, Suslikov, of course. He really *did* make a hole into Europe. He wanted to break down the whole wall, but they prevented him doing that.'

'Why?'

'Because the rotten influence of the West would have swamped us with such force that we couldn't have stopped it.'

'But why stop it?'

'If we didn't stop it, this is what would have happened.'

And with that the mighty knee of the Central Committee of the CPSU gave Suslikov such a blow under his bottom that he flew straight into the hole to the West. And Suslikov-York dissolved into dust.

COMMENTARY

The reader, again, may well doubt the truth of the dream we have just recounted. How, he may ask, do we know that Suslikov saw this or that in a dream? There are at least two reliable sources of evidence. The first is the account given by the dreamer himself. When Suslikov was at Party school he quite often took part in drinking sessions with the intellectual élite of the Central Committee. Usually he was silent, governed by the rule *Keep quiet, you fool, and then you'll seem smarter*! But when he did open his mouth in order to draw attention to his existence, he used to tell everyone about his dreams. He had nothing else to talk about. The second reliable source of evidence about the dreams of Suslikov (and of those like him) was his speeches. At bottom, they consisted of what the common people were wont to call 'raving nonsense', or, as the Russians say, the delirium of a grey mare. And it may well be asked where *could* such nonsense come from except from rubbishy dreams?

CONFERENCE IN THE CENTRAL COMMITTEE OF THE CPSU

The Partygrad/Lighthouse/Democratization Operation was Suslikov's first large-scale project since he became a CC Secretary. And he intended to make it an example of a new style of thought and action. On the next day he set up the conference.

'In order to implement the measures we are instructed to implement,' said Pyotr Stepanovich, opening the conference, 'we must distinguish between the internal and external aspects. From the point of view of the internal aspect our task consists in converting Partygrad into a model of perestroika such as will become a lighthouse for all the rest of the country. This means that we must conduct perestroika in such a way that, as a result of it, our communist social order becomes even stronger than before. I think that none of you are exactly novices in the Party and that you understand what I have in mind. It is an open secret that in recent years we have somewhat weakened our political educational work and let go the reins. Every kind of irresponsible person, subject of course to rotten Western influence, has taken advantage of this. Now we have to let these people know that we will not allow the roots of our social organization to be undermined. We can permit much. But there's a limit to everything. Perestroika will succeed when, in the course of it, we are able to strengthen the roots of our society and faith in our ideals.

'From the external political viewpoint,' continued Pyotr Stepanovich, 'our task lies in demonstrating to Western people, by means of concrete examples, the substance and progress of our perestroika. Western people are ideologically and politically underdeveloped. Their heads are crammed with sex, pornography, violence and the pursuit of profit. One has to spell out everything to them literally with one's fingers.

'Comrades, we have begun to live in a new way. There is nothing that we need to hide. We shouldn't disguise our shortcomings, but we needn't hide our successes either. Let the foreigners take a look at the institutions in which bureaucratism and corruption flourish as well as those ones where traces of the past have already been surmounted. Let them look at a real live bribe-taker. We could show him to them in court. Western people like such spectacles. We will show them that we now have as much freedom of expression as they have. Let them meet whomever they want to meet. And talk to whomever they want to talk to. No holds barred! But we mustn't allow it all to happen haphazardly. We must conduct educational work with our own people so that they are imbued with a spirit of responsibility and show themselves to be politically mature citizens of our socialist society.

'At the present stage of our development' – Comrade Suslikov was coming to the end of his speech – 'friendly relations with the West are extremely important to us. With the West's help we will overcome the temporary difficulties that have arisen faster and better. It is with this aim in mind that we have decided to convert Partygrad into a weapon of our external policy.'

At the conference a special commission was established whose task would be to offer help to the Partygrad administration in the matter of preparing the city and the oblast for their role as a perestroika lighthouse. At the head of the commission they put Comrade Corytov, Suslikov's right-hand man and a man most experienced in the methodology of the Communist Party of the Soviet Union. At the same time a conference was being held within the KGB. Comrade Pyzhikov, one of the deputy chairmen of the KGB, began his speech by reciting to his subordinates the current popular parody of Pushkin's epistle to the Decembrists.* 'Believe me, comrade, it will pass, this glasnost thing that you so like, and then the KGB will strike, and you'll end up the biggest ass.

'You see, comrades,' Comrade Pyzhikov drew the moral from

* The Decembrists were the aristocrats who in 1825 staged a liberal revolt against the new tsar Nicholas I.

this joke, 'our people still love and respect us in the old way. But at the same time perestroika obliges us to perfect our methods of work, to exhibit suppleness and to deliberate on our experience in a creative manner.'

At the conference they considered a whole range of subtly interconnected questions: the structure of Western tourist groups and delegations; the participation of Western spies in them; the infiltration of Soviet people into them; the recruiting of foreigners into the Soviet intelligence service; control over foreigners; the relationship between foreigners and Soviet citizens; help to be given to the Partygrad section of the KGB and militia in terms of personnel, information and technical aid.

A keen discussion broke out on the second question. One half of the conference (the 'liberals') insisted that only half of the foreigners would be Western secret service agents, while the other half (the 'conservatives') held that 100 per cent would be. But when it came to discussion of the third question, the conference was up against a difficulty. Somebody said: 'If we infiltrate our own people into foreign groups in advance in the West, or recruit a foreigner into our spy service, than it would not be correct to say that 100 per cent of the visiting foreigners would be foreign secret service agents.'

'The contradiction is only an apparent one,' ruled Comrade Pyzhikov. 'You are making metaphysical judgements on the principle "either . . . or". But why do you think that because somebody serves in one secret service, he doesn't serve in another? We have to make a dialectical judgement on the matter, as Lenin taught us. That is, on the principle of "either . . . and". Our people can be agents of foreign services. This we will not forbid. We will even recommend it. As for recruiting foreign spies to our side, there's nothing difficult about that. We sometimes even have to beat them off. Comrade Andropov taught us another thing. He said that when the chiefs of foreign secret services turned up at the Lyubyanka to study our past work, we could sleep in peace.'

Before the commission set out for Partygrad, Suslikov had a confidential talk with his aide, Corytov. Suslikov stated his ideas, using the haziest and most ambiguous expressions. Corytov understood them to mean this: 'It is easy to criticize the previous leadership for its mistakes. But just you try to avoid mistakes when you have to take historical decisions and when all the academic institutes in the world put together can't manage to predict the course of events even for the next decade. Before we embark on a radical change in our political strategy we must give a clear answer at least to the following questions: (1) Can we from our own resources and without the help of the West overcome our difficulties or not? (2) Can we defend ourselves with the weapons we have or not? (3) Will there be an economic collapse in the West in the next few years or not? The answer to these three questions was No. That's why we embarked on perestroika.

'We didn't go after perestroika because we were doing well. It meant a retreat. Unfavourable circumstances made it necessary. We could not overcome the difficulties which had developed in the country during the period of stagnation by using the old methods. This would have made a bad impression in the West. But without the West's help we cannot pull ourselves out. Moreover, our own people wouldn't support us. They're tired and in a very bad humour. Somehow we have to make it look as if we're rearranging the country in a Western manner, and indeed the time has come to start out on this road.

'But the passing of time makes us correct our calculations. Even now it's becoming clearer and clearer that we shan't get aid from the West on the scale we'd hoped for. In addition, when it aids us the West ties us down to forms of life which harm our society. We've overestimated the West's defensive strength. With the weapons we now have we'll remain a deadly dangerous adversary of the West at least for the next decade.

'We've gone too far. Perestroika has had unintended results which threaten the very roots of our social order. Its minuses are already obvious, while the promised pluses are still in question. If things go on like this the Party will lose the trust of the mass of the population. That's what it is beginning to look like now in Poland.

But the all-important fact remains that we cannot overcome our crisis without using our own methods, however much aid the West gives us. Here China has shown us the way.

'What conclusion should we draw from all this? I think you've already guessed the answer: to stick to our old course is to end up with catastrophe. We have to prepare a change. But cleverly, so that not a thing can be said against it. Outwardly everything should look as if perestroika is increasing its tempo and strength. So maximum press publicity! For the West the most important thing is not what we do but what we say. Let us all chatter about everything we like – the more it's heresy the better. People should have the chance to talk themselves silly to the point of absurdity. Then they'll feel themselves what their precious friends could end up with. We should give great prominence to the soviets.* Well, they're the highest organ of power already, aren't they? Gradually we should make them responsible for absolutely everything. Let them play at being parliaments. Meanwhile we, the Party apparatus, should retreat for the time being into the shadows and prepare ourselves for a new policy change, for the end of the deviation and for a new Party attack.

'We must unobtrusively strengthen the Party cadres with reliable people. The KGB will be taking a back seat too. Let the militia be responsible for public order. Let the public criticize the KGB in the press and even demand that we disband it. In fact the KGB needs new and stronger cadres. And more of them. Who will check up on this? Who will believe it if there are rumours of it? The press is stressing that the militia is the organ of the soviets. All right, let the public get fed up with them! But all the time the KGB must watch everything and remember everything. We shan't forget anything, we shan't forgive anything. Our business is, bit by bit, to make the people discontented with borrowed Western forms of life. We must sponsor informal rallies and movements to defend the true ideals of communism. We should begin to slip stuff into the press about the negative consequences of perestroika. Not

* Soviets are supposed to be popularly elected councils that are independent of the Party. Suslikov, during the Party's time of retreat, wishes to highlight this hitherto bogus independence.

loudly, of course. Rather, in the form of workers' letters. As criticism of the excesses of perestroika.

'Special attention to youth, schoolchildren and students. It's they who will eventually be deciding the fate of their country. But we are the people responsible for the direction in which things go. Everything must be done without hurry, quietly, confidently. No hullabaloo!'

THE THOUGHTS OF CORYTOV

As an old Party apparatchik Corytov knew that Suslikov couldn't say such things at his own risk. He was expressing the views of certain forces in the Party. But which forces? Or was the view an agreed compromise? Not a clear one; a silent one, but a compromise all the same? It was Corytov's guess that for the moment nothing at all was defined in the Party, that everyone was waiting on events; that minds were secretly fermenting. From the ferment more or less clear ideas would eventually emerge and, with them, intentions and decisions.

He, Corytov, was being given the opportunity to fix his own position. If he were in power, he wouldn't allow perestroika. The unmasking of Stalin in Khrushchev's time had been a crass error. Perestroika was an even more serious mistake. It could even be an irretrievable one. If they didn't correct the mistake now, everything could end in catastrophe. In short, as a Party member devoted to the ideals of communism, as an old apparatchik and Russian patriot, he, Corytov, would act as his conscience told him to act.

COMMENTARY

We have used the word 'conscience' in vain, for of course Corytov has never had a conscience. Moreover, our assertions regarding his freedom to define his own position may appear exaggerated. How can the obscure Corytov dare to do such a thing when the great Suslikov cannot? Simply because, we may reply, he *was* the obscure assistant of a great man. For it is the Corytovs, in their utter mediocrity, who form the minds and will of the Suslikovs.

THE EMISSARIES OF THE REVOLUTION

Next day the members of the Commission flew off to Partygrad; an unprecedented event in Soviet history. In Brezhnev's time there would have had to be several months of conferences of every sort, after which the whole commission, complete with household staff, would have flown off for a rest in the Caucasus or the Crimea. And indeed why fly to this Partygrad at all if everyone knew in advance that these flagships of perestroika were utter bullshit? Because their very *raison d'être* is to throw dust in the eyes of Soviet people as well as of foreigners.

But then we all know very well how to do that without the help of a commission from Moscow. That's what Brezhnev's bureaucrats and professors would have thought. But Gorbachev's innovators and initiators think differently. They have decided to accomplish the mission entrusted to them solemnly on the highest perestroika level.

TO PARTYGRAD

While our Muscovite Commission is making its way to Partygrad, it may be of some use to acquaint ourselves with the town's past and with its situation at the moment of the Commission's arrival. Expressing oneself in the language of high philosophy one might say that, until recently, Partygrad had no history whatever. It existed somewhere and somehow; things happened in it, but absolutely nothing that was worth calling history. Or one could even say, what happened there was worth calling 'not history'.

And not even what actually wasn't worthwhile but, more precisely, only that which would have been considered as not being worthwhile.

In Partygrad one could discover America or the atom, invent the bicycle or even the motor car without anybody paying the slightest attention. The Partygraders knew this better than anyone else. They reckoned that nothing they had or which had anything to do with them could be worthy even of their own attention. Even the discovery of America or the motor car they would have regarded as rubbish in comparison with the invention, say, of a gadget that perforated eggshells invented in Germany. And yet there was a sort of chain of events in time in Partygrad which one might call its tiny little history, or thin historylet.

THE ORIGIN OF THE TOWN'S NAME

Partygrad's original name was Knyazev, which is mentioned in the very earliest Russian chronicles. According to these, Prince Oleg of Kiev, while commanding an armed force against the Khazars, spent a few days in a certain town which was afterwards called Knyazev. On his return from the victorious campaign, Oleg visited Knyazev again. There he was bitten by a snake which had come from God knows where. Oleg died of the bite. Now, in the most conspicuous place in Partygrad's museum of folklore, there hangs a picture painted by a local artist, portraying Oleg at the moment when the snake bit him. The picture follows themes from Pushkin's famous poem: 'The Lay of the Prophetic Oleg'.

Certain progressive Soviet historians reject the hypothesis of the death of Oleg in Knyazev on the grounds that no snakes have ever lived in the oblast of Partygrad. Even more important, a snake could not have bitten Oleg because he was wearing chain-mail. But those who support the snake hypothesis refute the arguments of the opposing school with the following counter-arguments. First, there weren't any oblasts in those times. Second, the climate then was milder and snakes were to be found even north of Moscow.

Third, the snake could have been slipped in by Oleg's enemies. And as for the iron trousers, the snake could have caught Oleg at the moment when he had taken them down in response to a call of nature.

The inhabitants of towns around Partygrad believe that the snake did not bite Oleg in Partygrad but where *they* lived. In France several inhabited places claim to be the birthplace of d'Artagnan, while in Spain there's a dispute about that of Don Quixote. In Russia, as you see, people quarrel about the place where the snake bit the legendary Prince Oleg. Do you appreciate the difference? Incidentally, many Russian towns quarrel about where the former Empress Maria was strangled. In connection with this there is one amusing curiosity. They appointed the former Second Party Secretary (namely the Secretary for Ideology) dean of Partygrad University's historical faculty. Speaking at a session of the learned council about the problem we have mentioned, he said: 'The majority of inhabited places in the oblast are engaged in socialist competition to be named the town in which Prince Oleg was bitten by the snake and the Empress Maria was strangled.'

Under Gorbachev they nominated this man for Party work again, and with promotion too; that is, to the oblast level. They nominated him as an outstanding scholar in order to raise the administration's intellectual level.

At the time of Ivan the Terrible they changed the name of Knyazev into Tsarev, because the Muscovite Grand Duke had received the title of Tsar. After the October revolution of 1917 the town was renamed Trotsky. In the twenties Stalin began his struggle against the Trotsky personality cult and they called the town after a hero of the civil war, Tukhachevsky. When Tukhachevsky was shot as an enemy of the people, they gave the town the name of Stalin's colleague, Yezhov. After he had been liquidated Stalin called the place Djugashviligrad, after himself. But this name lasted for only a few years. After Stalin's death they called it Grazhdansk or Citizengrad. But this name held for only a few years too, and then they named the place Khrushchev. After Khrushchev's fall the town didn't have any name for quite a time. Brezhnev then insisted that it should bear the name of his front-line friend, Marshal I.S. Rukosyev, who had been wounded at the end of the war by a stray bullet and died in the town's hospital.

When Brezhnev came to an end, for some unknown reason and without somehow realizing it they renamed the town Brezhnev. When Andropov became General Secretary of the CPSU he ordered that the town should be given its present name in honour of the Party, as Partygrad, thinking that this would be a genuine continuation of an old Russian tradition.

It's hard to say how long this name will last. Gorbachev's Partygrad toadies have more or less applied to Moscow for the town to be renamed Gorbachevsk. But the answer came back that Gorbachevsk was already reserved for Stavropol. It's most likely that Partygrad will be called after Suslikov who, as we have seen, had a Partygrad career, rising in it from the rank of ordinary spermatozoid to that of First Secretary of the oblast Committee of the Party. Soon Suslikov, already a secretary of the Central Committee, will be a member of the Politburo. Then he will have the full right to have a town called after him.

THE PREHISTORY OF PARTYGRAD

Archaeological 'digs' were never carried out on Partygrad territory. Nevertheless it was here that the most sensational discoveries were made in the whole of Soviet archaeological history. This happened in the following manner. As early as the thirties they had pulled down the town's main cathedral, intending to erect on its site (as they had intended in Moscow) a very large building in which all the Party and governmental institutions of Partygrad could be reaccommodated. They excavated a huge hole for the foundations. But then they abandoned the building for the same reason that they abandoned the scheme in Moscow; where instead of building a Palace of the Soviets on the site of the demolished cathedral, they built a swimming-pool. After the war, when the authorities had no intentions in regard to the Partygrad hole, or simply the intention to make a deep hole, they discovered the skeleton of a prehistoric man. The scientists established that the skeleton was the oldest anthropoid being on earth. They called him 'Partypithecanthropos'.

Partypithecanthropos had a flattened skull slightly larger than a chimpanzee's. It moved as a quadruped, standing only occasionally on its hind legs. The same scientists advanced the hypothesis that the human being arose spontaneously in the Partygrad oblast from the local flora and fauna (as the newspapers reported). It did this arising, moreover, considerably earlier than in London, Paris, Rome and *a fortiori*, New York. However, the old people in Partygrad were convinced that the skeleton was that of a well-known pre-war local drunkard who actually did have a flattened skull on account of his frequent fights and falls.

The said drunkard usually moved from one drinking-point to another on all fours and stood on his hind legs only at the bar to get vodka or beer. This drunkard was supposed, too, to have fallen into the foundation pit during a powerful drinking bout and to have been sucked down into the slime. As proof of their contentions the old people pointed to the fact that Partypithecanthropos had lead fillings in his teeth and that nearby was found a Voroshilov sniper's badge. But since the declarations of the old Partygraders did not accord with the Supreme Leadership's then position in regard to Russian superiority over the world in all matters, including the process of turning monkeys into men, they put the old men into a strict-regime prison for slandering the Soviet social order. The old men succeeded in one respect: the camp was on oblast territory, and so they ended their life's journey, so to speak, at home.

Then the creators of the Deep Hole discovered pieces of birch bark with unintelligible inscriptions. The scientists deciphered the inscriptions and explained that writing on Partygrad territory long antedated that in Ancient Greece or even Egypt. The first words of the ancestors of the Partygraders were swear-words, a fact that greatly pleased Soviet intellectuals and connoisseurs of Soviet society in the West who study the Russian language in dictionaries with uncensored contents. The progressive Soviet linguists (the structuralists) developed a whole theory on the basis of the Partygrad discoveries to the effect that the Russian *Mat** system was the most ancient form of language in the history of mankind. The scholarly avant-garde went even further; they discovered the be-

* A swearing system comprising sexual obscenities.

ginnings of *Mat* even in Partygrad cows, sheep and hens. But since these ideas cast doubt on the Marxist thesis that men are descended from monkeys, they criticized these theorists in the local press and sent them to the local psychiatric hospital for treatment.

As we have already related, the first reports of Partygrad are to be found in the very oldest Russian chronicles. But on the other hand no mention is made of the place in scientific documents. Not long ago the Partygrad scientists revealed that there never ceased to be a life rich in events in Partygrad even in those years of which strictly nothing is known about the place. In particular, in connection with the recent Christian millennium of *Rus*, they explained that the Partygraders were baptized two weeks earlier than the inhabitants of Kiev. The Kievan Prince Vladimir was hesitating between adopting the Christian or the Muslim religion: he didn't know the difference between them. Having learned that the Partygraders had accepted Christianity, he was annoyed by this impertinence and gave himself priority as First Christian.

It was in Partygrad that the baptism took place of the legendary Prince Igor, the nephew of the legendary Oleg who was bitten by the legendary snake. According to the newspapers, this Igor was a reformer in the style of Gorbachev. Thanks to his reforms, Partygrad rose to the level of the highest achievements attained in the world of that time, inasmuch as the then summit of progress was feudalism. Partygrad had the task of catching up with the leading feudal countries in economics, politics and culture. On the Prince's palace was painted the slogan *Long live feudalism, the radiant future of the whole of humanity*! And on the first Christian temple they hoisted a banner which proclaimed *Forward the victory of serfdom*! Town criers were appointed who went around the town shouting information about the world and Partygrad, adding to the strength of the sound by cupping their mouths with their fingers. It was then that the word *glasnost* first appeared in world history. They formed it from the word *golosit*, which signified a kind of wailing or howling that made even the dead turn in their graves. Long before Peter the Great, Prince Igor was thinking about cutting a wall through into Europe. But he didn't yet know where Europe was and cut it through on the wrong side, that is to say into Asia. As a result Partygrad was submerged in darkness and fog. And so the period of stagnation lasted there right up until Gorbachev.

At the time of the Tartar/Mongol invasion the Mongols (or was it the Tartars?) missed out the oblast of Partygrad. Only once did a detachment of Mongols-Tartars appear on the far bank of the river which separated not only Partygrad from the outside world but the outside world from Partygrad. The inhabitants opened the gates (a figurative expression, because there weren't any), shitted into their trousers (also a figurative expression, because Partygraders didn't yet wear trousers) and brought out a huge amount of bread and salt, preparing for an unconditional surrender. But the Tartars/ Mongols, appalled by the stench that emanated from the town, and thinking that the bread and salt was some kind of Trojan horse, galloped away. As a result, the Partygrad prince, Pustaslav, had to spend a whole year pestering, or literally, in the Russian phrase, 'hovering on the threshold of' the Golden Horde with his request to offer tribute from the oblast.

It was from that time, they say, that the Russian idea of paying a five-year tribute in four years originated. The expression 'to hover on the threshold' is used here in an exclusively aesthetic sense, as neither Tartars nor Mongols had of course any thresholds on which to hover.

In the time of troubles at the beginning of the seventeenth century a detachment under the False-False-False Dmitry got to the edge of Partygrad. But an unknown peasant by mistake directed the Poles further on to a neighbouring oblast where he handed them over to Ivan Susanin. Then this peasant, who was told that someone had written an opera about Susanin, bitterly regretted that he himself had not sent the Poles into the local quagmire or marsh. But it was too late. Much later, and quite independently of Partygrad, the Poles sank up to their necks into the quagmire of socialism. And even the Pope, whom the Americans appointed so as to return Poland to the bosom of Western civilization, had to come to terms with this historic fact.

Until Peter the Great the Partygraders went around without any trousers. Peter ordered them to stop this barbarism and sent foreigners to Partygrad for them to copy. The Partygraders drove the foreigners out, having first taken their trousers down and given them a hundred strokes with a switch on their bare bottoms. Peter then flew into a rage and threatened to cut off the sexual organs of anybody in Partygrad who went around without trousers. The Partygraders bowed to the will of the great reformer and began to wear homespun breeches, which they never took off, even when they were answering the call of nature.

The French invasion of 1812 didn't touch Partygrad either. Until now the historians have been racking their brains as to why Napoleon retreated from Moscow by the same road as the one on which he arrived, and they advance the most brilliant hypotheses. If they had known of the existence of Partygrad, the need for such hypotheses would have subsided. The French were simply panic-stricken lest, if they deviated from the road they knew, they ended up in the Partygrad oblast, then a *guberniya* or government area where the quagmire would have sucked them down and they would have disappeared without trace from the pages of history. Rumour had reached them that the Partygraders lived off dried cockroaches and that they crushed bed-bugs and drank the blood. And this increased even more the fear that these foreign robbers had of the Great Russian Unknown.

All the great events of Russian history passed Partygrad oblast by, or were swallowed up in it without trace. In other oblasts there were peasant rebellions, but in Partygrad, in response to them, the whole population was flogged. Besides, they flogged everybody in Partygrad in the normal course of events just to teach them a lesson. When the 'liberal' period came and the official floggings were postponed or reduced, the population of the oblast itself took the initiative. The men took their dirty trousers down, the women cast off their dirty skirts and everyone thrashed everyone else's emaciated bottoms with the switches which grew in such abundance in the oblast.

COMMENTARY

Dear Reader, if you imagine that the sketch we have given you of the pre-revolutionary history of Partygrad is a satire in the spirit of Saltykov-Shchedrin,* you are gravely mistaken. There is nothing

* His *The History of a Town* (1569/70).

satirical in this sketch. If we have simplified matters a little, that is inevitable in any short sketch of a huge history. In my time I happen to have given lectures at Partygrad University. There I met the local historian. He used to swamp me with excerpts from the book he was writing in several volumes on the pre-revolutionary history of the town and the oblast. He produced the most meticulous evidence in order to exhibit the grandeur of the process of history in this particular part of the planet.

My hair stood straight up on my head when I read how much gruel and cabbage soup the Partygraders ate from the moment when the human species originated in these parts until the October revolution, how many birch-bark sandals and coats they wore out, and how much excrement they wrenched out of themselves and threw on to the surrounding land. If there had not been any historical hurricanes which carried off millions of people and compelled the survivors to swallow garbage, the Partygrad oblast would have fouled the whole planet to such an extent that even with the help of Reagan, Thatcher, Mitterrand, Kohl and all the West's other political operators put together, Gorbachev would have been unable to cut through a window even into Asia, let alone into Europe. There was, we assure you, not a single element of satire in the compilation of our little history; no exaggerations; no distortions; no embellishments. There was only the naked truth. (Then I said to myself: 'Spare me, Lord God, the spectacle of the *naked* truth!')

THE REVOLUTION IN PARTYGRAD

Although the idea of communism was invented in the very centre of civilization, the West, it was on its periphery, in Russia, that a real-life communist society made its appearance. Even now Westerners may sometimes permit themselves to speak of a communist earthly paradise; but actually to live in this paradise, *that* they grant to non-historical peoples, in the first place to Russians. The latter, after all, have long been accustomed to living like swine.

Although the socialist revolution took place not in Partygrad but in Petrograd, the capital of imperial Russia, the new society it generated reached maturity above all in the Russian provinces, in places like Partygrad. Nor was there anything accidental about this. Socialist (or communist) society has proved itself to be provincial through and through.

Until the revolution there were no revolutionaries in Partygrad. Not a Bolshevik in sight. It was the local exploiting classes themselves that established the power of the soviets in Partygrad immediately after the February revolution; that is, earlier than in Petrograd or Moscow. They did this out of political illiteracy of course. When Lenin ordered them temporarily to remove the slogan *All power to the Soviets* in Partygrad, they didn't obey him. They didn't obey him because not one of them had ever heard of Lenin. Secondly, a lot of red cloth went on slogans, as well as an ocean of paint, and these cost a lot of money. Moreover, when some student had painted the slogans, he simply disappeared. So there was nobody to write new ones.

The transition to the new social order in Partygrad happened without noise or bloodshed. The town authorities simply called the old institutions by new names, made them ten times larger and filled them with upwardly mobile common folk.

Having fulfilled their historical function, the former exploiting classes sent their envoys to Lenin. But he wouldn't receive them. He simply couldn't believe that Soviet power had come to Partygrad earlier than to Petrograd; and without Trotsky, to boot!! And where was this Partygrad anyway?! This was just somewhere that Lenin hadn't heard of. The Partygrad envoys took to drink in Petrograd. The Partygrad exploiters left for Paris. And then Soviet power set in, good and proper. All things considered, it set in for ever, because it was beyond anyone's human imagination to think up anything else for a place like that. And now it's hard to believe that there was ever anything else in Partygrad but Soviet power. Well, *was there*? It looks as if throughout history the power there was always Soviet, only it called itself by another name.

The civil war passed Partygrad oblast by because both the rival armies, the Whites and the Reds, were frightened of being bogged down in the great Partygrad swamp and losing their way in the woods, where there were packs of hungry wolves who ate Whites and Reds quite impartially. After the civil war ended, the Bolsheviks entered Partygrad. Some reports say they came from starving Moscow; others that they were military deserters who had been hiding in the marsh ever since 1914. After Lenin's death the rumour reached Partygrad that a call, 'Lenin's Call', was summoning everybody to join the Party. Then tens of thousands of Partygraders tried to join it. If Moscow had not sent an instruction to check the rush into the Party of every Tom, Dick and Harry, every adult in the oblast would have become a member. When Moscow sent its signal, the reverse process began: absolutely everyone began to *leave* the Party. If the authorities hadn't then begun to arrest the fugitives and stick them in corrective labour camps, Partygrad would have remained a non-Party town.

The trouble was that everything happened either later or earlier than in Moscow. Lenin's New Economic Policy started in Partygrad when it had finished in Moscow. But it failed to get going then after collectivization had begun. On the other hand Partygraders *were* in the vanguard of progress: they put into collective farms everybody who could be counted as Kulaks. Again Moscow thrust its oar in: and they drove even the poor peasants out of the collective farms. So they too had to have their own collective labour camp built for them.

When industrialization began, the peasants tried to get into the towns, leaving behind them nothing but dreary land. So alongside the camp that we've mentioned there was now a need to build a new one and fill it with fugitives from the country. And then they began to put people in both camps quite indiscriminately: and, what is more, from other oblasts. And so these camps became the first undertaking in the oblast which had real republican standing.

In the thirties they arrested twice over every person working in the district offices and three times over all those working in the

oblast offices. But there's no evil without good. The presence in the oblast of a large number of prisoners did contribute to industrial and cultural progress. Even before the Soviet-German war they built five factories in the oblast which were of all-Union significance, more than twenty enterprises on the oblast scale, a university, five institutes, three technical schools, a branch of the Moscow Conservatory, an opera-house, two theatres for drama, a ballet school, three scientific research institutes, and a psychiatric hospital of all-Union status. And the number of schools, hospitals, sports complexes and other institutions which by then had become an indispensable part of the Soviet way of life is simply incalculable.

Outside the town they began to build Europe's largest chemical factory.

THE WAR

During the 1941–1945 war with Germany the Partygraders began to prepare themselves for enemy occupation by studying the experience of other oblasts already occupied. They earmarked people who should work with the Germans. They allotted the most comfortable of their own labour camps to be German concentration camps. They formed powerful partisan detachments. For these they established substantial bases in the quagmire where the partisans could sit out the whole war and then inform posterity of their heroic exploits.

The man who was appointed head of the partisan movement was Mitrofan Lukich Portyankin, the future First Secretary of the Party obkom and a secretary of the Central Committee.

As a cover for this highly responsible assignment, they made Mitrofan Lukich commander of the garrison's Bath and Delousing Centre. But this post was an important one in its own right. A good many military schools were evacuated into the district. The authorities also set up base camps and depots for sending personnel to the front. So the Bath and Delousing Centre began to play a role which was just as important as that of the other institutions, military and civilian. Later on, Mitrofan Lukich followed

Brezhnev's example and published his war reminiscences under the title *In the Enemy's Rear*. But his august rival pointed out that the title of the book had a doubtful meaning: the oblast had stayed *our* rear, not the enemy's. And so the book was quietly withdrawn.

Partygrad profited from the war. To it they evacuated a whole series of military factories, institutes and scientific foundations. The Germans did not in the event encroach upon the oblast, and the usual Partygrad poverty seemed an oasis of peace and plenty in wartime. And so a mass of culture operators and other enterprising people who had no particular wish to block out the embrasures of enemy pillboxes with their bodies or throw bunches of grenades under enemy tanks, did their best to get to Partygrad. It was they who destroyed Partygrad's historical innocence. Although these people all vanished back to Moscow after the war, thanks to them Partygrad tasted the delights of a many-faceted, intellectual, spiritual and moral debauchery and thenceforth began its journey of adaptation to world civilization.

THE POST-WAR PERIOD

They finished building the chemical factory even in Stalin's time. There were no raw materials for it in the oblast. So they had to build several railways and tarmac roads and a row of other factories. Each of them dragged another after it, and soon there were bicycle factories, refrigerator ones and places for the manufacture of washing-powder, aeroplane parts and God knows what else. As the witty local intellectuals had it, they had turned the oblast, formerly a backward agricultural area, into a backward industrial zone.

When Stalin died, the Partygraders went into a double drinking bout. The first one was from grief. It lasted two weeks. The second was from joy. It also lasted two weeks. After Khrushchev's unmasking-of-Stalin speech at the Party congress the authorities emptied the Partygrad labour camps, but they decided to keep them temporarily in being. For a whole month they carried the works, busts and portraits of Stalin out into the quagmire, where they disappeared without a trace. It was as if Stalin had never existed. Stalin Square and Stalin Prospect were renamed Lenin Square and Lenin Prospect. They converted Stalin's statue into a statue of Lenin.

Under Khrushchev and Brezhnev the flood of general progress swept ever onwards over Partygrad province. The average height of the inhabitants increased by two centimetres and the average height of their homes by two storeys. One could compare this tempo of increase to that of New York, Tokyo or New Mexico. The young people started to wear jeans and beards. Now they had a legal basis for wearing jeans because they were made locally. During the period of *détente* the government bought a factory for making jeans from the United States. And now the Soviet Union competes successfully with the United States in third-world markets: not of course in jeans but in covers for tanks, aeroplanes and rocket-launchers.

They've renamed jeans 'young people's sporting trousers'.

Someone wrote in the newspapers that jeans in Soviet society (but not of course in the rotten West) helped the building of communism and that in every Soviet youth, even dressed in jeans, there beat 'the flaming heart of the Komsomol'. What the press didn't say was that jeans were worth a lot on the black market, where they were perfectly accessible to youths who did no work whatsoever. At first beards worried the oblast authorities, who turned to Moscow for instructions. The reply came that, for the time being and at this time of cultural development, beards were allowed, but only on condition that they did not hide decadent thoughts and moods.

The girls of Partygrad began to lose their innocence three years earlier than before the war. At the same time they became pregnant only half as often; this although contraceptives were available only to those on special lists and only on revolutionary holidays. However, the number of extramarital pregnancies increased many times beyond the pre-war figures. The young women rid themselves of the fruit of their sin by 'the methods of their grandparents' (to quote the press); that is to say, by the method of abortion.

Agriculture began to pick up. It was at this time that Yevdokia Timofeyevna Tyolkina started her career as manager of the agricultural division of the obkom of the Party and was known as 'Maotsedunka'. At a conference of agricultural leaders she voiced a winged phrase which immediately flew round the entire oblast and brought to Maotsedunka real popularity. 'Thoss year,' she said, 'oor harvest in the USA promises to be grand.' If this phrase wasn't winged, how did it fly around an oblast the size of an average European country?

In the seventies they modernized the military factory. Now it is no longer a matter for shame to show Western spies obsolete technology. They built a factory by adopting the latest technology stolen from the West. In a word, by the time Gorbachev's perestroika began, the single oblast of Partygrad had a greater industrial production than the whole of the Russian federation at the end of the twenties.

THE ASSIMILATION OF MARSHY LAND

On the territory of Partygrad oblast there stretched the largest quagmire in the whole of the Soviet Union, perhaps even in the whole world. A great quagmire is not simply a swamp or place flooded by water. Indeed, no water is to be seen in it. From outside, a quagmire looks very attractive: grass, flowers, berries, shrubs, little clearings. Frankly, paradise. But if in ignorance or carelessness you wander *in* there, you will discover that the heavenly appearance disguises a bottomless, slimy pit. By then it will be too late and you will be unable to warn anyone at all about the hidden danger. And nobody will be able to help you. You will disappear for ever and without trace.

They don't even guard the neighbouring corrective labour camps on the side of the quagmire or the ultra-secret atomic, chemical or bacteriological factories either. The quagmire is more reliable than any defence. Not one prisoner so far has been able to escape by that route. Nor has any inquisitive person managed to penetrate the secret zone via the quagmire.

Local intellectuals with a critical disposition regard the quagmire as a symbol of the new social order. For so doing they are sometimes punished by being exiled from the town into the above-mentioned secret factories and camps. The Party leaders of the oblast, gripped with concern for the welfare of the people, have more than once made attempts to begin to 'assimilate' the quagmire (or, as the newspapers called it 'the quagmire-lands'). Having duly received rewards and promotion for their attempts, the authorities would abandon the undertaking. Afterwards the same newspapers would write: 'Attempts to assimilate the quagmire-lands were swallowed up in the quagmire of bureaucratism.'

It was Pyotr Stepanovich Suslikov who made the last and largest effort, when he was First Secretary of the Partygrad obkom of the Party. In recognition he was awarded the title of Hero of Socialist Labour. After that, Pyotr Stepanovich began to prepare himself for the flight up to the summit of Party management in Moscow, so he abandoned his efforts about the quagmire. Like his predecessors. But in distinction from them he paid attention to one positive value of the quagmire, thanks to which it can play an outstanding historical role: since the quagmire is able to suck into itself absolutely everything without any trace, it is able to suck in the sediment from atomic explosions, poisonous chemical substances and death-dealing bacteria. If the most powerful hydrogen bomb were to explode above the quagmire, the effects would be no stronger than those of a gas escape such as happened not very long ago at Partygrad in a ten-storey block of flats in the new housing estate. After a couple of days the quagmire would look as if there hadn't been an atomic explosion at all. While the consequences of the gas blow-out couldn't be removed in a whole year.

When Suslikov was head of the Partygrad oblast, he said that, 'in the event of atomic war the whole population of the oblast will be resettled in the quagmire and will build there an even grander and more brilliant house of communism than the one which the Western imperialists have prevented us from building on dry land'. And Maotsedunka, whom we've already mentioned, declared that the oblast in the quagmire would produce such mountains of carrots, potatoes, cabbage and other agricultural products and of such quality that even the swine wouldn't eat them. The phrase 'produce mountains of' was one that Maotsedunka adopted after her first meeting with the Donbass miners.

The Partygrad intellectuals used to comment wittily on Maotsedunka's declaration, saying that the pigs would indeed not eat this food for the simple reason that pigs disappeared from the oblast long before Maotsedunka was made Heroine of Communist Labour for her outstanding agricultural achievements in the oblast. Despite this, what did flourish in the oblast was an all-embracing and all-engulfing swinishness. As to the quagmire, quite noiselessly and without any aid from sensational journalism, it began to be used as a garbage tip for atomic emissions and chemical effluent.

ATOM

When Moscow took the decision to build the first atomic factory devoted to peaceful purposes, it chose the Partygrad oblast. In this it was guided by the following considerations. The oblast held first place in the country for density of corrective labour camps. One could use the prisoners for work which was most secret and most harmful to health. The Partygrad quagmire was the most convenient place in which to bury atomic waste. The oblast was a long way from Moscow and hidden from foreigners. Nothing happened there that could attract the attention of the public. They were building or planning many secret factories which, in case of war, would be needed as an energy-base that would be independent of the normal sources of energy.

The name Atom somehow became attached to this construction. It crept into newspaper articles and official documents. When building was over and the factory went into operation, the whole district was officially given the name Lenin. But the population persisted in calling it Atom.

The most improbable and contradictory stories slipped out regarding the life led in District Atom. Some said it was a paradise on earth; full communism, where everything was plentiful and almost for free. Others said that Atom had drafted in prisoners who were either long-term or condemned to death. In the case of the last the authorities had commuted the death sentence into labour for life in conditions of high radiation.

In fact Atom contained both worlds: the paradise seen by ordinary inhabitants of the oblast, and the hell of which these same citizens didn't wish to think. On the one hand there was the life of the best specialists and qualified workers. They were on double wages and lodged in flats the like of which people couldn't even dream of elsewhere. They had double holidays and many other privileges. Their material luxuries and general way of life were superior to those in the town. On the other hand they lived under continual surveillance and in isolation. They could spend their leaves only in specified places, where their freedom of movement was strictly limited. But what was most important, they quickly began to experience a lowering of all their basic vital functions: apathy, depression and repeated sensations of alarm and terror.

Not long after the nuclear factory went into operation a catastrophe happened. How it ended was a closely guarded secret. That there had been a catastrophe was evident from numerous indicators. (You can't hide an awl in a sack.) Whole villages were evacuated. The hospitals filled up with strange-looking patients. Child monsters began to be born. Unfortunately for Partygrad, nobody then had thought of perestroika or glasnost. Moreover, the wind was blowing the wrong way and so the radioactive fall-out was blown not into Europe but into Siberia. (If the wind had blown from the East, perhaps the glasnost period would have started earlier, and Partygrad would have been made famous all over the world, as Chernobyl was to be later.)

The rumour arose in Atom as a result of the catastrophe that mutants had been seen who were able to live in conditions of heightened radioactivity; it was said that they wanted to breed them specially for military purposes and for work in contaminated areas. But it was said too that the mutants had revolted and had to be destroyed. But few people believed this rumour. In the opinion of the Partygraders, there couldn't be any mutants because the climate and the grub were not right. Probably in Atom some pipe broke or roof caved in. That sort of thing often happens in our country. But, most likely of all, the workers had built an apparatus for making hooch within the reactor, had got drunk and had a fight. There are, in any case, quite enough healthy people in our country to work in contaminated places without using mutants.

Atom became a normal element in the life of the oblast. Many graduates from institutes and technical colleges were sent to work there. And they were most willing to do so, being tempted by the favourable conditions. From Partygrad itself the authorities sent to Atom people who were slackers and even 'internal émigrés'. This was the name they gave to all those who had succumbed to the corrupting influences of the West and were in a state of conflict with the Soviet social order, its ideology and its system of power.

Certain peasants from the Atom region started to appear in the market with vegetables and dairy products which they sold more cheaply than other peasants.

Sometimes alcoholic wrecks would appear in the restaurants with thick packets of roubles and spend them all in one evening. The militia would fish them out, or rather pick them up in the street and send them back to Atom. These debauchees would tell how, at times, for one hour's ultra-secret work, they would receive two hundred or even five hundred roubles. True, one hour's work made them impotent; or lost them their hair; or their appetite. Or they developed agonizing pains in the stomach, chest or head. But on the other hand they could also afford one glorious day of life 'in the communist way'; by which they meant spending all their money regardless with the first rogues they met.

PARTYGRAD AND MOSCOW

The relations between Partygrad and Moscow are complex and even contradictory. On the one hand Moscow is Partygrad's highest supervisor and divine authority. On the other hand Moscow's role *vis-à-vis* Partygrad is like that which the West plays *vis-à-vis* Moscow. For in Moscow people get up to something hoping that it will be noticed in the West. In Moscow even the high leadership, before blurting out some rubbish or other, has formed a view via its spies of how the venal Western press and conservative Western politicians will react to it. And when the Muscovite leaders wake up in the morning, the first thing they do is to look for their ugly mugs in the Western press. In Partygrad too they do things not unlike this in the hope that rumours of them may get as far as Moscow. If in Moscow they start to grow small beards, in Partygrad they will be growing them down to the waist. If people are sentenced in Moscow to three years for undisguised free-thinking, in Partygrad it will be five years for implicit scepticism. In Moscow the authorities called a new region 'New Cherry' although no cherry trees had ever grown there. In Partygrad they called a new residential quarter 'New Limes', although not a single lime tree had ever grown there.

The Partygrad pavement drunkard who tried to earn himself a drink by wheezing a few of his own songs to a guitar was named 'Bard', as they name them in Moscow. When they removed him to Atom as a 'layabout' it was rumoured that he had gone to Paris in order to win himself world fame.

Indeed, the wish to tag along behind Moscow takes pathological form in Partygrad. There, people are even proud of Moscow's harsh bellow. If Moscow rumbles at the Partygrad authorities, the Partygraders will tell each other that 'our Boss' (meaning the first secretary of the Party obkom) 'has got it in the neck in Moscow. That means he'll be going up in the world'.

Moscow's influence on Partygrad is many-sided. Here are two examples of it. One respected civil servant was refused a tourist trip to Bulgaria because his closest friend and boon companion had said, as a joke, that the respected civil servant was intending to ask for political asylum there. It was obviously a joke: everyone knew that to ask for political asylum in Bulgaria was exactly like hiding from the Partygrad KGB in that famous building on Dzerzhinsky Square which is called the Lyubyanka. But the KGB took the joke for some kind of signal and forbade the journey.

The civil servant regarded the veto as unfair and began to shout about the lack of freedom of conscience in Partygrad. They then explained to him exactly what freedom of conscience was. Then he baptized his son in protest, for that fashion had made its appearance in Moscow and awakened Western hopes of a religious revival in Russia; and indeed, of the collapse of the regime because of lack of faith in Marxism. This earned the civil servant a strict reprimand from his Party boss.

In intelligentsia circles, always inclined to verbiage on any subject, people said about this case that it was indeed up to Partygrad to play a leading role in the religious revival in Russia.

However, the head of the Church in the oblast rejected this

rumour in the Party press. At the same time he condemned the President of the United States as a warmonger. After this affair, our civil servant was given the duty of spending a whole year engaged in intense anti-religious propaganda in order to purge his reprimand and to regain the reputation of an old and politically reliable communist.

Yet another example. A woman in Moscow, who had been longing to go the West but had failed to get an exit visa for a number of years, chained herself to the gate of the American embassy. The foreign radio stations with programmes to the Soviet Union beamed the news of this escapade to the Muscovites. They even heard about it all in Partygrad as well.

And the Moscow woman had a follower in Partygrad. Because the john leaked and wasn't fixed for half a year, he chained himself to the lavatory-pan in his flat for a whole year. His neighbours told the militia. The militia decided that the matter had a whiff of politics and got in touch with the KGB. The KGB arrived in four motor cars, dispersed the crowd of idle gapers, broke down the door into the lavatory, disconnected the pan from the plumbing system (which was easier than filing through the chain) and removed the protestor together with his lavatory-pan. The Western press paid no attention to the valiant exploit of the Partygrader fighting on behalf of human rights. Because there was no interest in him, he got only a year in prison for hooliganism. When he came out, his lavatory-pan was still leaking.

PARTYGRAD AND THE WEST

Although there were no real dissidents in Partygrad, the town had not managed to escape the West's corrupting influence. Many Partygraders heard Western broadcasts, saw Western films and read Western books. Some people travelled to the West or knew people who'd been there. Foreign goods were sold on the black market. The Westernizing initiative was coming from above, from the children of the privileged Soviet class: in other words, from the children of the big shots.

The Partygrad administration and the ideologically healthy section of the population saw the danger of Western influence and took measures to contain it. But opinions were divided over all this. Some people wanted interdictions and repressions. Others looked at the problem in a more liberal manner. Let them console themselves with Western rubbish, they thought, provided they don't get into politics. But the 'conservatives' believed that this 'rubbish' was more dangerous than politics. In our country there are defences against deviation: ideology and the KGB. But, they said, against American jeans, chewing-gum and heart-rending rock wails there is no defence at all.

Gradually various currents began to flow into Partygrad in the sphere of human freedoms and human rights. And that was the fault of the leadership itself. In the network of political education and propaganda it had become so insistent on explaining that there were more of these blessings to be found in the oblast than 'in the famous West'. All this stirred up an unhealthy curiosity among the people and unfounded hopes. One old woman spent two weeks queuing in the Party obkom in order to ask for 'twenty-four hours of these rights and freedoms'. Otherwise it would be too late, she would soon be dead. And before that she wanted to taste what they were like. They put the old lady in a home for very old people and didn't let her out until she was dead. But she became nevertheless the founder of the movement for the defence of human rights in Partygrad.

The old lady died. But her cause stayed alive. Another lady who worked in a research institute received, for services rendered, a free trip to Japan as a tourist. The news really shook the town. In the whole history of humanity not a single Partygrader had ever been in Japan. But the Party raikom* didn't give the lady its recommendation (which is indispensable for any trip abroad), on the grounds that this scientific worker, with her huge dimensions, would not be able to squeeze into miniature Japanese toilets and would therefore ruin the reputation of the Soviet Union. The lady, aghast, declared the right to travel abroad was an innate human right and did not depend on the dimensions of one's behind. The chairman of the commission replied that the right to travel abroad

* Party district HQ.

was *not* an innate human right, for the reason that there had been human beings before there were frontiers. The scientific worker was impressed by that argument and took back her words about rights. But it was already too late: they had expelled her from the Party.

DISSIDENT-FREE ZONE

During the years when Mitrofan Lukich Portyankin ruled Partygrad he often used to talk to his son-in-law, Pyotr Stepanovich Suslikov, about problems of importance to the State. 'Look 'ere, Pyotr,' Mitrofan Lukich would say, pouring vodka into the presentation crystal glasses that Mitrofan Lukich had acquired as a war trophy at the collapse of Nazi Germany when he was on a mission studying the bathing and delousing arrangements in Nazi concentration camps, 'look what they're cooking up in Moscow! The bastards have got out of hand. But we 'ere 'ave peace and plenty. Whoy?'

Pyotr Stepanovich kept his servile gaze on his highly placed father-in-law. The latter was emptying his glass into his gaping maw, which glittered with gold caps. He coughed his appreciation. He made a few jokes about his first glass. Then he poured out a second one, because a sincere Party conversation could, in his view, take place only at a high degree of alcohol.

Mitrofan Lukich proceeded with his discourse, tucking into a few *zakuski* (sturgeon, a touch of caviare, to go with his second glass). 'Because we've got our heads screwed on our shoulders. That's whoy! No dissidents show up in our oblast for the same reason whoy southern fruits don't grow in the cold north. What's the point of southern fruits growing in the north?'

Mitrofan Lukich interrupted his speech in order to pour out the next 'little glass'. Pyotr Stepanovich waited in obsequious silence, realizing that Mitrofan Lukich did not expect an answer from *him*. Mitrofan Lukich asked questions so that he could answer them himself: a rhetorical technique he'd already adopted in the years when he commanded the garrison's bathing and delousing. It was his habit then to station naked soldiers in the street in front of the bath-house and put strategic questions to them, such as 'Can we overcome the enemy if we 'aven't overcome the louse?' And then give exhaustive answers in the spirit of the speeches of his beloved Stalin.

'For southern fruits to grow in the north,' continued Mitrofan Lukich, 'special 'ot-houses are needed. And in order that foreign fruits should grow in Partygrad, fruits called dissidents, there too there would 'ave to be special 'ot-houses. The main thing is to see there ain't any. So, no greenhouses, no fruits growable in 'em, eh? Got it?'

Suslikov nodded assent. But Portyankin, having downed his third glass, plus again appropriate *zakuski*, poured out his fourth and continued to give the young rising generation in the person of Suslikov the benefit of his own long experience.

'We 'aven't got any foreign embassies 'ere. There are no Western journalists. A few foreigners work in our factories. But what sort of foreigners? Italians. They don't count. It's true some people listen to Western broadcasts. Well, let 'em listen to their hearts' content. That nonsense can't 'arm us. These Western human rights and democratic freedoms are no good to us – loike a concertina to the Pope, an umbrella to a fish or a saddle to a cow!'

When Suslikov became First Secretary of the Partygrad Party obkom he swore an oath to his protector, Portyankin, to turn the oblast into a dissident-free zone. In this operation he was governed by certain principles. To squash dissidents wasn't a clever thing to do. Not let them appear, that's what one should aim at. Then there's no need to squash them. But if they do appear as a result of an oversight, one must neutralize them, discredit them and destroy them by all available means. When they are destroyed or have disappeared or have been made harmless or even made useful, one can allow them. In this Suslikov followed the example of Stalin, who was ready to abolish shootings when the last 'enemy of the people' had been shot. In order to accomplish his programme, Suslikov proposed to disperse the intelligentsia so that they had no chance of arranging unauthorized meetings. He then set up a special ideological commission which purged all the libraries in the town of any literature that had even a suspicion of a criticism of the Soviet social order or ideology. He took firm measures against speculators on the black market, against those who distributed *samizdat* and foreign books and he set up a close check on duplicating machines and radio receivers.

In short, the results of Pyotr Stepanovich's wise administration were not slow to materialize. Every morning when Pyotr Stepanovich arrived at his office at Obkom the first thing he did was to ask his personal assistant Corytov: 'Well?' 'Clean' was Corytov's report.

'Well, thank God for that,' Pyotr Stepanovich would murmur. 'Then connect me with the Centre.' And Pyotr Stepanovich would report to Mitrofan Lukich in Moscow that there were no dissidents in the oblast entrusted to him. 'Keep it like that' was the answer he would get.

A BLACK DAY

Then the black day arrived when to Comrade Suslikov's usual question his faithful Corytov failed to pronounce his confident 'Clean'. Nor did Suslikov himself report to Moscow about the perfect order reigning in the oblast entrusted to him or hear the encouraging 'Keep it like that'. In a grief-laden voice he whispered incoherently to Portyankin about how there had been a little slip-up; that they hadn't yet got to the bottom of it; hadn't yet assessed the matter thoroughly; that they had taken a liberal approach.

Then Suslikov heard the icy voice of Mitrofan Lukich: 'Comrade Suslikov, I am a simple man and a sincere one. But when there are threats to the conquests of the October Revolution, don't expect any mercy from me. If you don't put the matter right, you can hand in your Party card. Got it?'

That night lights burned until dawn in the buildings of Partygrad's responsible institutions. The armed forces of the region were on red alert. Army and militia patrols thronged the town. But what had actually happened? It transpired that four citizens of Partygrad had gone to Moscow and tried to get in touch with Western journalists in order to describe the ulcers of Soviet society. The appearance in Partygrad of its own home-grown dissidents was totally unexpected, but in a special way.

Partygraders had of course known for a long time that certain oddballs existed whom people had begun to call by the sophisticated foreign name of 'dissident'. There had always been such oddballs around. But until then they had been merely something to make fun of. The KGB knew about them. But they too weren't much worried because they knew what these dissidents were worth.

To put it briefly, the situation was this: the phenomenon existed, everybody knew about it but pretended that it didn't exist, because there had been no official notification of its existence. And therefore it sort of couldn't quite exist.

TO PUT IT ANOTHER WAY

Although the phenomenon existed empirically, it didn't rank as something socially significant; it existed below the social threshold that divides existent phenomena into two groups – those which sort of exist and those which exist without the 'sort of'.

And what happened then? An order came from Moscow to regard the Partygrad dissidents as existent without the 'sort of', because they had manifested themselves on the level of the world press. It was just after this that Suslikov reported to Portyankin about the dissidents' appearance in the oblast. Now the threshold of social significance had been moved. The new social phenomenon with the foreign name of 'dissident' had received the right to an officially recognized standing.

The Partygraders who were now counted as dissidents included a real communist, an hereditary proletarian, a quintessential Ivan and a student who had organized an illegal journal called *Glasnost*. Their names didn't matter: the Western journalists who wrote about them didn't call them by name. They referred to them in passing as 'dissidents from the provinces'. The West, you see, was unwilling to take cognizance of the existence of Partygrad even in such a negative form.

There are two kinds of communist: the natural one and the pedant. The natural communist is a Soviet man who has learned to live in Soviet society and to get along somehow in it. He is ready for everyone and everything. Communism for him is not a distant paradise (in which he doesn't believe) but an actual implacable reality from which one must extract for oneself the largest piece of meat one can lay one's hands on.

The pedant communist is hardly different from the natural one in his normal way of life, but he has no following. He has chosen the role of a man who is better and more devoted to the ideals of communism than other people. And so he turns himself into a small pedant when it comes to interpreting the ill-considered remarks of the classical authors of communism. For example, one of the classical authors chattered something about civil servants' pay being no higher than workers' pay. So the communist pedant demands a maximum pay scale for the Party. What is more, he is ignorant of the fact that most Soviet civil servants' pay is lower than that of qualified workers.

Another communist 'classic'* blurted out something about cooks governing the State under communism. The communist pedant takes this idea up with the Party organization, despite the fact that there hasn't been a trace of cooks in the old sense for ages. Another 'classic' raved about workers running factories themselves. The communist pedant stands up for self-management in the factories, although today you couldn't get the workers involved in such idiocies even by force.

In other words the pedant communist considers that communism is badly run in the Soviet Union and that the recommendations of the classics of Marxism have not been implemented. In short, if Lenin had been alive everything would have been different.

The greater number of pedant communists stay on the oddball level. They are tolerated in the collectives and sometimes even encouraged. But some individual pedants go so far that they

* Lenin, actually.

become a scourge in collectives and the institutions, which they attack with a relentlessness born of paranoia. These people are usually dealt with in the most merciless fashion: they are put in lunatic asylums or exiled to far-off regions. Nobody comes to their defence. Who worries about real communists! Serves them right!

One communist of this type had already annoyed the power organs in Partygrad. They pushed him out of the Party and out of his job. But they weren't in any hurry to send him to the psychiatric hospital, because they thought he was half-witted. This was obviously a mistake, for he was one hundred per cent crazy. Profiting from the KGB's blunder, the genuine communist rushed off to Moscow with the intention of telling the Western journalists that communism in Partygrad was incorrectly implemented and to petition the rulers of the Western countries to urge the Soviet government to correct Soviet communism and establish it in the Party in its genuine form.

THE HEREDITARY PROLETARIAN

In the oblast there was a yet more dangerous enemy of the Soviet social order: a locksmith/plumber who called himself an hereditary proletarian. His job was to install and repair foreign baths and WCs in the flats belonging to the Partygrad Party aristocracy. He was clever enough to record on cassettes the noises emitted by the governors of the oblast when they were in the toilet. Hundreds of copies distributed in the town had a great success: especially the 'anal declarations' of Maotsedunka and of Suslikov himself. Moreover, those who heard the cassettes were always able to identify the sounds. Panic broke out in the oblast government circles. Only Maotsedunka seemed to take the matter calmly. 'Let them come to see me after dinner,' she said, slapping herself on her immeasurable bottom. 'I'll give them a stretch of music which will make their Beethovens and Picassos shut up shop.' They told Maotsedunka that Picasso was a painter and not a composer. Quite undisturbed by this she replied that, as far as she was concerned, painters could be shat on too.

Suslikov, however, saw a threat to his career in what had happened. The chairman of the oblast direction of the KGB, Gorban, said that if the bathroom sounds of the high leadership were widely advertised, Soviet power wouldn't last out the year. Besides, nobody would prevent the Western sociologists who were looking out for the most ulcerous places in the Soviet social system from taking note of the opinion of the head of the Partygrad KGB.

All of the KGB and the militia were thrown into the search for the culprit. Sensing the danger, the hereditary communist escaped to Moscow with a sack of cassettes on which was inscribed *Anal Speeches of the Rulers of Partygrad*. He intended to publish these speeches in the West and earn from them both fame and millions just as other Soviet dissident writers did.

THE END OF THE PROLETARIAN DYNASTY OF THE IVANS

Ivan Ivanovich Ivanov proudly called himself 'Three Times Ivan'. His father was Three Times Ivan too. He was a factory worker and, when the war with Germany broke out, he volunteered for the front and quickly perished. The second Three Times Ivan followed in his father's footsteps and he too became a factory worker. After the army he married and brought into the world a son whom he also called Ivan. Three Times Ivan No. 3, unlike his forebears, was reared at a comparatively benevolent time and in a benevolent family. Ivan No. 3 did very well at school, where he was especially proficient in mathematics. His teacher judged him to be a future star in the field of science.

But an event occurred which shattered all the dreams and plans of the Ivanovs. Brezhnev himself visited Partygrad. Among the factory workers who had been selected to shake Brezhnev's hand was Three Times Ivan No. 2. As he shook his hand, Brezhnev suddenly remembered that at the beginning of the war he had issued a Party membership card to one Ivan Ivanovich Ivanov. Wasn't this man the son of the said Ivanov? The director of the factory, not waiting for Ivanov to reply, said Yes; the Ivanov dynasty of factory workers was famous all over the oblast. Three

Times Ivan No. 2 lost his head and blurted out that his son was also Ivan and would follow in the footsteps of his father. Brezhnev said how remarkable it was that the children of workers followed their father's profession; the most respected profession in the world. This should turn into a universal tradition. In the newspapers they printed a photograph of Brezhnev shaking the hand of the second Three Times Ivan, what Brezhnev had said and the hasty promise of Ivanov.

There then arose the movement started by the second Three Times Ivan. Three Times Ivan No. 3 would have tried to put a spoke in his father's wheel, but the authorities leaned on him and forced him to sign a circular to the children of factory workers, exhorting them to continue in the profession of their fathers. They gave the Ivanovs a two-roomed flat out of turn. They gave a medal to Three Times Ivan No. 2. In the factory they then began to hate him and to do him every sort of rotten turn. Three Times Ivan the Third's children got beaten up more than once by the children of factory workers who were forced to work there, so that for the first time a militiaman accompanied him to the factory.

Although Three Times Ivan No. 3 was a conscientious worker he dreamed of only one thing: to get himself out of the working class as soon as he could and, for a start, to get his promised place in the institute's correspondence course department.

But then and there, fate, implacable fate, interfered with his life. The campaign, whose sacrifice he was, came to an end. The authorities forgot about the working dynasty of the Ivanovs. The workers provoked Three Times Ivan No. 3 into making a speech about disorders in the factory. For this he was thrown out of the Komsomol, sacked from the factory and sent to Atom as a layabout. From there he ran away to Moscow, threatening to burn himself alive in Red Square.

THE GLASNOST COMMITTEE

But what alarmed the Partygrad authorities most was that an illegal journal called *Glasnost*, produced by students at the university, had begun to circulate in the town. It was explained in the journal that a Glasnost Committee was being formed with the task of informing the Partygraders about those events in the oblast that were not reported in the newspapers. Who could have imagined then that within a few years the glasnost idea would have been taken over by the country's highest leadership, while at the same time its actual originators would disappear without trace in corrective labour camps?

The fighters for glasnost prepared the first number of the journal which produced evidence of corruption in the highest reaches of the oblast's administration and of abuse by officials of their office. In particular, the paper reckoned that Suslikov had an amount of money at his disposal to amass which a man earning even as much as a thousand roubles a month would have needed to do a century's work at least. The editor of the paper went to Moscow with the intention of sending the journal to the West.

THE END OF DISSIDENCE IN PARTYGRAD

The Western journalists in Moscow saw no special significance in the Partygrad dissidents. One of them apparently even denounced them to the KGB, saying in justification that he had taken the dissidents for KGB *agents provocateurs*. All the same something did appear in the Western press to the effect that the dissident movement was hotting up in the Russian provinces, especially in Partygrad. And this short article was quite enough to make Suslikov come out in a cold sweat and have pains around the heart.

They arrested the Partygrad dissidents in Moscow and handed them over to the Partygrad authorities. At a session of the bureau of the Party obkom, Suslikov reported that 'as a result of the rotten liberalism of certain officials, the weakening of ideological education and of the pernicious influence of the West, there had recently been certain signs of dissidence. However, these had been detected and obliterated'.

Some time passed and then Corytov, in answer to Suslikov's 'Well?' would say 'Clean'. Suslikov reported to Portyankin that the position in the oblast had been sanitized and heard his long-awaited 'Keep it like that!' Could Suslikov have imagined that a few years later the whole of Russia would be flooded with dissidents of a new type and that he would almost be a dissident himself?

THE STORY UNDERNEATH

But everything that we've been talking about in the Soviet period made up only an insignificant part of the real story of Partygrad, moreover a part of tenth-rate importance. It was only the scum of the history of Partygrad, not its deep stream. The last was what one might call the social life of the mass of the population: more particularly it consisted of the various social procedures, rituals and measures that formed the customary elements of people's everyday life: the acceptance of novices into the Oktyabrata Pioneers* and the Komsomol; the Komsomol rallies; the same within the Party; social work; general and professional assemblies; meetings and demonstrations; propaganda circles and seminars; Komsomol and Party schools; universities of Marxism-Leninism; sessions of the power organs and administration at every level from the basic collectives to the highest instances of oblast power; governmental conferences, directives, control. In sum: the essence of the communist way of life.

That means everything a person does as a communist citizen. All the rest is, so to speak, only the raw material and the modalities of communist social life. Factories in the Soviet Union are not built in order to achieve some abstract production, but most of all as a means of organizing people in communist collectives. Only in the last resort are they instruments for the creation of objects of use and, more generally, of material things. Cultural work is not done for the sake of culture itself, but only as a means of educating people and controlling their behaviour and their state of consciousness. And the most important thing in the activity of the author-

* Organization of children of pre-school age.

ities is whatever enables them to preserve the unity of the social whole and to canalize the normal course of its social life.

If one could calculate the sum of the human efforts that were made in the oblast towards maintaining its social aspect, one would arrive at figures that would put in the shade all the official indexes of Soviet society's actual production (extraction of coal, output of steel, the harvest, the number of television sets and so on). The most rough-and-ready calculation of the number of people who pass through the Pioneers and the Komsomol, of those received into the Party, of participants in demonstrations and conferences; of the number of assemblies, conferences, speeches, resolutions and other things in official life; of the number of participants in propaganda groups and lecture tours and so on. All this would give a picture that would make your hair stand on end. And if the calculations were spread over the years and the different levels of the hierarchy, you would feel the very essence of the progress that Partygrad had experienced during the period of Soviet power.

THE FORGE OF CADRES

In the light of these notions it becomes understandable that the main growth of production in the Partygrad oblast lay in the production of administrative cadres. Look at the highest instances of Soviet administration in Moscow, at the apparatuses of the Central Committee, the Communist Party and the KGB and the top governmental and cultural institutions! What do you see? Above all, you will see rogues from places like Partygrad. From Stalin's time onwards rogues from the provinces were continually capturing the country's high leadership, and this corresponds with the provincial essence of communism itself.

Not long ago the recently retired Secretary of the Central Committee, Mitrofan Lukich Portyankin, who started his brilliant ascent to the very heights of power in Partygrad, gave an explanation of the phenomenon. 'It happens like this,' he said at a triumphal meeting on the occasion of the unveiling of his bronze bust in

Partygrad. 'Because Partygrad lies in the bowels of the people, in the depths of the people, at the centre of the people.'

Mitrofan Lukich said that Party State cadres do not simply grow on trees in Partygrad. Rather, they are *forged* there. So Partygrad was in the first instance the forge of Party/State cadres and only secondarily the milking-machine of the country. The expression 'milking-machine' was invented by Maotsedunka analogously to the way in which certain other oblasts call themselves the bread-bins of the country. According to national accounts, the Partygrad oblast feeds the whole country with milk, while the district of Stavropol does the same with grain. (In actual fact it supplies the milk just as badly as Stavropol supplies the bread.) By the way, the district of Stavropol has begun to change from being the bread-bin into being the forge: for under Gorbachev it is competing most actively with Partygrad in the production of cadres and has even surpassed it.

Partygrad gives the country not only the practitioners but the theorists of government. Here indeed the formula was developed that generalized the experience of people-management throughout the whole period of Soviet power. It was expressed by none other than Pyotr Stepanovich Suslikov, who replaced Mitrofan Lukich in the post of First Secretary of the Partygrad obkom and was, as we have seen, later Secretary of the Central Committee. 'Our greatest achievement', he said in his speech to the Party conference where he was nominated to the Central Committee, 'is not only that we, the Party administrators, have learned to rule our people, but that our people have learned to be ruled by us.' But the rumour was circulating that it was the same Maotsedunka who invented this formulation. She is supposed to have said, downing her tenth glass of vodka, that the most important rule in the business of governing the people was not to prevent the people from being governed by us.

In the same speech to the Party conference Suslikov provided some data regarding the forging of Party cadres in Partygrad. During the period of Soviet power in the Partygrad oblast there were forged 25,346 Party leaders on the regional level, 16,131 on the oblast level, 5,141 on the republican level and 1,797 in the sphere of central government! So in case of communism's victory throughout the world, Suslikov joked, Partygrad oblast alone would be able to provide the whole world with Party cadres. As the same Maotsedunka said after twenty glasses of vodka, to forge Party blatherers is not like growing potatoes and little pigs; in that sort of forging we can outdo absolutely everyone.

These emigrants from Partygrad and places like it in Russia bring to the central power apparatus a determination to defend the conquests of October unbendingly. But they do it in such a way that it looks like progress and like the struggle between young, educated, enterprising 'doves' against very old conservative illiterate 'hawks'. But once they've established themselves in the central apparatus, the provincial doves invariably turn into metropolitan hawks.

SOME HISTORICAL INFORMATION

The most outstanding personalities forged in the Partygrad smithy of cadres were undoubtedly Portyankin and Suslikov.

Portyankin, Mitrofan Lukich: of peasant stock. Education: technical school; courses for young political officers; NKVD school; oblast Party school; correspondence course at the Highest Party School. At the age of twenty-two Party member. During the war political officer to a partisan detachment and commander of the garrison bath unit and delousing detachment. He arranged drunken orgies with loose women for the high military command. The women were signallers, anti-aircraft gunners and nurses. And the orgies occurred in the special bathing department. Brezhnev steamed away more than once in Portyankin's baths. Finished the war with ten decorations and the rank of lieutenant-colonel.

After the war, Party work. Became the First Secretary of the Party obkom. For his successful accomplishment of his task of delivering dairy produce to the State, he was honoured with the title of Hero of Socialist Labour. There was a rumour at the time that he bought up butter in neighbouring oblasts and passed it off as Partygrad produce. They made as if to bring a charge against him but somehow or other someone halted the scandal.

During Portyankin's time there was a great industrial development in the oblast; including the above-mentioned Atom and the country's largest chemical complex. Portyankin himself had nothing whatever to do with these matters, as the construction was on the national scale. But he was always one of the first to receive an award. Brezhnev by then was head of the Party and State. He remembered how he had steamed in Portyankin's baths and took him into the Central Committee, where he became divisional leader, secretary, candidate member and full member of the Politburo. He was regularly elected deputy of the Supreme Soviet of the RSFSR and of the USSR. He was awarded innumerable decorations and medals. For his book *In the Enemy's Rear* he became a Laureate of the State Prize. In connection with the thirtieth anniversary of the victory over Germany, Portyankin became Hero of the Soviet Union for his outstanding services and for his personal heroism during the war.

In the post-Brezhnev years Portyankin failed to reorientate himself in the new situation, and under Chernenko came to look like a conservative. Under Gorbachev he was accused of corruption and bureaucratism and they retired him on a pension. His book became the subject of a satirical article, which ended with the question: who was it that Portyankin called his enemies, if he spent the whole war in Partygrad oblast drinking himself silly?

The oblast wasn't ever occupied by the Germans! After that, Portyankin died of a heart attack and a stroke simultaneously. He was not up to the Novodevichy cemetery. So they buried him in the Donskoi monastery in a graveyard which wasn't at all for big shots.

Suslikov, Pyotr Stepanovich: From a working-class family. Education: technical school of the food industry. Agricultural institute. High Party School. During the war a student. Komsomol activist. Informer to the Organs. Unmasked a group of 'defeatists' among his fellow-students, for which he was awarded a medal 'for daring'. Married Portyankin's daughter. At the age of twenty-four became a member of the CPSU. Engineer. Undertook Party work. Full-time Secretary of the Party committee of the Atom complex. Studied at High Party school. After his studies became the Second Secretary of the gorkom and later obkom of the Party, finally First Secretary of obkom. Made acquaintance of Andropov, who was taking a cure in the oblast. Acquaintanceship and friendship with

Gorbachev. For his reclamation of quagmire was awarded gold star of Hero of Socialist Labour and Order of Lenin. Transferred to the apparatus of the Central Committee of the CPSU. Under Gorbachev, he was nominated Secretary of Central Committee and candidate Member of Politburo. Active supporter of perestroika and 'left hand' of Gorbachev. Regularly nominated to Supreme Soviet of the RSFSR and the USSR. Laureate of the Lenin Prize for his direction of the reclamation of the quagmire-lands.

When they gave Portyankin his second gold star as Hero they erected a bronze bust of him in Partygrad. Next day a four-letter word of three letters appeared on the forehead of the bronze bust. They washed it off, but it appeared again. In the end they gave it up as a bad job and the swear-word was attached eternally to the forehead of Portyankin and everyone got quite used to it and could not have imagined the statue without the swear-word. They say that Suslikov will soon get a second star as Hero. Then they'll erect a bronze bust for him too. And on his bronze forehead somebody will also write the same four-letter word. And the Partygraders will sigh with relief at the sight of this symbol of the unshakeable continuity of their communist way of life.

TYOLKINA, YEVDOKIA TIMOFEYEVNA

After Portyankin and Suslikov came Yevdokia Timofeyevna, who ran the agricultural division of the obkom of the Party, Deputy to Supreme Soviet of USSR and Heroine of Socialist Labour. Formerly called 'Maotsedunka', because of her passion for voluntaristic* methods of administration. Now follower of Bukharin and so nicknamed 'Bukharik', alluding to her ardent love of Bukharin's ideas (which she knew only by hearsay). Known the length and breadth of Russia for her passionate support of the general Party line. Once she was an ardent Brezhnevist. Now she is an even more ardent Gorbachevite. Her perestroika fervour even surpassed Yeltsin's.

* A term designating popular participation in administration which, in Stalin's time, often resulted in the liquidation of bureaucrats via denunciation.

She proposed to disband the collective farms and to switch over all the oblast's enterprises to self-financing; to open Partygrad's frontier to the West; to turn the Party organs into soviets and to rename the Communist Party the 'National Party'.

Among other personalities, is a writer who in Stalin's time praised Stalin and received the Stalin Prize; in Brezhnev's time praised Brezhnev and won the Lenin Prize; and in Gorbachev's time praised Gorbachev and was declared to be a victim of both Stalin's and Brezhnev's terror. Alongside this writer was a painter who achieved world-wide fame. Under Stalin he made a daub of Stalin and won a Stalin Prize. Under Brezhnev he painted Brezhnev and received a Lenin Prize and under Gorbachev painted Gorbachev and was duly declared a victim of both Stalin's and Brezhnev's terror.

Besides the writer and the painter there were a theatre director and a film director who also won world fame. . . .

During perestroika all these people became People's Deputies and members of the raikom, gorkom and obkom Party bureaux. The writer became a member of the Central Committee of the CPSU and a deputy to the Supreme Soviet of the USSR. For this he was elected a member of a whole row of international organizations and received many Western prizes.

KHRUSHCHEV'S PERESTROIKA

The first attempt at a perestroika, it is sometimes forgotten, took place in Khrushchev's time. Khrushchev and his liberal assistants officially recognized the evident and undeniable shortcomings of Soviet society and decided to effect a comprehensive reorganization of the country. This more than a quarter of a century before Gorbachev's 'innovation'. They decided to perfect the work of Soviet enterprises, beginning to transfer many of them to the same 'self-financing' and 'self-supporting' which the Gorbachevites trumpet all over the world as a discovery in Soviet economics. As a direct result, the number of unprofitable enterprises grew and they forgot about the slogan 'self-supporting'. Then they began to talk about 'self-accountancy', which was an abbreviation of the equally senseless 'economic self-support'.* They perfected the working of the management system. They introduced new organs called 'soviets of the people's economy',† and so the bureaucratic apparatus grew too. Then they liquidated them and the bureaucratic apparatus grew once more. They divided, united, recombined and renamed ministries, committees, administrations, trusts and so forth. And the bureaucrats continued to multiply. In those years the Soviet people made a joke, that the ministry of railways had been divided into two: the 'there' ministry and the 'back' ministry.

It was the maize-growing policy of Khrushchev that provoked the most malicious jibes. After he and his assistants, advisers and relatives had visited the United States, Khrushchev decided to catch up the leading capitalist countries and introduce full communism even 'in the life-time of the present generation', with the help of maize. The Partygraders bowed to Moscow's order and sowed a whole field of American maize. What came up made the oblast shake with Homeric laughter.

Khrushchev and his accomplices earned for themselves the derisive name of *Kukuruzniki* or Maizeites. It was in the Khrushchev years too that they hatched the sensational idea that government officials shouldn't sharpen their own pencils because their precious time and creative forces were needed for more important efforts. The authorities printed a million copies of a brochure that had come from an American manager.

Offices were beautified by glasses full of pencils sharpened by their secretaries. They planned a special machine for pencil-sharpening. Of course the thing remained a project. And the Soviet managers, having released their energies from pencil-sharpening, switched them to a yet more powerful bout of corruption and careerist intrigues.

Khrushchev's perestroika ended without bloodshed. His colleagues betrayed their leader in good time and became Brezhnevites. By means of treachery and lackeydom these people took regular steps forward in their own careers. None more successfully than Portyankin, Suslikov and Maotsedunka.

* In Russian, *chozraschot*.

† In Russian, *sovnarchozy*.

THE PERIOD OF STAGNATION

Under Gorbachev people began to call the Brezhnev period of Soviet history 'the period of stagnation'. It never occurred to the Partygraders that their normal life, lived according to the laws of real communism, was itself a deviation from all sound norms and was itself nothing but stagnation. They simply didn't notice the stagnation.

Actually more was done in the oblast in those years than in all the previous ones. The standard of living rose in a way that could never have been dreamed of before or after the war. One separate flat per family became the rule. Each family had its television and refrigerator. Many people got themselves motor bicycles and cars and built country houses. Clothes became better.

Of course this progress stood no sort of comparison to Western affluence. But then the West had not yet become the standard of valuation of Soviet society. Partygraders knew about the defects of their own way of life. But they regarded them as an inevitable evil. They spoke of them, made jokes about them and told stories about them. They made fun of them and of themselves. But they understood that all this was a permanent part of the Soviet scenery and each person tried to screw out of the system as much as he could. Taken together, the aggregate of these 'screwings out' constituted the course of Soviet life. And everyone would still be living like that now if Moscow hadn't cooked up perestroika. The people would never have thought up anything like perestroika; they simply wouldn't have hit upon it because their instinct was, always, to avoid unnecessary and senseless worries. They knew the old wise saying: 'What you've got may well be nothing but a heap of shit, so it's better not to stir it up. If you do, you won't be able to live for the stench.' The people looked on Gorbachev, for the most part, as an idiot who had destroyed this fundamental rule of life.

Now we must return to the city of Partygrad as it was at the moment when the perestroika unleashed by Gorbachev reached it.

Despite the developments and achievements we have described, the Partygrad oblast was still reckoned to be the most provincial part of Russia. By no means everybody in the Soviet Union knew of its existence, let alone those in the West. Soviet people knew that it existed mainly from obituary notices to the effect that such and such a distinguished corpse was a scion of the working class, the working peasantry or indeed the working intelligentsia of the Partygrad oblast.

One of the stories told was this. Brezhnev wanted to get rid of one of his enemies and ordered that he should be put to work in Partygrad, convinced that this place was somewhere in Yakutia, Kamchatka or even Mongolia. Imagine his surprise and anger when, on a visit to Partygrad, he saw this disgraced Party worker standing among the rulers of the oblast.

At first the Partygrad authorities regarded Gorbachev's declared perestroika programme as a routine campaign and just another piece of eyewash. Every new Soviet government had had its perestroika. A little time will pass, so thought the local rulers, and perestroika will come to nothing and everything will then return to normal, as has happened several times before. So we must make every appearance of taking perestroika seriously and make our best efforts to implement it. The Partygrad government therefore seethed with activity: assemblies, conferences, speeches, resolutions, appeals and initiatives. They made changes in the power apparatus, moving people from A to B and back again. They pensioned off those who, even without perestroika, were heading for the graveyard. They unmasked the corruption of those who were already accused of it or had already been put in the camps.

All the same, the whole business did seem much more serious than usual, and so the oblast rulers entered a state of real confusion; because in Partygrad they could find nothing seriously wrong, nothing that could have been worthwhile restructuring. Life in the town and in the oblast in general was simply proceeding in its normal orderly manner and it seemed that there was no force in the world capable of compelling the people to live and work in a new way; that is, faster and more effectively, as Moscow was demanding.

In obkom the local rulers gathered at the first perestroikist conference to work out the open and hidden possibilities of perestroika. It was perfectly clear to all of them that almost no such possibilities existed. Military factories did not lend themselves to perestroika. They were receiving their raw materials steadily. The sale of their products didn't depend on Soviet customers. Productivity and quality depended not so much on the Soviet labour force as on Western technology, on Soviet spies and on those countries that the Soviet Union supplied with arms. The chemical complex, the bacteriological centre and the atomic plant were so ultra-secret that even the head of the oblast's KGB knew nothing about them. As to schools, institutes, hospitals and other institutions, they were working perfectly normally and no radical improvements were needed, a few technical details aside. The same could be said about the transport and mass-information system, as well as the innumerable institutions within the governmental apparatus and the power organs.

However, they were all well aware that they had to obey Moscow's directives in one way or another. Some officials thought feverishly about only one thing: how they would avoid losing their jobs during the perestroika antics. The First Secretary of the obkom of the Party, Zhidkov, sweated blood to set the oblast entrusted to him on the perestroikist path. But his efforts met with boundless obstacles. The obstacles were neither the conservatives nor the bureaucrats, as Gorbachev hypocritically complained or as the Western newspapers sincerely wrote, but the whole population of the oblast itself and everything that organized its life.

The trouble was that everybody immediately became perestroikist in their words. Everyone started to criticize the conservatives and the bureaucrats and to exhort them to 'think and act in a new way'. But when it came to action, absolutely nothing emerged except an ever-deepening confusion, chitter-chatter and eyewash. The oblast's most cunning and cynical careerists and rascals came to the surface. Disorder broke out even in the oblast government. In order not to press the charge of conservatism against the communist order itself, the authorities tried to find scapegoats who could be accused of conservatism, bureaucratism and corruption; and upon whom they could shunt off the blame for the first failures of perestroika. The topmost leadership of the oblast met and debated all night various candidatures for the role of those 'who were a hindrance to our movement which was striving along the road to perestroika'. Weary but content, with agreement reached, 'the commanders of the oblast' dispersed to their villas, flats and dachas.

THE FIRST STEPS

The new epoch in Partygrad began without thunder and lightning. On that day in Partygrad town, as throughout the whole of the country, the usual heroic working life followed its normal course. During working hours the workers scoured the shops in search of consumer goods, buying everything that chanced to be still on sale. In the drinking establishments they were after consolation too, swallowing up everything that poured. But outside working hours their activity was exactly the same, though with redoubled intensity. On that day 80,000 man-hours were lost in the town without good reason; there were 50,000 cases of fights in factories; 2,000 citizens, unconscious from drink, were swept off the streets in carts. There were 8,000 acts of hooliganism and 400 major robberies. There were at least 10 attacks by bandits with either murder or grievous bodily harm, 800 abortions, 2,000 sentences to long or short terms of imprisonment, 20,000 bribes were given and taken, and 10,000 Komsomol or Party speeches delivered. In short, it was a valuable day of Soviet life, full of joy and bitterness, successes and failures, gains and losses.

But when the Partygrad workers finally got their newspapers, which were for some reason late that day, and opened them, they were first amazed and then burst into irrepressible laughter. On the first page of every paper was the speech of none other than Comrade Zhidkov, First Secretary of Partygrad's obkom of the Party. 'In our oblast,' the speaker said, 'deliveries of food have worsened.'

'How could they get worse,' the chortling Partygraders asked each other, 'if they have always been worse than anyone could imagine?' 'In the oblast,' Zhidkov had said further on, 'work discipline has deteriorated.'

'More rubbish.' The Partygraders split their sides with laughter. 'It has always been on a level from which it was impossible to sink.'

Finally, Zhidkov said that drunkenness was increasing in the oblast. At that the Partygraders ceased to be able to laugh. They could only groan their overwhelming internal spasms and swallow the tears that ran down their faces in rivers.

'What on earth are the idiots up there thinking of?' wheezed some of them when the spasms of jollity had slightly abated. 'Drunkenness in the oblast reached its highest peak long ago and then went higher. In so doing it reached a level so high that nobody, however much they might wish it, could ever raise it more. That would be impossible even if all the rocket sites, all the aeroplanes and all the submarines were turned into stills for making hooch, and even if all the grain imported from the West and all the grain produced at home were turned into vodka. Perhaps the alcoholic consumption could be raised a bit by bringing in the dead? For the time being they don't drink, do they? They don't drink because nobody offers them a drink. The country after all hasn't yet got to full communism. It's still only developed socialism here. When full communism comes, the dead will all be given half a litre a day. My God, what a rejoicing there will be then in our overcrowded cemeteries! That's when our old Bolsheviks who were burned in crematoria will be sorry they got stuck on the hook of Marxism!'

At the end of his speech Zhidkov counted all the oblast's plants and institutions which had 'not yet launched themselves seriously into perestroika'. He also gave the names of the 'conservatives' and 'bureaucrats' who were throwing spanners into the wheels of the new Party programme.

But meantime they were deciding in Moscow on the very highest level to appoint somebody or other as enemy of the people in all the localities. Pyotr Stepanovich Suslikov, who had never cared much for Zhidkov, proposed him for that role. Gorbachev was ready to promote his supporter, Krutov, and seconded the candidature of Zhidkov for scapegoat, Krutov to become First Secretary. On the next day *Pravda*'s leading article on the front page enumerated the various regions that 'had not yet engaged themselves seriously in perestroika'. Prominent among them was the Partygrad oblast. Now Zhidkov himself was instanced among the 'conservatives' and 'bureaucrats' who were sticking spanners in the wheels of the Party's new programme. Zhidkov's fate had been decided in advance.

In Partygrad they immediately called a meeting of the bureau of the obkom of the Party. There they subjected Zhidkov himself to fierce criticism. In this Maotsedunka was especially to the fore. (At the last meeting she had upheld Zhidkov most cordially.) The obkom Second Secretary (the one for ideology) said that rumours were being endlessly repeated in the Western press about 'powerful local opposition to the Soviet government's new programme'; and that 'we must fully demonstrate our fidelity to the decisions of the Party Congress and to the personal directives of Comrade Gorbachev'. Zhidkov was carried out of the conference-room to hospital with a massive heart attack; and they didn't take him to the one reserved for the oblast's high personalities either, but to the most run-down one in the whole district.

Next day the newspapers announced that 'Citizen' (no longer Comrade) Zhidkov had been removed from his post for conservatism, bureaucratism, the suppression of criticism, corruption, moral disintegration, dismissed from the Party and handed over to the judicial authorities. On the wall, which the day before had been adorned by a touched-up portrait of Zhidkov, there now hung a caricature of the same man sticking spokes into the wheels of Gorbachev's perestroika.

REVOLUTION FROM ABOVE

According to Marxist-Leninist teaching, a social revolution is a jumplike break or overturn in society's development and as such is quite different from the gradual or evolutionary process. Revolution occurs when the lower classes of the population (the masses of the people) no longer wish to live in the old way, while the higher or ruling classes can no longer govern in the old way. Soviet intellectuals who have lost their faith in Marxism-Leninism (if they ever had it) have a shorter and more salacious version. Revolution, they say, occurs when the bottom no longer wants and the top no longer can. It is the masses of the people, then, who bring revolutions about, led by revolutionaries. The latter chuck out the former rulers, take their place and conduct the transformation of society.

However, recent Soviet history has introduced a substantial amendment to this Marxist-Leninist theory of revolution: it discovered a new form of revolution which doesn't correspond with the description adduced above, namely revolution from above. Or rather the Western mass media discovered this form of revolution. It was discovered by people without the slightest notion of Marxist-Leninist teaching about revolution and with even foggier conceptions of what was really going on in the Soviet Union, which they called 'revolution from above'. But when the West talked of 'revolution from above', the Soviet leaders up at the top with Gorbachev found this appreciation of their own reforming flimflam so much to their liking that they call it a revolution too.

Gorbachev's revolution differs from Lenin's one in 1917 in this matter of tops and bottoms. This time the situation is that the tops don't want to govern in the old way, while the bottoms no longer wish to live in a new one. The dirty-minded intellectuals formulated it like this: those on top no longer want; those underneath no longer can. The high leadership of the country conducts this sort of revolution at the head of the masses of people and compels them to transform society. The leaders kick the conservative rulers out of their jobs and put their own supporters in instead. If this type of revolution is to be called 'revolution from above', then Lenin's type must be called 'revolution from below'.

The news that Moscow had decided to regard perestroika as a revolution from above arrived at Partygrad in the middle of the night. It reached the editor of *Partgradskaya Pravda*. The editor got in touch immediately with Krutov's assistant, who at once rushed off to Krutov himself and got him out of bed. At the word 'revolution' Krutov went into a state of panic. Right from his school bench he knew that revolution meant the dethronement from power and the expropriation of the privileged classes. And Krutov certainly had something of which to be expropriated; indeed, rather more than the Governor-General of Partygrad province had before the 1917 revolution.

But when his assistant told him that the talk was about a revolution of a new type, he calmed down a bit. And he put himself at the head of the Partygrad revolution. At the extraordinary meeting of the obkom of the Party he said there was nothing terrible about this revolution, which was simply the next stage of perestroika. But they, the Party, had to do some work to clear up the workers' minds. Otherwise, when they heard about the revolution they would buy up all the soap, salt, matches, cotton goods and other things of general use; they would start to bury their valuables and some would try to run away abroad. Looting and violence could begin. . . .

And so obkom set about clarifying. But the effect was the opposite of what they wished. Everything they wanted to avoid happened and at twice the strength.

KATASTROIKA

The authorities raised the price of booze and limited its sale. The already empty shops were emptied. Queues lengthened. Prices soared in the market. At home, in queues, in buses, at work, at meetings, the people openly abused perestroika. They told endless jokes. Somebody thought that the translation of the word *perestroika* in Greek was *katastrophe*, and so the new word *katastroika* was coined.

Retired people and old Party members regarded perestroika as counter-revolution and a betrayal of Lenin's work. The glasnost campaign developed into a debunking of all communism's ideals. The appearance of 'unofficial' groups, considered earlier to be the result of the pernicious influence of the West and then prosecuted as such, caused indignation in the average man. And when the authorities began to dismiss senior government workers and close certain institutions and plant as unprofitable, as a manifestation of the struggle with bureaucratism and in order to raise productivity, panic broke out in the oblast.

At the extraordinary meeting of the obkom of the Party the leaders of the oblast reported on the real situation and asked Krutov to tell Moscow the whole truth in order to avoid a catastrophe. But Krutov was afraid that in exchange for this 'whole truth' they would sack him from his position as a conservative and 'opponent of perestroika'. So he fidgeted and fiddled and called for calm and for 'a creative approach to the process of the revolutionary transformation of society'. As an experienced Party worker, he knew that the main thing in these situations is to be patient and wait until 'everything sorts itself out'.

The Partygraders would find their alcohol somehow, even if they had to root in the earth for it. The sacked bureaucrats would be reabsorbed and find a new nest. The unprofitable factories that had been closed would reopen under another name. People were used to food shortages and had survived much harder times before. The young people would get this out of their system and then calm down. After all, you cannot live on rock music and chewing-gum alone. One has to be educated, get a job, make a career, improve one's living conditions: in short, one has to live by the laws of real life and not by temporary slogans.

DRUNKENNESS AND COMMUNISM

In Partygrad, as everywhere else, perestroika began with the struggle against drunkenness. The fight against drunkenness began on the very first day after the 1917 revolution. Some historians even hold that it began before October. There is even evidence that

Lenin sent a telegram on the subject to the revolutionary staff in Petrograd on the day before the revolution broke out when he was hiding from the agents of the provisional government in the Gulf of Finland. In the telegram he more or less asked the Petrograd proletariat to cut down temporarily on drink in case they should sleep through the revolution or do it the wrong way round. But Stalin apparently hid the telegram, saying that if the proletariat stopped drinking, they could all say goodbye to socialism.

Towards the end of Stalin's time drunkenness in Russia was on such a scale that it became a threat to the very social order it had helped establish. The Party then began by degrees to develop its line about the restriction on drunkenness. However, the venerable working-class drunkards stuck to their guns. After all, over many decades they had won the right to unrestrained drunkenness. And their ranks steadily increased.

Even during the years when Pyotr Stepanovich Suslikov was head of the oblast he used regularly to sit on the terrace of his dacha with his friend Gorban. They would drink vodka, nibble caviare, sturgeon and other good things from the privileged food-shops while they held an unhurried conversation about matters of State.

'But Grigory Yakovlevich, you know our workers will drown communism in drink if we don't do something about it. The day will come when you won't meet a single sober worker in working hours in our factories. Think of the fights and the damage! And the stoppages! And the theft! And the hooliganism! Strictly speaking, the whole lot of them should be prosecuted, the bastards.'

'I know, Pyotr Stepanovich, I know! But what can one do? The people are a force – you won't get rid of it with a few pep talks. Prison? You can't gaol everyone. Our people haven't yet arrived at a state of communist consciousness. Look at you and me! Here we are. We're drinking, but we don't lose our heads. The main thing is to drink in moderation and have a bite with it. After work, of course. What do *they* do? They drink without eating anything. And the swine drink at work, dammit!

'I think our scientists should invent a vodka which retains all the positive qualities of our vodka but eliminates the negative ones.'

'Our people wouldn't drink vodka like that. What sort of vodka would it be which didn't upset your stomach and didn't break your head to bits and didn't make you want to hit somebody?'

'You're right. But we've got to do something. The people are going down, they're drinking themselves to perdition. Anyway, here's to the sober life!'

Pyotr Stepanovich and Grigory Yakovlevich clinked glasses, emptied them, took pot luck with the eats and parted, both pleased that they had done their duty to Party and people.

SOBRIETY IS A NORM OF LIFE

Gorbachev's campaign against drunkenness went further than any other of its kind in Soviet history. The authorities adorned the roofs of Partygrad with slogans such as *Sobriety is the norm of our life; Sobriety is our weapon; Build communism on a sober head.* They decorated the shop windows with placards showing the dismal consequences of drunkenness. What made a specially strong impression was the graphic rendering of an alcoholic's liver. On that day the workers drank twice as much alcohol as usual. Thousands of boys and girls joined the drunkards' ranks. In three days the police detained more than 5,000 citizens who had been drunk during working hours. The militia searched 15,000 homes and confiscated 20,000 stills for making hooch. This showed that in some families husband and wife each had a separate still. In the most intelligent families the children apparently had their own little stills. The town's leading drunks appeared on television and appealed to the workers to drink water only.

But there was no decline in drunkenness. And crime increased steeply in line with the prohibitions of drunkenness and with the drunkenness in the teeth of the prohibitions. That year three times as many people were tried in court for small embezzlements made in order to get drunk as had been charged at the start of the campaign. The number of poisonings from stupefying toxic liquids rose too. But the thing that distressed drinkers and non-drinkers the most was that the price rise in vodka had struck a blow against the special kind of culture that was based on the old prices: a blow from which that culture could not recover. A half-litre of vodka cost three roubles. The drunks would fork out a rouble each and buy half a litre. That gave rise to the expression 'make up a threesome' and the custom of going round in threes. On the basis of this sort of clean arithmetic there were many jokes and stories. Here are two of them.

Question: 'How can you divide eight hundred by three and have nothing left over?' *Answer:* 'Three hundred grams of vodka divided by three leaves nothing over; and any drunkard will divide the remaining half-litre into three parts for you without leaving anything over.' Three American spies were dropped into Russia by parachute. One of them buried his parachute in a wood. All OK; no KGB about. He went into a village. Two men came up to him and said: 'Here's our third'! And the spy confessed.

But drunkenness in its whole cultural aspect didn't wither on the vine, so to speak. The great Russian people's talent found a new sphere of application: the invention of new ways of becoming stupefied. They began to make preparations of toothpaste, of carpenter's glue, of washing-powder and even of old gramophone records. So people would say: 'We're off, let's knock back some Shalyapin.' Or: 'Yesterday we tried to finish off that Sobinov.' And people began to use new specifically perestroikist expressions such as 'perestroik your ugly mug', 'I'll give you glasnost' or 'talking Gorbacrap'.

THE STRUGGLE AGAINST BUREAUCRATISM

The campaign second in significance after the anti-alcoholic one was the campaign against bureaucratism. And it was senseless and fruitless at first.

The anti-bureau campaign began immediately after the 1917 revolution. A special organ was created for it called the Workers' and Peasants' Inspectorate: WPI for short. Stalin was at the head of it. But the fiercer the struggle became, the stronger was the growth of the State bureaucratic apparatus. This wasn't a deviation from certain healthy norms. On the contrary it was the natural result of the new social order itself.

Partygrad was no exception from the general rule. There, too, the battle was waged against bureaucratism. As in other places it enabled some people in the power system to crush others and take their place. It was a struggle within the bureaucratic apparatus which only from the outside seemed to take the form of a struggle against it. Scapegoats were found. Their punishment, often more imaginary than real, gave the impression of serious policy.

This time the scapegoats were chosen from among the 'mafia' of Zhidkov. In public they were accused of every mortal sin, including bureaucratism. It emerged that it was their fault that there was a shortage of consumption goods in the oblast. All the faults in housing, transport, schools and hospitals fell upon them too. The authorities lumped the blame on them even for things with which they had no connection, such as the catastrophe in Atom, the droughts and the rains.

Changes took place in the staff of oblast government. They changed the three secretaries of obkom, gorkom* and raikom. They changed the chairmen of the soviets. In the whole bag of tricks they changed more than two hundred officials. Some they retired. Yet the majority of them stayed on all the same in the power apparatus in some capacity or other. Naturally *all* of them became perestroikists and critics of the period of stagnation.

THE CRISIS IN GOVERNMENT

However, the general crisis in the Soviet power and government system did grip the government of Partygrad. Krutov was thirsting to please Moscow in order to retain his post. But he saw that Moscow was split. In his instructions from Suslikov and his discussions with him, he felt all the time that everything had a double meaning. They were asking him to pursue perestroika ever more energetically, but at the same time they were hinting that he shouldn't exert himself especially, that he should, as a communist, keep the experienced cadres intact and should not forget to edu-

* Party HQ for the city.

cate the population in the spirit required. Krutov found a way out of the quandary by involving himself less and less in the workings of those parts of the system that were already under somebody's control, and in the institutions and factories that were similarly under control. Potyomkin villages,* against which a determined war had been declared by the Centre, took new and more refined forms. The villages seemed to have become genuine, but in fact the deceptions had even deepened. And something similar happened on all levels: in the towns, in the districts, in individual enterprises and institutions, in the smaller collectives and in the behaviour of individual citizens. Instead of the perestroika declared on high there was at the lower levels only an imitation of it. It was a grandiose imitation all right: so grandiose that many people took it for the real thing.

The interesting point was that the crisis in the power and government apparatus took place despite the fact that the representatives and heads of the various subsections of the apparatus constituted a mafia on the personal level; one closely welded together by collective guarantee and mutual assistance.

The formation of the mafias had even helped to bring about the crisis in the apparatus. If the First Secretary of the Party obkom drinks in the same gathering with the Chairman of the oblast soviet, that does not mean that the system of administration forms a harmonious whole. When they part, these people act independently of one another; and their familiar relationships and shadowy joint deals give them greater reason for ignoring one another.

The Partygrad governing apparatus met with a hazy resistance from the broad strata of the population over the reforms thrust upon them from above. The apparatus had known all along that these reforms could not be realized in the way that Gorbachev and his colleagues wanted. So the Partygrad bosses began deliberately to make an imitation perestroika look as much like the real thing as possible.

The frontiers of the permissible had gone, so that when the bosses started to imitate perestroika's positive intentions, they caused a real crisis in the oblast. People came to believe not so

* An historical term for 'eyewash'.

much that the reformed society would lift itself up to a higher level as that the stupidity of the leadership would cause society to fall to the very lowest level. It was as if the crisis had been unleashed gratuitously by the central power into Partygrad and had never risen spontaneously from the oblast's own life. Partygrad was gradually being dragged into a crisis which had somehow arisen in Moscow from routine discussions about reforms.

GLASNOST

The age of glasnost began earlier in Partygrad than in Moscow. Strictly speaking, Moscow made its first experiment with glasnost in Partygrad. And it was only when the Centre had convinced itself of the use of glasnost that the high leadership decided to introduce it right through the country.

It all seems to have started with a perfectly ordinary event. A new block of flats in Robespierre Street blew up because of some fault in the gas supply. The explosion was tremendous. It was heard all over the town. The whole population ran to look at the damage, including invalids without any legs and drunkards who happened to be lying around at the time.

It was rumoured that five hundred had perished in the explosion. Rumour and gossip lovers multiplied the casualties by two and then by three. A few dissidents would have rushed off to Moscow to communicate the information to Western journalists, but they were caught on the way to the station.

The rulers of the oblast met in extraordinary session at the Party obkom. Krutov made a personal call to Suslikov, who advised him to cut off the lying rumours. Krutov interpreted that as advice to publicize the facts and make capital out of them. This he did. The authorities printed the information, reducing the number of casualties and casting the blame on the bureaucrats of the previous administration. Because the number of dead seemed immense even after the figure was heavily reduced, the West interpreted the information as the beginning of glasnost.

An absolute hurricane of glasnost blew into Partygrad about the unmasking of drug addicts, prostitution and homosexuality. Although there weren't any drug addicts in the oblast, the campaign against them went to such extremes that even Moscow was envious. The authorities had to bring in some drugs from Central Asia to teach their 'unstable elements' to use them. There were demonstration trials of 'dealers in death'. More than five hundred people were condemned to long terms of imprisonment in strict-regime camps. But when it came to prophylactics against drug addiction, the official policy came unstuck. The Partygraders who had become hooked on drugs no longer wished to stop taking them. And then the *real* dealers in death came on the scene, against whom the militia and the KGB were powerless.

Until perestroika, prostitution didn't exist in Partygrad either. This is not to say that chastity and continence in sexual relations flourished in the city. Quite the reverse. What did flourish there and throughout the rest of the country was promiscuity, and in its most primitive forms. There was no prostitution in the sense that there were no women earning their livelihood by selling their bodies. The Partygraders used their sexual capabilities to get what they wanted, but this was not prostitution in the strict sense. All this fitted in with communist morality.

When the glasnost era started, the authorities began to publish 'unmasking' material about all sorts of hidden vices. It was then that a journalist from *Partgradskaya Pravda* hunted out two old whores who spent their time with drunken invalids (of which Partygrad was full) or with soldiers. The journalist treated the old bags to real vodka and extracted confessions from them. So a feature appeared in the newspaper which shook Partygraders and provoked a mass of letters to the national press. After that a sizeable number of young girls decided to become prostitutes and these, according to the newspapers, earn more than professors, engineers, stewardesses and even pilots of aeroplanes.

A whole series of Partygrad enterprises switched to self-financing. They were given a freedom of operation unheard of until then. The automobile factory was the front-runner in economic perestroika. The factory managers became quickly involved in foreign orders and trips to the West. They wished to get hold of new technology and to find markets to place their goods. The trips were successful. The managers returned weighed down with foreign goods such as computers, videos and other gadgets, which they then sold almost legally for crazy sums of money. And this not counting the cars from foreign firms which had made profitable contacts with the Soviet enterprises, bypassing the authorities.

The factory managers were especially proud that they'd bought an ultra-modern assembly belt. They didn't buy it (the price was symbolic) so much as receive it as a gift, in gratitude because the Soviet government had agreed to accept from this Western country an interest-free loan with no date attached. Western technicians installed the assembly belt themselves. Knowing full well that the Russian botchers and slackers would let through defective parts, they set up a robot on the assembly belt whose function it was to pick up the faulty parts and throw them off the belt as rejects.

The assembly belt was set triumphantly in motion. Suslikov's assistant, Corytov, flew from Moscow for the ceremony with a whole crowd of Western and Soviet journalists. The foreign technicians demonstrated the assembly belt using the components they'd brought from the West. The effect was overwhelming. The economists calculated that the productivity of the factory would increase by more than five times; and that the factory's net economic profit would equal that of the world's leading automobile factories. In addition, five thousand workers would be 'released' from the factory, to go to Siberia or to the north of the country. The rulers of the oblast reported to Moscow that a Gorbachevite economic reform had been successfully realized.

But the components that had been made in the West were one thing and the domestic ones another. The triumph was over and the public sensation over the assembly belt faded while the sensational debate in the Supreme Soviet took over the limelight. The foreign technicians had gone home. Soviet-made components were allowed on to the belt. And then something happened which they'd tried not to think about earlier. The robot started to grab one Russian part after another and throw it off the belt on to a heap of rejects. Panic in the factory. The management went into extraordinary session. What was to be done? The robot wasn't a person. You couldn't get it drunk with vodka; you couldn't suborn it with bribes or prizes; you couldn't pick holes in it at a Party meeting. You couldn't sack it. Who knows how this story would have ended if the engineers hadn't jokingly turned to a drunken worker who was passing by and asked him to lend a hand? The man didn't say a word. All he did was produce a dirty piece of rope and tie up the robot's hand so that the robot continued its grabbing movement but at the same time left the rejects on the conveyor belt. And the belt was working at full power. So the problem was solved. The motor cars were of course defective. But that wasn't the point. The main thing was that the productivity of the factory had risen to Western levels.

The engineers were rewarded for their good work. They duly sacked the workman for being drunk during working hours and sent him out of town to Atom. They tried to replace the cord with a metal chain, but that didn't work. They had to return to the old cord, and hire the drunkard again. For some mysterious reason the robot obeyed only the cord with which the drunkard tied it up. The country's best scientific brains couldn't solve this riddle. The USSR Academy of Sciences proposed that the robot should be reorientated so that it would throw out the *good* components. This was a reasonable idea. But they didn't dare take the risk. In the end the defective motor cars produced in Partygrad were eagerly snapped up for a song by an Italian firm that specialized in the recycling of old cars.

The factory that made, among other things, artificial limbs, followed the example of the motor factory. It decided to start producing miniature automobiles. They were to be invalid carriages, but at the same time the vehicles could be used by non-invalids too. They decided to buy the little motors for the little automobiles in a German factory for children's toys. The wheels would come from a Japanese factory for children's bicycles. An Italian firm offered to supply the bodies, using the rejects from the Partygrad motor factory. And once again scores of workers from the factory, together with men from the KGB and the GRU, trundled off abroad with empty trunks, hoping to fill them with objects of Western comfort.

Very quickly all the Partygrad enterprises were included in the accelerated development of the economy on the basis of free enterprise and self-financing. There was a joke about this in the town. To the question 'How is accelerated development different from ordinary development?' a Partygrader replied: 'In the same way that diarrhoea differs from ordinary defecation. It's the same old shit, but speeded up.'

A PARTYGRAD CHAADAYEV

Krutov lived in perpetual fear that glasnost would dig up the dark secrets of perestroika, and that he would become the butt of the liberated press. So he was ready to petition for retirement on grounds of health. But his assistant, who had been Zhidkov's assistant before, advised him not to take such a rash step.

'Sidor Yegorovich, if you ask for retirement, they'll immediately stamp you a conservative and pin all the sins of perestroika on you. I'll take you along to see a man I know. This man has a small position. He is only the manager of a vegetable depot. On the other hand he has a good head on him. One could say he was a genius. In the West he would probably have been a financial bigwig or company chairman. But in our Russia he has had to stay stuck in a lousy vegetable depot, which didn't even have any vegetables. In a word, like Chaadayev.'

'And who was Chaadayev?' asked Krutov.

'A friend of Pushkin. He was close to the Decembrists. He wrote letters about the situation in Russia. Because of that they declared him to be mad.'

'In short, he was a dissident. Well, now they're rehabilitating the dissidents. Dissidents are doing useful work. OK, show me your own Chaadayev.'

Thus came about the meeting between Krutov and the Partygrad Chaadayev; the man called Grobyka, who was manager of the big vegetable depot.

The meeting took place in Grobyka's suburban villa. From the outside, the villa looked like an ordinary dacha of an ordinary Soviet rascal of middle rank. But when he got inside it Krutov understood that he, the first person in the oblast, was simply a pauper in comparison with Grobyka. After a dinner that impressed Krutov by its truly imperial abundance, they went into their host's study.

'So this is the library,' exclaimed Krutov, when he saw the huge number of books.

'Yes, I've been collecting all my life,' said Grobyka with pride. 'Now the books are priceless. If they were sold on the black market, one could cover the whole of the oblast's financial needs. Only one shouldn't do that.'

'But why not? If you did that we would award you with an order and sing your praises in the newspapers.'

'I don't need honours. I'm not vain. And I'm not greedy. That isn't the problem. Difficulties never stopped anybody from living. Once you get rid of your difficulties, new ones appear which are even heavier. So it's best to live with the old ones one is accustomed to.'

After a few hints the conversation went on to economic reform and the position of the oblast in general.

'You, Sidor Yegorovich, are not in your first year of administrative work,' said Grobyka. 'It's not for me to teach you. This reforming business isn't hitting us for the first time. And what of the result? Well, this time the result will be the same. And what's the snag?'

'Well, *what's* the snag in your opinion?'

'Well, it's this. That our leaders and theorists do not keep in mind the specifics of our social order. Look at my depot! From its very beginning it's been self-financing. As a matter of fact it finances someone else too.'

Grobyka didn't specify whom. But Krutov himself knew that all the rulers of the oblast used the services of economic geniuses like Grobyka while pretending they knew nothing of them.

'In Stavropol, where Mikhail Sergeyevich himself was in charge for many years, they produced five times more vegetables than we did. But they were feeling the deficit even then. We didn't *have* a deficit. And now we're managing somehow. How do we do that?'

'Indeed, how *do* you manage?'

'Instead of vegetables, put me in charge of automobiles, computers, boots or novels. After six months I'll have sorted them out so well that Moscow will be baying with pride. Agreed, the boots and the novels will be bad by Western standards. But what of it? Actually they don't matter to our country. Nothing special will happen if a novel is boring or a car breaks down every kilometre.'

'Well, where does the secret lie?'

'We need order and confidence. People must think that they've either got, or can get, everything. In Stavropol and Moscow they think that there aren't any potatoes or cabbages. So they shout about it and everyone suffers and looks at the West. They remember that under the tsars there *were* enough cabbages and potatoes. Among us in Partygrad people think: Thank God we've still got some. And they keep quiet.'

'What, do you think we should turn the screws on them again?'

'Forget about screws! I'm not against perestroika. But how should one understand it? If we follow the newspapers, the thing has failed already. The first thing, Sidor Yegorovich, is to stop reading the newspapers. Let your assistants read them. That's their job. But yours is to rule. And tell the Moscow government to clear off and the Moscow blatherers too. Spit on the whole lot of them!'

'How am I to do that?'

'Like this. Shout: "To hell with all of you and everything!"'

'For that they would be after me . . .'

'Not at all. It wouldn't cost you a thing. They would think more highly of you. They would come to you with orders. But you would say: "Bugger your orders!" Then they would come back with reprimands. "Bugger your reprimands!" you'd say. Then they'd start scolding you. But you'd stick to your guns. To hell with them!' Then immediately you'd feel that things were coming right and gradually everything would settle down.

'And, by the way, I never go near my own base or to the collective farms which supply me with vegetables. Nor in the markets either. Never! Everything works of its own accord. The main thing is not to prevent anything happening in the way it can and wants to happen. If something doesn't come about, no amount of forcing will compel it to happen as you want it to.'

The longer Grobyka spoke, the happier and more peaceful became Comrade Krutov's soul. In it there arose hope for the success of the reforms and of perestroika in general. And when the Partygrad Chaadayev hinted about the possibility of furnishing Krutov's dacha with foreign furniture, hope became confidence.

'Your Chaadayev has certainly a good head on him,' said Krutov to his assistant after the meeting. 'But how about moving him to an administrative job?'

'He wouldn't go,' answered the assistant. 'Why should he, if he's ruling the oblast already?'

THE RUSSIAN ECONOMIC MIRACLE

Strangely enough there wasn't any of Lenin's New Economic Policy in Partygrad. As soon as the private traders managed to get going, they were put in prison.

But after NEP was over, some activity did start in the private sector. This happened on the private plots of the collective farmers and in the dacha gardens of the town-dwellers where fruit and vegetables were grown and sold in the 'collective farm markets' in the town. Also there were private tailors, cobblers, doctors and coaches for exams. All the time under Stalin and his successors illegal private enterprise sprang up on a fairly large scale.

From time to time the entrepreneurs were unmasked and put in prison. For quite a few years a factory flourished in Partygrad that produced 'foreign goods' such as ladies' blouses, jeans, shoes and handbags. Of course all these things were made in Partygrad, but the makers stuck foreign labels on them and sold them for large sums on the black market.

The authorities turned a blind eye to this because they took bribes from the rogues which far surpassed their salaries. The former First Secretary of the Partygrad obkom, Zhidkov, himself protected the operations of the rascals. His wife actually became the head of the oblast's conspiratorial mafias. Besides the factory we've mentioned there flourished an illegal 'rest-home', which was in fact a brothel for the privileged classes. Everyone in the town knew about the existence of such gangs and wrote letters to the newspapers in Moscow, to the KGB and the Central Committee of the CPSU. But to no avail, because Zhidkov was an old friend of Brezhnev himself. It was only when the regime changed that the authorities unmasked and arrested the whole band of 'illegals'.

Gorbachev's plans to start a 'New Economic Policy' – that is, to spread private enterprise – put the Partygraders in a difficult position. Those who were capable of carrying through these new instructions from Moscow with a will and with success were all in prison. And for the time being there was nobody who wanted to follow their example except a few rascals. For nobody believed that the new instructions were intended seriously. From their own experience they knew that to be a 'private entrepreneur' in Soviet conditions meant to be a swindler. And the orders from above had only to change (and they *would* soon change) for all the 'privates' to be unmasked and sent to prison.

In order to please Moscow the Partygrad authorities decided to give some of the former private traders and speculators early release from prison. In particular, they let out the organizer of the underground garment factory that had made 'American' jeans. Innumerable small workshops for repairing domestic utensils, shoes, clothes, watches, now turned themselves into 'private enterprises'. In addition, they opened a private restaurant and private dental and homoeopathic clinics.

The workshops had always been centres of crime. They brought in a derisory revenue to the State, while those who worked in them made a mint of money. So they were regularly unmasked and put in prison. Then new honest cadres would be put in to 'clean them up'. But after a few months they would turn into out-and-out crooks too.

When the authorities turned these workshops into private enterprise their idea was that the 'private traders' wouldn't steal any more than government servants did and that they would be better swindlers. For a while it seemed that the calculation was going to prove right. But very soon the power organs were inundated with the population's complaints. The 'privates' were the greater thieves and did their job not a whit better than their predecessors.

Nor were things any better in the 'private sector' on the collective farm market. The KGB arrested one old woman who had been clever enough to sell on the market from her own personal plot more vegetables, meat and dairy products than four collective farms employing over two hundred people. The local progressive economists, who were now granted a hitherto unheard-of freedom of expression, wrote a whole heap of articles in the newspapers about the value of a 'reasonable approach to private initiative'. They wanted to make the high-producing old woman into a Heroine of Socialist Labour, but the obkom Party Secretary had ideological doubts about whether private enterprise could be counted as socialist.

Moscow was consulted. The avant-garde of Muscovite official thinkers explained that, in certain circumstances, private enterprise could be considered to be socialist if it served the cause of socialism. So the high-producing old woman would have become a Heroine of Socialist Labour if members of a gang of crooks who had been channelling collective farm meat, vegetables and dairy products through her hadn't quarrelled and denounced each otner to the KGB. The KGB arrested both the old woman and the crooks, who were all chairmen of collective farms. The arrests frightened other private dealers, who at once suspended their dealings.

Comrade Krutov had a discussion with Moscow and proposed to the oblast government to free the old woman for the time being and to conduct a propaganda campaign throughout the villages. The idea was to persuade the peasants that they could safely bring their own products to the town markets.

But what brought the oblast most fame, and most worry, was the activity of two private enterprises: the workshop for metalware and the private lavatory. The last was a Soviet-German joint venture.

The private workshop for metallurgical goods (nails, screws, nuts, drawing-pins, paper-clips, hinges, doorknobs, locks and so forth) developed, literally in the course of a few weeks, such economic efficiency that it beat the highest world indicators, including the Japanese ones. As head of the workshop they appointed an old Party member, the previous director of a section of a mechanical engineering factory. In Partygrad they spoke of the 'Russian Economic Miracle', putting it alongside the Japanese and German ones. An article with this title even appeared in the

Muscovite press and in *Kommunist*. The country's leading economists, including Gorbachev's closest adviser, Academician Crackpot, wrote comprehensive works with extremely ingenious explanations of this economic phenomenon.

What happened to this private workshop in Partygrad had a great deal to do with the decision of the highest leadership to switch enterprises over to self-financing or self-support because the workshop not only supported itself but enabled the successful self-financing of a whole series of other enterprises in the town, including the mechanical engineering factory which we previously mentioned.

The private lavatory was an even greater success. The former director of the main food shop was in charge of it. Five years ago he had been condemned to ten years in a strict regime camp for major theft. But he had been let out early for 'exemplary conduct in the place where he had served his sentence'. He was even given back his Party membership without loss of seniority. The toilet was the most exemplary enterprise in the town. A lighthouse of perestroika in the highest sense of the term. In its financial return the toilet surpassed the workshop for metalware and was ranked among the town's most important enterprises. But the main thing was that the toilet was in direct contact with West German firms which had provided it with equipment of top world class, as well as toilet-paper and various kinds of cosmetics and bathroom accessories.

They wrote in the newspapers that toilets of the Partygrad private kind could be seen only in the world's best hotels and in millionaires' villas; that even Prince Charles and Lady Diana's lavatory and bidet were not as good as the Partygrad one.

In front of the toilet a private shop opened where one could buy toilet accessories of the highest world standard. Besides that they opened yet another private enterprise. There they taught the citizens how to use correctly the achievements of toilet civilization. There was a private infirmary dispensing even more exciting medicines, and also something which everybody knew about but did not mention for fear of being accused of conservatism.

When the information reached Partygrad (not a rumour, but actual information) about cases of Aids in Moscow, the toilet enterprise bought a hundred million contraceptives in West Germany at a knock-down price. The Germans were about to throw them on to the rubbish heap as old stock. The Partygraders didn't use the contraceptives. As the newspapers said, Russians hadn't yet reached that level; as a result of Stalin's terror and the years of stagnation, they had lagged behind the West. But they eagerly bought up the contraceptives. Given the inflation of the rouble, the contraceptives circulated in Russia as hard currency along with dollars, Deutschmarks and the Bible. 'If perestroika goes on for another two years,' remarked the head of the toilet enterprise, taking draughts of Bavarian beer, 'we'll take over the whole economy of the oblast. And then, with God's grace, we'll get rid of Soviet power. In the obkom I'm in touch with people who'll back me over this. We'll bring in the parliamentary system. We'll put in Sakharov as President and Yeltsin as Prime Minister.'

'What use are parliaments to us?' exclaimed his wife. 'We Russians aren't educated enough to be parliamentarians. It would be better to introduce monarchy. The papers say they've found the Tsar's bones. It seems as if one of them survived. They're up to something there!'

'A good idea! But whom will we make Tsar?'

'Solzhenitsyn, of course. Who else?'

'Then that's decided. We'll hang his portrait tomorrow above every standing and sitting point in the public lavatories. We'll found a committee to arrange his return to the Motherland. We'll put you at the head of that.'

'Vanya, I want to be a People's Deputy.' 'OK. Fine! We'll put your name forward. We'll put pressure on Chancellor Kohl and Genscher. They'll see to it.'

THE GOVERNMENT'S WORRIES

A triumphant article appeared in *Partgradskaya Pravda* about the 'Russian Economic Miracle'. After that the KGB and the militia engaged in a serious study of the secret of this 'miracle'. Gorban met Krutov and they had the following conversation.

'The situation in the private sector', said Gorban, 'is not only criminal, but super-criminal. The value of its production is as much as that of the WMG* for half a year.'

'Aha! More than came from the automobile factory.'

'Yes. And look, one thousand men work in the factory and only fifty in the workshop. Take a sheet of paper and do a bit of division if you haven't forgotten your arithmetic. And if you have, ask your grandson. He'll do the sum for you in a flash.'

'Alas, he won't be able to. In Russia, as in the West, even professors of mathematics don't know their multiplication tables.'

'Well, you see what's happening? This WMG should be supplying the whole oblast with nails, an avalanche of nails. But where are they? You try to find them in the shops!'

'Where?'

'Where, my arse! These swindlers followed the Moscow directive and found their own retail market for their production. They're selling them to people who are building themselves private dachas, and moreover at prices ten times higher than the State price. The swine are selling them even in the Baltic and the Caucasus. What can be done? I must inform Moscow about all this.'

'Wait a minute. Don't rush things. In Moscow they're looking at all this in a different way. Perhaps we'll be able to slow everything down.'

'I don't agree with you. Do you know how many letters and denunciations we've got already? Our people have nothing to eat, but they're quite happy as long as they can send complaints. The swine even write to Moscow. But the workshop isn't such a disaster. Worse is the matter of the toilet company. I can tell you, my friend, we aren't going to escape bad publicity in the Moscow press. We've got glasnost now, and if they smell something they'll tune in to us. The whole country will be in stitches. In the private toilet there are only four sit-down lavatories and seven stand-up *pissoirs*. Now these are the accounts audited by the government: the *pissoir* without soap charges fifty kopeks. With soap, a rouble. With comb and use of a mirror, two roubles. The sit-down lavatory without paper costs a rouble. With paper, two roubles. In order that the toilet, even at these fleecing prices, should produce a revenue like that, it would mean that the whole of Partygrad would have to occupy the sit-downs for a second and the stand-

* Workshop for Metal Goods.

ups for two seconds. But according to the reports of the KGB, the toilet stays empty. Nobody uses it except the relatives and friends of the 'privates', and they don't pay a thing. Well, tell me where all the income came from. Tell me that, for God's sake!'

'Well, I'll tell you.' And Gorban painted Krutov a picture of organized crime on an international scale such as he had heard of only from his son who read Western books and listened to Western radio stations. In Krutov's consciousness the word combination 'capital punishment' was surfacing, of which he had spoken not long ago in connection with the affairs of his predecessors. But then he remembered his conversation with Grobyka.

'We won't act in the heat of the moment or get into a state of panic. These people are doing a useful job. It's well worthwhile giving them a talking to.'

So Krutov and Gorban had their talk with the private entrepreneurs. From the workshop they each received a gold cigar-case and a necklace for their spouses. The private toilet company gave them the very latest West German lavatory and bidet. These were visible signs of progress in Partygrad.

LIBERALISM IN PARTYGRAD

The first Partygraders interpreted the concept of liberalism as Russian tradition would have them interpret it. From the camps and the prisons the authorities released a number of broken people who called themselves dissidents. At the same time they inaugurated such an educational campaign that, when it was over, the Partygraders even stopped telling stories they'd invented during the years of Brezhnevite terror. The Partygraders were used to the fact that, when a lot of talk about freedom began, it always ended with arrests. The authorities started, on various pretexts, to weed out unstable elements from offices and institutions, especially young people. The militia, together with the people's vigilantes, raided places where they sold forbidden books. In the streets they began to detain young people with transistor radios which were tuned in to Western radio stations.

But quite quickly Moscow authorized a relaxation. 'Informal' groups appeared. The best known of them in the town were the 'New Limers' and the 'Metallists'. The first were young people from the New Limes region. Usually they were merely children from more or less well-off families who had not managed to get into decent high schools. They worked intermittently anywhere they could. They speculated on the black market in foreign 'goodies' such as books, cassettes, transistors, jeans and cigarettes. Taking after the same crowd in Moscow, they formed groups and declared the movement's aim: 'Cultural self-expression and passing the time independently of the Komsomol and of Marxism-Leninism.'

The Metallists differed from the Limers in their life's programme only in that they dressed in uniform; foreign jackets and jeans adorned with metal accessories, and shaved their heads like Western punks. They came from working families and counted themselves as 'working class'. Gorban, head of the oblast's KGB, said of them all: 'Our people can't even succumb to corrupting influence and go to pieces in a decent manner.'

The Party's obkom decided to 'revive' the dissident movement, but in a form that would fit perfectly into the channel of perestroika. They found one clapped-out and worthless writer, the publication of whose totally talentless novel had once been held up, and wrote an article about him in the newspaper describing him as a victim of Brezhnev's 'terror'. The writer had once spent fifteen days in prison for drunken hooliganism. And then the authorities credited him with having been suppressed for his criticism of Brezhnevite bureaucratism and corruption. They also found a talentless painter who had served some sort of sentence for the seduction of minors. They decided to write an article about him too as a 'victim of Brezhnevism' and to arrange an exhibition for him and recommend him to foreigners as a dissident.

Krutov said: 'We must see to it in such a way that the prisoners of conscience who've been freed shouldn't take it into their heads in their joy to praise our society instead of portraying its ulcers. That wouldn't do at all.'

Even in Brezhnev's time movements of Slavophiles and Westerners had sprung up in Partygrad which followed Moscow's example. At the start they were united because all wanted progress.

But there was this difference. The Slavophiles drank vodka and wheezed with pleasure, while the Westerners also drank vodka but hankered after whisky and Calvados, which they'd read about in Western writers' books. But then one day the leader of the Westerners made a slighting reference to Russian kvass.* Although kvass had long disappeared from Partygrad, the leader of the Slavophiles declared that he could not tolerate such an insult to the reputation of the Russian nation. And then all hell broke loose. It ended with a complete break and mutual opposition.

The Westerners began to insist on Partygrad's adoption of jeans, beards, tights, transistors, Hemingway, Bergman, Antonioni and everything else that was an indispensable attribute of the cultured man's life at the end of the twentieth century.

The Slavophiles accused the West of having no soul and summoned everyone back to the roots of Russian national life. They praised *chastushki*† to the skies, the ceremonies of the people and the whole heroic past.

The leader of the Slavophiles published an article entitled 'The West doesn't give us orders'. In it he called for the revival of the ancient custom of smearing a bride's gate with tar, if the bride had lost her innocence before marriage. The article made quite a stir. The popular mass, in the form of one deaf and dumb woman aged a hundred, supported the proposal. But it proved hard to implement. People pointed out that the town had no gates and no tar. That wasn't so very serious. But then it was explained that there weren't any bona fide people either. So they rushed out into the country. There every home had a refrigerator and a television set. All the young women wore tights: they even slept in them. The boys without exception wore jeans with American labels.

* A slightly alcoholic drink made from cereals and stale bread.
† A sort of limerick: often obscene, with a long tradition.

After that the Slavophile movement went into a decline. And then, of course, the Westerners terminated their existence too.

But when perestroika began, these traditional lines of thinking rose up again and on a scale that would have been unthinkable in Partygrad and in Russia in general. To continue the Slavophile tradition the patriotic movement, 'Patriot', appeared, while for the Westernisers there was the internationalist movement, 'Democrat'. The split between them from the very start had to be political because it was hard to buy vodka in the shops, and expensive too; so both lots drowned themselves in home-made hooch.

THE PATRIOTS

The patriots, following the example of *Pamyat** in Moscow, began to concern themselves with the preservation of the monuments of olden times. In Partygrad there were a few monasteries and churches which had no architectural value whatever. These were already being looked after by a few enterprising clergymen. Otherwise nothing. So there was nothing to preserve. And then the patriots made a discovery that shook the Partygraders with its implacable logic: that the monuments of the Russian past were not being preserved because they had been deliberately destroyed by Zionists, masons and cosmopolites, who had found soft spots for themselves in all the country's institutions. These dark and sinister elements were, in general, responsible for all the misfortunes of the Russian people. It was perfectly possible that it was they who in days of yore had put the snake under the legendary Prince Oleg when he was answering a call of nature outside the walls of the future Partygrad Kremlin. And it was they, naturally, who had hampered the building of the Kremlin, sending the money to Israel.

In general the Partygraders responded to the summons of the patriots and gave them encouragement. But they did meet certain obstacles when it came to implementation. Unfortunately there

* A sort of chauvinistic, anti-Semitic society.

were very few Jews in Partygrad oblast. And those who were Jews had forgotten that they were Jews. The patriots interpreted this fact as a sign of the cunning of the Jews. Anyway, Jews wouldn't want to live in such swinish conditions. Obviously, only the long-suffering Russians could live in them, whereas the Jews had entrenched themselves in Moscow in the plushest places and rather nearer to the West. Anyway, in all the Party positions in Partygrad there was not one single Jew.

Then the Patriots let out the rumour that Zhidkov himself was half Jewish; and even wholly Jewish; that his real name was not Zhidkov, but Zhidov;* and that even if he wasn't a Jew, his wife was an obvious Jewess; and that even if they weren't Jews themselves, their children had 'Jew' written all over them.

The patriots put forward candidates at the elections to the Council of People's Deputies. Among them were the writer and painter mentioned previously and also the wife of the chairman, as the manager of the toilet joint venture was now called. Anna Spiridonovna, known to the people as 'Nyushka'. Having constituted the committee for the elevation of Solzhenitsyn to the Russian tsardom, Nyushka became a popular social worker in the oblast. Her platform at the election had one single plank: the issue of soap for every single bottom in the population every month. Since nobody could get soap in the town for love or money at that time, Nyushka's platform had a wild success. She received ten times more votes than the communist candidate, who was none other than the Second Secretary of the obkom of the Party. In the West they were already speaking of communist defeat in the parliamentary elections. The greatest Kremlinological expert concluded that the country was at the beginning of the post-communist era.

THE DEMOCRATS

From the start everyone who had been put in a psychiatric hospital in the years of stagnation or had been sent to Atom joined the

* *Zhid* is an insulting word for Jew.

democrats. At their head stood that marvellous student who in his time had prepared the first number of the illegal journal *Glasnost* and miraculously survived. They released him from his camp on the undertaking that he would act in the spirit of the perestroikist directive for glasnost and democratization.

The democrats began to issue a journal called *Democrat*. When the movement's membership reached the hundred mark, a number of university lecturers joined up together with researchers in scientific research institutes. One of them was a senior lecturer of a famous Moscow college thirsting for world fame. He pushed the student leader out and took command of the movement himself.

However, the democratic movement went further than the government had intended. Or, rather, the government itself began to get up to tricks which even the dissidents couldn't have conjured up earlier. One of the members of the bureau of the Party's obkom accused Krutov himself of inconsistency and indecision in the implementation of perestroika, left the bureau's staff and joined the democrats, kicked the senior lecturer out and took command himself. At the election of the People's Deputies he headed the poll, established a parliamentary opposition group and spoke of the formation of a new Democratic Party.

The group set up its platform with the following demands: (1) all power to the Soviets, which themselves would be turned into an institution of the parliamentary type; (2) end of the single-party system; (3) ownership of means of production to go to the workers; land to the peasants, factories to the factory workers; (4) government organs to relinquish their command function; (5) the oblast to become a federation of independent districts; (6) everyone forbidden henceforth to throw bottles on to the grass, spit on the ground, to crush bed-bugs and cockroaches or to let off hydrogen-sulphide at night; (7) reform of the legislation regarding standing in queues; (8) Partygraders to be permitted to travel to the West and come back at any time of the day or night without official permission; and, bypassing Moscow, to set up direct communication with all the capitals of the world.

After the democrats' platform had been published, Partygraders plunged into the sort of discussion that hadn't happened in the country for twenty years. In particular, the following problems came to the fore. What if the soviets don't take supreme power into their own hands? What if the workers don't want to join other parties? Anyway, who is a worker and who isn't? Which means of production should be given to teachers, doctors, musicians, artists, millionaires, accountants, soldiers or officers? Who will actually be in command of the production if the governmental organs aren't? Who should own the railways, the airlines and other large-scale enterprises? What about the army and the secret service? Who would own the prisons and labour camps?

The discussion obsessed the minds and feelings of the Partygraders to such an extent that they forgot not only about raising productivity but even about keeping it up to its previous level. Drunkenness assumed dimensions never seen in all the 'years of stagnation'.

THE NEO-COMMUNISTS

What made the Partygrad government tremble most was the formation of a student group of neo-communists with branches in the senior classes of high schools and among young working men. The neo-communists declared that, for them, perestroika wasn't a revolution but a counter-revolution from above and a betrayal of the ideals of communism. They protested against the practice of spitting on the country's past and said the present government had just as many shortcomings as that of Brezhnev and of Stalin. The neo-communists organized a demonstration several scores strong and moved on the Party's obkom with slogans as *Long Live Communism!* and *We shall defend the positive conquests of Soviet history!*

Maotsedunka came out of the building to meet them. To encouraging laughter from gaping bystanders she asked the neo-communists ('milksops', as she chose to call them) what positive conquests they actually saw in Partygrad. The demonstrators made as if to answer the question but they weren't allowed to speak. On the orders of Maotsedunka these 'hooligans' were carted off to prison, where they remained under arrest for fifteen days. When they got out they wrote and distributed a New Communist Manifesto which stated that the struggle for the ideals and achievements of communism was the basic form of social struggle of the present epoch.

The Soviet press treated the declaration of the neo-communists as a provocationist sally on the part of the conservatives. In the West they didn't mention them much and, if they did, they called them neo-Stalinists. The neo-communists were quietly removed from the town and sent to Atom. Once more the main enemy of real-life communism had turned out to be the communist idealist.

THE RENAISSANCE OF CULTURE

According to official reports and newspapers, there was an intensive cultural life in Partygrad. The town had everything that Moscow had, but on a smaller scale and at a lower level of quality. The Union of Writers had a section there, as did the Union of Artists and the Union of Composers. For instance in Partygrad there are now more writers than there were in all tsarist Russia at the time of the 1917 revolution. Then the place had its own Tolstoys, its Chekhovs, its Gorkys and its Mayakovskys. Now times had changed and the Partygrad writers preferred to think of themselves as the local Hemingways, Ionescos, Dürrenmatts, Steinbecks, Graham Greenes and Updikes. There are even candidates for the local Agatha Christie: and, what's more, it's usually a man. And the local artists are now all Picassos, Dalis and Kandinskys. And after the book traffickers had brought the albums of Western artists into Partygrad, all the tendencies of Western painting and drawing developed there. The abstract painters were especially fashionable. Even amateurs who had never held a paintbrush in their lives suddenly seemed able after a few days to rustle something up that put them immediately into the ranks of the most progressive artists in the world.

Of course this state of affairs wasn't reached in a day or without struggle. Both the authorities and the masses of the population put up a long fight against these new cultural influences.

After the new 'waves' had been routed in Moscow, and of course in all the provincial cities, the high leadership decided to allow them to some extent. As a result, a former Partygrad Dali became head of the Partygrad division of the Union of Artists, a Partygrad Stockhausen became head of the Union of Composers and a Partygrad Camus took over the Partygrad division of the Union of Writers.

It was from Western radio stations (or 'voices') that Partygrad learned that a cultural renaissance had begun in Partygrad. The stations began literally to choke with rapture at the freedoms conferred upon the practitioners of Soviet culture by Gorbachev's administration. For this reason the government stopped jamming Western radios broadcasting to the Soviet Union. On Partygrad screens the authorities showed a number of exceptionally bad Soviet films which the 'voices' claimed to be cinematographic masterpieces, for which reason, of course, they had been banned by the reactionary leadership of Leonid Brezhnev. At the same time books, no less rotten than the films, appeared in the bookshops which, according to the same 'voices', were literary masterpieces (for which reason they had of course been forbidden by the reactionary Brezhnevite government).

The Partygrad theatres, it was proposed, should decide their own repertoire and fix the prices of the tickets. During the first week, theatres that had been empty became half full, although ticket prices had doubled. The proponents of the Gorbachevite policy were absolutely delighted. The newspapers extolled in dithyrambs the wise decision of the Central Committee. But the very next week the theatres emptied completely and for good. The Partygraders had become convinced that the plays which had been forbidden earlier were even more boring than those which had been permitted and decided that they wouldn't waste their money on the theatre. Then the authorities started to sell the tickets in the town's institutions and factories, compelling Komsomol and Party members to buy them in the line of duty. Although the trade-union organization was offering a 50 per cent discount, the communists and the Komsomol refused to buy them, relying on the Gorbachevite directive that democracy should be pushed to the limit.

And since there were no foreigners in Partygrad who, as in Moscow, would take the bait of the 'cultural renaissance', the theatrical renaissance found itself in a quite disastrous situation. The artists and directors, who had been thirsting for freedom of creation, began to ask to be put back under the 'iron control of the censor'. But this wasn't allowed. 'It was freedom you wanted,' Obkom told them, 'so now get yourselves out of the shit on your own steam.'

Then those actors who were held to be the most talented and the most persecuted formed their own Independent Theatre. One dud time-server of a writer who had pretended to be a victim of the Brezhnevite terror promptly rewrote a play by a writer living in the West who'd been expelled from his country during the years of stagnation for having criticized Brezhnev. The play was published in the West and won a sensational success for the Partygrad pillager. The Soviet writer living in the West started stuttering about plagiarism. But the Partygrad swindler declared he'd written the play twenty years before and that it had been distributed in *samizdat* and that the émigré writer had borrowed stuff from *his* play. This explanation was eagerly accepted in the West. The play had no success at all in Partygrad. On the other hand, when the Partygrad theatre took it on tour in the West, it had a triumphal reception. (However, the truth was that the West was in raptures over Russians in the same way that it was in raptures over Papuan art, slapping them on the shoulder and giving understanding winks.)

It was the same with the Partygrad painters. The inhabitants of the town stopped going to their exhibitions altogether because they hadn't been educated in all the Western 'isms' which had earlier been forbidden but had recently been permitted in Partygrad.

There could be no question of anyone buying any of the pictures, because the basic purchasers of decorative art were the State foundations and enterprises who preferred portraits of the country's leaders and eminent citizens and scenes from Soviet society's working and militant life. And there weren't any foreigners in the town who could have spent hard currency on the daubs of Partygrad modernists and avant-gardists. Then the authorities decided to send the modernists with their daubs to the West after the theatre. And there they had a *succès fou*.

Finally, they allowed the writers to form an independent co-operative with the right to publish books at its own discretion. The co-operative tried to publish the creations of the Partygrad writers that were supposed to have been written and banned in the Brezhnev time. But when the Partygraders had read two or three of these wretched little books, they came to the conclusion that the authorities had been absolutely right to forbid such rubbish. And they just stopped buying the books.

Then the co-operative started publishing Western detective stories and pornography. And business improved. And then they opened a canteen at the co-operative, where they sold ravioli and hamburgers at bearable prices. This type of production had a much greater success than the books.

The members of the co-operative began to acquire flats, villas and cars to travel in the West and bring back videos, computers and other Western gadgets for which there was a demand in the black market or in second-hand shops.

A group of young writers tried to get the co-operative to publish a collection of their own work. But they were hurled out, neck and crop, and sent off to the State publisher. There the bureaucrats refused to print their work and advised them to return to the co-operative. The beginners sent their work to the West. But there too they were refused. They were told that such creative freedom as the Soviet Union now had, the West itself lacked. And if an independent literary co-operative at home in Russia didn't want to print their concoctions, it meant that they weren't fit to be printed.

THE RELIGIOUS REVIVAL

Before the revolution the oblast of Partygrad was very God-fearing. To this day there are traces of this piety. If the Western press is to be believed, the tradition will serve as a base for religious rebirth in Russia. Here is a characteristic example of the deep piety of the Russian people.

In a communal flat in New Limes, Partygrad, there lived two old women. They loathed each other and did everything they could to do each other in. And my God, what dirty tricks they dreamed up! To throw disgusting pieces of soap into the stew-pot was the most innocent of their little games. And then one old woman died. The other gloated: 'Well, God has punished the deceased for her evil ways, and I'm still alive!'

'You've no occasion to be happy, old crone,' said the still living hag's neighbour (to whom the housing committee of the district soviet had promised the hags' room after their death). 'In the other world the deceased will be complaining of you to God, telling him how you chucked soap into her soup. And God will send her to heaven, but he'll send you to hell.'

'It wasn't me who threw the soap into the soup it was her,' wailed the angry old woman. 'Well, I'll show that bitch where she gets off. I'll tell God the whole truth about her!'

The old woman decided to get to the other world as soon as she possibly could in order to justify herself before God and to play some dirty tricks on her hated opponent. And she died that very evening, clutching a piece of 'domestic' soap in her bony hand – the cheapest and most disgusting soap that ever existed in the history of mankind. As he read the burial service over hag No. 2, the priest said the departed had shown the world a striking example of steadfastness of faith. The funeral of the old woman turned into something like a demonstration. Talk began about conferring some kind of sacred rank on her: the rank, I think, of martyr.

Until the revolution all the houses in Partygrad were hung with icons. They were to be found even in the barns and sheds. After the revolution almost all of the churches were shut down and icons lost their value even more. Anti-religious propaganda plus 'dekulakization' of the peasantry led to a glut of icons. People burned them in stoves, boarded up windows and doors with them and used them to plug holes in walls and fences.

But then the rumour crept into Partygrad that in Moscow icons were rising in price. This was happening already after the war. A number of enterprising peasants, loaded with sacks of icons, took them to Moscow and sold them for what to them seemed good prices; and they went home dead drunk and contented.

After that there came the icon boom. People collected tons of icons in Russian villages and carted them off to Moscow. Prices went up and up and up and up. This started the rumour that God himself was about to be rehabilitated, that the leadership in Moscow was being baptized secretly 'just in case', and so on.

When the authorities repaired the Partygrad monastery and

opened the church in the town centre, the religious rumour acquired the strength of authenticity. All Party organizations had been sent a secret letter, on the basis of which the propagandists had conducted a broad propagandist explanatory campaign. But nobody any longer believed that religion had been revived because it was part of culture, or was connected with *détente* in the world. The magnetic quality of religion itself increased every day.

Finally, young people with beards appeared in the town, festooned with crosses and trying to imitate the old Russian way of speaking. The beardies established close relationships with the local priests and believers. They occupied a whole house on the outskirts of the town. They travelled across the whole oblast. They returned to the town only at night. Nobody saw with what. Spiritually it was the most enlightened and radiant period in the history of the oblast. The head of militia built himself a new dacha. Many workers in government offices got new cars. Fashionable foreign goods filtered into the town; foreign radios were heard. More and more often one heard English expressions like 'Goodbye', 'OK', 'Girlie' and 'Boss'. In the West people began to speak of a religious revival in the very bowels of Russia.

Suddenly there was a clap of thunder. The bearded youths were discovered to be crooks who were buying up icons in the country for a song and selling them in Moscow to foreigners for hard currency.

The religious movement then went into a decline and would have been swallowed up altogether if perestroika had not begun.

PERESTROIKA IN THE CHURCH

The authorities handed over to the clergy a monastery which bore the name of Lenin and contained a museum of atheism. The monastery was named after Lenin, as a museum and not as a monastery. But it retained its title even after the Soviet authorities turned the monastery partly into a real monastery and partly into a theological seminary.

The monks were obliged to preserve that part of the monastery that contained the anti-religious museum in apple-pie order. And to give them their due, they kept their word. The Partygrad bishop spoke on the subject when he attended a meeting in Moscow with religious emissaries from Western Europe. He said that Marxist teaching in no way contradicted religious teaching.

The monks restored the monastery, indeed almost created it anew; moreover, with full respect to Soviet historical concepts, Soviet ideology and to the international situation. The restoration was done with the aid of the latest technology, including computers. For example, if a tour leader wanted to show you an underground room into which at some time or other in the past they had shut up some personage of the royal type, he pressed a button, the floor opened and before your very eyes a stone well appeared. At the bottom of it you would see the dummy of the unfortunate princess attached with a stout chain to the wall. Water would begin to cover the floor; huge stuffed rats (cybernetics!) would clamber up on to the shelf on which the princess lay on straw. . . . Or the tour leader might be asked to illustrate the position of the working class in pre-revolutionary Russia. Once again he presses a knob. The wall of a room slides aside. Through a bullet-proof, transparent barrier one sees the body of a worker hanging on the rack. Another press of the button. The worker is hoisted upwards, his arms pinioned behind his back. Executioners standing on each side of him begin to beat him with rods while others roast his heels. And during this you will hear the icy, emotionless voice of the tour leader: 'Well, that's how the workers lived in our oblast before the revolution.'

And now we shall make a turn of 180 degrees! Press the button again. And before you lies the panorama of the town bathed in a clear light. In the distance are the factories. In the sky aeroplanes and rockets fly around. Students are on their way to the university. Healthy children bathe in the swimming-pool and play in the children's little square. In cross-section, the smart flat of an ordinary citizen. Fertile cornfields. Plump herds of domestic cattle. Shops full of goods. Although the visitors know that all these are simply the product of the imagination of the raikom's propaganda division, the spectacle moves them all the same. And they leave the monastery called Lenin with the hope that they will perhaps really see a sausage or a herring in the shops.

The opening of the monastery and the seminary was an imposing occasion. It was attended by representatives of the Central Committee of the Communist Party of the Soviet Union and of many cultural organizations, including the anti-religious society called 'Religion: The Opium of the People'. All friendly churches and religions sent their representatives as well as Amnesty International. The Pope did not come as he was on a planned visit to the Galápagos Islands. For this he was unanimously criticized. Many speakers said it was time that the Vatican began its perestroika and that it was time that the Pope was elected from at least two candidates. Nor need they be Catholics or even believers. Indeed, the time had come when a Soviet person could be elected as Pope. Everyone agreed that the first Soviet pope should be Gorbachev, or at least Yeltsin. The last would be even better, as he was then to all intents and purposes unemployed. And he would put the Vatican through such a perestroika that within a year it would forget how to cross itself.

Finally, rumour had it that Gorbachev had been baptized in order to attract the Orthodox Church to the side of perestroika; and that he had been circumcized in order to win the friendship of the American Jews and Israel; and that on the insistence of his wife, who was a Muslim, he had become a Muhammadan in order to get the whole Arab world on his side.

Committees were formed in Partygrad to agitate for the construction of mosques and synagogues in the town and also to promote universal circumcision. Members of the Party and of the Komsomol were allowed to attend church, to carry out religious ceremonies and to baptize their children. It was especially recommended that citizens should observe the Great Fast. The society 'Religion: The Opium of the People' proposed that the Fast should be made twice as long. If all the inhabitants of the Soviet Union fasted for six months in the year, the newspapers suggested, the food problem with agriculture would be halved.

PERESTROIKA IN THE MORTUARY

The Funeral Complex in Partygrad was the name for the cemetery, the morgue, the crematorium, the columbarium and the workshops for the preparation of funeral installations (tombstones, railings and crosses, urns for the ashes of the deceased and flowers real or artificial).

Partygrad cemetery is one of the most remarkable in all Russia. In the middle of it there is a crematorium like the palace of a rich nineteenth-century landowner. This produces a surprising impression. Comrade Suslikov, who in his time had been First Secretary of the Party obkom, declared in his speech at the official opening of the crematorium that 'when one looks at such a majestic building, one experiences the joyful feeling of having built a new society'. The newspapers wrote that we have created in our town a new enterprise for the processing of the remains of deceased workers 'which is unrivalled in Europe both in capacity and in beauty'. Beyond the crematorium is the columbarium. That is remarkable too. In it the deceased occupy exactly the same position in society as they did when they were alive.

The burial ceremony for the crematorium was so accurately and artistically worked out that the Second Secretary of the obkom of the Party (namely the Secretary for Ideology) said it was on the same level as the ballet of the Bolshoi Theatre. He even more or less suggested that the crematorium should go on a foreign tour as guest artist. But Moscow rejected this idea on the grounds that members of the burial squad would, to a man, defect to the West. In the words of the oblast's chief ideologue, the Funeral Complex had become 'a fundamental part of our way of life'.

Those who worked in the Funeral Complex were known as 'workers of the world beyond the grave'. They got regular prison sentences for swindling and bribe-taking. But at the same time the Funeral Complex was the only profitable enterprise in the oblast, if one didn't count the Church which of course had been separated from the State.

The workers of the world beyond the grave were the first people in the oblast to respond to the high leadership's appeals for new thinking and to join in the perestroika of the whole of the country's way of life. Although their business was not so much the way of life as the way of death, they, as one should expect from Soviet citizens concerned with the progress of their own society, decided to take the initiative and begin a thorough perestroika of the country's way of death.

One evening they met in the office of the cemetery. The table groaned under the weight of hors-d'oeuvres and alcoholic beverages such as even the food division of the Party's obkom never knew. They sat there long after midnight, all very jolly and contended. Everyone told the latest stories and anecdotes about Gorbachev, including the one about a hunchback* whom only a coffin could straighten out, as the Russian saying goes.

Between the jokes they also got down to business brass tacks. It was the manager of the Funeral Complex himself who suggested the abolition of the cumbersome and expensive graves. The deceased, he proposed, should be dismembered and buried in cellophane packets in small bits. The Secretary of the Party organization proposed that graves should be vertical instead of horizontal. In that way they would take up less space. Besides, the tree-planting machines recently imported from the Federal Republic of Germany should be used for digging the new graves. By this method the productivity of the grave-diggers would be increased several-fold and the Funeral Complex would be brought up to international standards.

The Komsomol representative proposed that the bodies of the deceased should be reduced by a pressing machine. In this way, if the machine pressed hard enough, they could even be accommodated in matchboxes. In compressed form the deceased could be placed in the columbarium. This would facilitate the work of the crematorium and cut down the demand for graves. The Chief Engineer introduced a most valuable proposal in line with the struggle with bureaucracy and corruption. Why not sack the cemetery guard who took bribes and replace him with a pair of really fierce dogs? Somebody added that then two kennelmen would have to be employed. The chairman of the local trade union said that his council approved the initiative about the kennelmen. But one couldn't sack the guard. It would be enough to change his job specification and call him 'door-keeper'. In short, on the next

* In Russian *gorbaty* = hunchbacked.

day all the Partygrad newspapers printed the appeal of the Partygrad workers in the world beyond the grave to all the grave and burial workers of the USSR to join the perestroika of the country's whole way of life in that sector of the construction of the community that had been entrusted to them.

But in spite of all this the authorities again put the workers in the world beyond the grave in prison. This time they were not sentenced for taking bribes but for a much more serious offence – one could say, a political offence. Of course they did take bribes. Who doesn't in this age? The peculiar criminality of the cemetery workers lay in the fact that, as some old retired communists wrote in *Partgradskaya Pravda*, the burial men 'made a fortune out of grief and fleeced the dead'. These veteran communists also wrote a letter to the Partygrad KGB in which they drew the attention of the Chekists* to the 'unhealthy atmosphere of the cemetery'. As was later explained, this 'unhealthy atmosphere' consisted of the following elements.

In response to the Central Committee's decision to increase productivity, the labour force of the Funeral Complex assumed the socialist obligation to double their own productivity. But, unfortunately for them, it became clear that the town's mortality rate had begun to fall. What was to be done? They found a way out: to bury the same deceased several times over and to get hold of buriable corpses by buying them in for cash from other centres of population. The result was that they were buying up all the corpses in the oblast and thus over-fulfilling the Complex's work plan three times over. On paper, of course. For this the 'workers in the world beyond the grave' received premiums and awards. But at the same time all the other cemeteries in the oblast under-fulfilled their plans; which brought the oblast's indicators down in general within the All-Union scheme of socialist emulation.

* The name of the KGB in Lenin's time.

They built the Old People's Home, called after N.K. Krupskaya,* in the immediate vicinity of the Funeral Complex. The choice of location was governed by the highest humanitarian concepts. As the newspapers put it: 'Soviet people should look towards the future with confidence and with their eyes open.' Certain practical considerations played a role too. Granted that very old people died more often than young people, their burial expenses, as the same newspapers said, were unproductively high. But as the Old People's Home was situated almost on the ground of the Funeral Complex, there was no need to build a special morgue for the Home or to spend a lot of money transporting the deceased to their place of burial.

The Old People's Home became an enterprise of 'republican importance' (again a journalistic expression). They put old people into it from all over Russia whom their relations wanted to get rid of. It wasn't so easy to get them in; demand exceeded capacity. Big bribes were needed. Besides, the Home's management used the place as an illegal hotel for every kind of rogue and speculator, and so the number of beds for the old was thereby reduced.

There was even less money available for the maintenance of the genuine inmates of the Home than for national servicemen.

The Home's staff robbed the old people in every conceivable way. Consequently they died like flies in autumn. This didn't upset anybody in the town because the old people came from elsewhere. Besides, things looked a lot better in the official report than they would have done if the inmates had all lived a long time: the value of the institution was assessed in terms of the number of people who passed through it. The municipality, which was in charge of the Home, received sizeable bribes from the Home's staff and for the time being turned a blind eye to what was going on. All the same the staff of the Home, like those of the Funeral Complex, were arrested for swindling fairly regularly.

When central government raised the slogan of 'accelerated development', the Home's staff responded with enthusiasm. They took it upon themselves to increase the throughput of the Home.

* Lenin's wife.

But they overdid things and so these perestroikist enthusiasts found themselves in prison along with the staff of the Funeral Complex.

Long before perestroika the inhabitants or 'patients' of the Old People's Home were engaged in speculation, the resale of stolen goods, pimping and the running of illicit stills; all this in order to make some sort of a living. They drew the staff into their petty machinations. In the last resort the staff took the reins into their own hands and so gangster bands of old men and old women were formed in the Home by the staff. From time to time these bands were unmasked. The staff received prison sentences while the old folk were dispatched to their graves. But new people were always ready to replace the fallen warriors and after a while the black market would spring into life with redoubled force.

When Gorbachev's anti-alcohol campaign started, the Home turned into one of the largest centres of speculation in alcoholic drinks and illicit stills. On one occasion the militia laid on a search of the entire Home. A machine for brewing hooch was found in almost every little room. The old people went into open rebellion when the militia tried to remove the apparatus. They barricaded themselves in and threatened to burn down the Home with everyone in it. After consulting Moscow the authorities decided to leave the old people in peace on the grounds that they would soon die anyway. The calculation was correct. Half of them were dead within a couple of days. The nervous tension had been too much for them.

And then they filled the Home up again with retired people who were still quite well. They turned out to be cleverer and more enterprising than the former inmates. Apart from private trade they organized a criminal syndicate with international links. The idea had certainly been born among them to cut, via Partygrad, if not a window then a hole into Europe, and to make Partygrad an open town for foreigners.

Communism didn't invent corruption. But it didn't obliterate it either. On the contrary it gave it new strength and new forms. One of the tasks of the organ mentioned above in its struggle against bureaucratism was the battle against corruption. By then corruption had already assumed unheard-of dimensions. There had been a systematic struggle against it throughout the whole of Soviet history. But nobody had succeeded in rooting it out. And this was no accident. In a communist society corruption had simply proved to be the appropriate method of distributing and redistributing the good things of life. In reality the distributive principle was not the principle of 'each according to his work', but the principle 'everyone has what he can snatch from society through the use of his own social position'.

Those persons operating within the system of power and government have to be corrupt not so much because of the opportunities that their position offers, but because of the inevitability of their being corrupt as a result of the system itself. A man who refuses to be corrupt cannot normally work for long in the Soviet system. One has to distinguish between corruption as a social phenomenon and corruption as a crime. It is surely only the deviations from the norms and rules of corruption which should be judged juridically, not corruption as such. Moreover, corruption happens on the basis of special directives from above or of agreed decisions taken by the local leadership.

When a campaign begins urging everyone to struggle against corruption, suitable candidates are chosen as scapegoats and then all the hullabaloo is about them. Accusations of corruption are also used as a means of discrediting opponents and rivals. For instance, when Gorbachev became General Secretary, he accused Grishin of corruption. But if Grishin had been made *Gensek,* he would have accused Gorbachev of corruption.

The main purpose of Gorbachev's campaign about corruption was to compromise former Brezhnevites, to throw them out of seats of power and put his own people in their place. The first victim of the campaign to fall was Portyankin. In Partygrad the scapegoat, as we have seen, was Zhidkov, a former henchman of Brezhnev. Into his place went the Gorbachevite Krutov, who, as far as corruption went, was at least twice as bad as Zhidkov. The new authorities wanted to arrange a show trial of Zhidkov. They wanted to sacrifice his 'mafia' on the altar of glasnost. But Zhidkov died. Newspaper articles about his unmasking had made no special impact.

A real live scapegoat was needed in Partygrad who would act the play in the necessary and proper manner. At the conference of the obkom of the Party they had a long discussion about who would make a suitable candidate. They wanted a candidate who would 'leave the wolves unharmed and the sheep happy'.* (It was Krutov himself who rephrased the old proverb, but he did it in such a way that it corresponded with the nub of the problem.)

Help came from the journal *Democrat*. Its first number ran an article on the Partygrad millionaires: people who officially received miserable salaries but in practice played a huge role in the oblast's life. The paper named ten people who were 'the real masters of the oblast'. Grobyka came first. But at the obkom meeting they passed him by in silence. Everybody present had been up to some business with him.

And Suslikov himself protected him. If anyone touched Grobyka, the scandal could spread all over the planet. All the highest leadership of the oblast would be compromised and possibly quite a few people in Moscow too.

The second secret millionaire on the list was the manager of the factory making artificial limbs. He also had something on scores of personages in the oblast, but at a lower level. Moreover, some of them could well be sacrificed. And the links between the factory manager and important functionaries were not so clear as in Grobyka's case. One could put a stop to them. One could reveal them only in so far as the particular political situation demanded. So they decided to make the factory boss the criminal scapegoat. It was his unmasking they decided to use as the instrument with which to demonstrate the full seriousness of the battle for the regeneration of Soviet society. For this they set up a special commission, which made the following revelations.

* Compare the old Russian proverb: 'Let the wolves have their fill and the sheep be unharmed.'

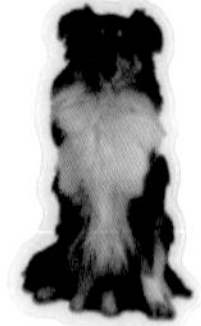

COMMUNIST CRIMES

There are crimes common to all times and all places. But there are also crimes that are inextricably bound up with a specific time, a specific people, a specific social order. The crimes which the commission of the Party obkom revealed were specifically communist crimes.

Every Soviet institution is decorated with busts and portraits of the classics of Marxism, of Party and government leaders and other well-known personages. Also to be seen are slogans, placards, reproductions and copies of famous Soviet artists, together with the classics of world art. The members of the Commission counted the number and reckoned the value of these ritualistic decorations in the factory. The figures they got were terrifying. There was the four-metre granite statue of Lenin in front of the main building. There were two other two-metre plaster Lenins inside the premises. One of them was painted in imitation bronze, the other in imitation marble. There were six four-pood busts of Lenin, eight three-pooders and twenty-four of a pood or less. There was one four-pood bust of Marx and three one-pooders. (For some reason the classics of Marxism were measured in poods and not in pounds or kilograms.)*

The number of portraits of the classics of Marxism, of Party and government leaders and every kind of famous and estimable personage ran into several hundred.

In addition to all this beauty which was on view, the capacious cellars of the factory were crammed full of the same sort of goods, either left over from the past or bought for an emergency. A huge amount of space was taken up with statues, busts, portraits and pictures representing Stalin, Beria, Malenkov, Khrushchev, Brezhnev and other operators from the past. It was striking that the 'artistic' productions devoted to Brezhnev were more numerous than those devoted to Stalin. And they were worth twice as much as the Stalins. There was a special cellar full of objects for demonstrations and festivals.

* The pood = forty Russian or thirty-six English pounds.

'Not a bad little museum at all' (the head of the Commission was summing up the members' impressions). 'In comparison the Louvre and the Hermitage are just small amateur collections. And what can they be stashing away in institutions larger than this?! And all over the oblast and throughout the country as a whole?'

The members of the Commission laughed till they cried as they looked at the portraits of oblast leaders, especially the late Zhidkov and the still flourishing Maotsedunka. The latter was depicted in the form of Mona Lisa against the background of a pigsty.

'You laugh too soon,' said the expert from the Union of Artists. 'In five hundred years' time that picture will be worth more than the Sistine Madonna. If it survives, of course. There was a time when people laughed at the Sistine Madonna. They found it by chance in some kind of shed.'

'And if it's shit, please excuse my coarse expression, why not bung it off to the West and flog it there?' remarked the chief of the militia. 'You'll probably find amateurs there who will pay large sums of money for it. And we *do* need hard currency.'

The factory manager had been cunning enough to steal huge sums of money at the expense of these ideological masterpieces. It transpired that the pricing system of the masterpieces was such that no uninitiated person could make head or tail of it. For example, a two-and-a-half metre statue of Lenin was a thousand roubles dearer than one of two metres and thirty-five centimetres. All that needed to be done was to put a pedestal under the smaller (and that was ten centimetres thicker) and cover it with a red duster and anyone would take the shortened statue for a genuine two-and-a-half metre one. And the factory manager was in cahoots with a crook from the sculpture factory, the two of them putting the difference into their pockets. Having fixed the deal, that is, with the directors and chairmen of the local trade unions and other initiated people.

It was even harder to see the difference between a three-pood and two-and-a-half pood bust of Brezhnev because the second was of the same size and it was only in the inside that the eight kilograms were missing. But the first was five hundred roubles more expensive than the second. Brezhnev's portrait (2.50 metres in a gold frame of one shape) was two thousand roubles more expensive than another portrait of the same Brezhnev (2.45 metres in another kind of gold frame, and hardly distinguishable from the first).

In short, after ten years' work in the factory, the manager had built himself a dacha, bought flats for himself, his son and his daughter in the co-operative, bought a car for himself and his son, and used to relax regularly in the country's best spas. He looked after himself all right, but he didn't forget his bosses, to whom he gave valuable presents. And they turned a blind eye to the machinations of the enterprising factory manager.

'This man will do,' said Krutov, when he had read the Commission's dossiers. 'An old communist, war veteran, met Brezhnev personally, got drunk with Zhidkov, went to Party school. He knows very well how to behave in court. We'll promise him a short sentence with a quick release after an amnesty. He'll do all we need. And the whole world will see how we are fighting against corruption and backing perestroika, with no respect of persons.'

'It would be no bad thing if we were to come out with an appeal to all the crooks in the country to join the struggle against corruption and support perestroika,' proposed Gorban.

'An excellent idea indeed,' cried Krutov. 'Millions of crooks all over the country will follow the initiative of the crooks of Partygrad.'

PERESTROIKA IN THE CRIMINAL SPHERE

One of the workers in the Party's obkom said in jest that in the criminal sphere we can compete confidently with the West. The head of the oblast's militia, Comrade Rylov, said what follows.

The criminal sphere is an exact copy of normal honest society. Each social type develops his own type of criminality with its own characteristics. And the whole world will see us as we struggle against corruption.

Properly speaking, the criminal sphere is in its way part of the economic system. But enough of theory. Let us be more concrete. One must make the distinction between communist and capitalist efficacy. If a tenth part of the crimes committed in Partygrad came to light, the place would rank as one of the most famous criminal towns in the whole wide world. But if ever anybody were to publish the work productivity of its criminals – namely, the reason why the crimes are committed – then Partygrad would become the laughing stock of the whole of humanity's gangsters. Let me give you just a few facts about this.

In fifty cases out of a hundred, Soviet crimes are *disinterested* crimes. One can say that these are crimes committed for the sake of crime or pure crimes, in the manner of art for the sake of art, or pure art. Under capitalism the percentage of pure crimes is insignificant, almost nil. The pursue of profit ('naked cash') has completely taken over the gangsters' sector as we know it.

Here are a few figures which characterize the disinterested character of our Soviet criminality. In the oblast during the last three months 516 windows were broken, 78 teeth knocked out, 25 arms and legs broken, plus 36 ribs. There were 18 black eyes and 987 cases of smashed jaws. All this done absolutely disinterestedly.

Sometimes the criminals pay for it all themselves. In 30 per cent of the cases the profits are no higher than 10 roubles. We call such crimes 'half-litre crimes' because ten roubles is the price of half a litre of home-made hooch.

Only in 15 per cent of criminal cases, continued Rylov, is the haul as much as fifty roubles. We call such crimes 'restaurant crimes' because the profit is drunk up in a restaurant. And in only five cases out of a hundred does the profit exceed a hundred roubles. We call these crimes 'pensioners' crimes' because in these cases the criminals can put aside ten to twenty roubles for a rainy day and for their old age. As everyone knows, our robbers do not as yet get an old-age pension because they have no documents to confirm their work record.

The total value of all theft in Partygrad during the last ten years was less than that of the gold-and silverware that one West German minister stole in a single night. During the daytime this minister fought battles in the Bundestag about the inalienable rights of man. At night his hobby was to steal from the local jewellers. That's what real democracy means.

Let us now consider the technological aspect of our Soviet crimes. There the years of stagnation had a greater effect than they did in our other sectors engaged in the building of communism.

Just a few data. Only six months before perestroika 137 people were hit on the head with a brick in the town. Of these 50 survived because of the bad quality of the brick. During the same period 207 people were stabbed with screwdrivers, scissors, forks and other household instruments; 48 people were strangled with cords, belts, stockings and other flexible objects and 37 people were drowned in a bath, washtub or other container of liquid.

There was only one case of an attempt to kill by pistol! The assassin fired sixteen shots at his own wife who weighed a hundred kilograms. And he missed, although he fired from a distance of only ten paces. He missed because the pistol didn't work. As a punishment for his careless handling of the weapon his certificate of 'Excellent Shot' was taken away from him. In short, we cannot compete criminally with the West when it comes to economic effectiveness and technological equipment.

But after a few months of perestroika Comrade Rylov had to make a fundamental change in his position. Every kind of contemporary criminality appeared in Partygrad. Crimes such as the town had known only from Western films and which everyone would have sincerely thought impossible in the country. The extension of the private sector gave rise to organized rackets. Many traders wanted to close their businesses down but it was too late; bandits forced them to carry on – or else! Other traders began to engage bandits and thieves to protect them against the mafia.

Then a new mafia came into existence to compete with the old mafia. After a series of bloody encounters the two mafias amalgamated and took the whole of the private sector of the town's economy under their united control. As a result, the working conditions of the private traders became worse than those in the State enterprises, while the material profit was reduced to a minimum. And so among the traders the ideas of Owen, Fourier, Proudhon and even Marx began to rise: a phenomenon which did not at all accord with Moscow's instruction to regard Marxism as obsolete.

The mafia took over the manufacture and distribution of drugs. They made the narcotics out of local raw materials, toadstools, bed-bugs, soldiers' puttees and atomic waste. These narcotics were unusually strong. One drop of them would put a man into a state of total stupefaction for a whole week. No preliminary adaptation was required for their consumption. In imitation of American 'crack', they called the stuff 'dreck'.

The mafia also monopolized the whole of the sex industry. It started courses devoted to the improvement of sex technology. They squeezed out all the homoeopathics, yogis and faith-healers. They opened a school for the training of highly qualified prostitutes, female and male, whom they called 'sexologists'. The number of people who wanted to go to the school was higher than of those seeking university places. Only those with a good report from the Pioneers or the Komsomol were admitted.

The quasi-legal publication of pornographic literature (called 'erotic literature') began. As in the West, monthlies started up with titles which included the names of the male and female sexual organs. Queues of purchasers of the magazines formed on the evening before publication. They were longer than the queues for perestroika journals such as *The Spark* and *Partygrad News*. Naturally a club for 'Intimate Meetings' opened. Westerners wrote about it, saying that the club was in the finest brothel traditions, which were combined with the achievements of world sexual engineering.

The mafia became enormously strong and famous and soon went into battle against the private company that ran the lavatory. To defend itself, the latter employed an armed guard. Battles began such as Partygraders had seen only in American films about old Chicago. There was shooting every single night.

Then the mafia began to kidnap people and demand ransom. The result was discouraging. Usually the relatives of the kidnappers were ready to pay only if the kidnappers would NOT release them. So this type of crime failed to establish itself.

The mafia also started to rob banks, shops and warehouses. But there too no decent tradition took shape. Inflation made money unattractive, and there was nothing to take in the shops: rogues of the old sort had cleaned them out already.

Nor did the thrilling craze for people chasing one another in motor cars take on in Partygrad. Private cars were still difficult to get hold of. Their owners preferred to hide them in garages or sheds for a whole series of reasons. Petrol was short, spare parts unobtainable. It was a pity to spoil a beautiful object. And the town's roads were full of holes, so no go for racing. So, if there were races, they were mainly on all fours. The newspapers wrote about one such race. In an underground factory where they worked illicit stills they invented a new drink called 'gorbachukha', one drop of which was enough to poison a European town of medium size. The militia was ordered to seize the distillers alive in order to discover the secret of the beverage. But having breathed in the vapour of gorbachukhas, the militiamen lost the use of their legs and had to pursue the escaping home brewers on all fours.

NO EVIL WITHOUT GOOD

But the progress in crime did have some positive consequences. Because dreck reduced the appetite, people began to eat less, and this was one of the reasons why the oblast's food position improved. Since they could no longer compete with the mafia, the old-style millionaires were ruined. Grobyka himself went bankrupt. In the material sense he fell lower than the historical Chaadayev because he lacked popularity as a thinker. He wasn't declared insane, but simply a fool.

There were now so many thinkers in the town that you couldn't avoid bumping into them. Everywhere one heard the names of Berdyaev, Rozanov, Solovyov and other sages of the past. Everyone forgave the thinkers for speaking and acting against communist Soviet society and even considered this a virtue. In his grief, Grobyka drank gorbachukha and nibbled handfuls of dreck. Bit by bit he sold his library on the black market at half price. The Soviet authors were sold by weight as pulp, from which they made the paper for the pornographic magazines and for *Patriot* and *Democrat*.

On TV they began to show a twenty-part serial film called *In New Partygrad*, all about the proliferation of gangsterism. The film gripped Partygraders' souls. At viewing time they chucked all business aside, including political gatherings and drinking and rushed to their TV sets. On these occasions it was like being in an Italian town with a football match going on.

The authorities drew practical conclusions from this. Whenever a factory went on strike they began to show gangster films on one channel right round the clock. The strikes were cut short because the strikers couldn't be torn away from the television, even with the promise of a free *chekushka** of gorbachukha.

'No evil without good,' commented Krutov. 'When all this perestroikist murk comes to an end we shall have a few weapons of our own left from it. When all is said and done, what do the people need? Bread and circuses. It was always so and will be till the end of time.'

PERESTROIKA IN THE LAWCOURTS

In Moscow there were raving discussions about the indispensability of liberalizing the system of jurisprudence. In Partygrad these ideas fell on most fruitful soil. This was understandable: at least a third of the adult population of the oblast consisted of prisoners or former prisoners, while another third were potential criminals for the future. The Partygrad press advanced, for deep consideration, ideas that had caused confusion even among people who were used to the views of Western specialists. Here are a few examples.

The principle 'He who isn't caught isn't a thief' is out of date. Now we have to think in a new way. Anybody who is caught at the scene of the crime should summon his lawyer. The latter will confer with the judicial organs. Meanwhile you, the defendant, can go and have a rest at a spa; expenses paid by the victim of the crime. Of course, after the trial, if there is one and if you are found guilty, you will be obliged to return part of the money to the victim.

The victim himself is obliged to present indisputable proof that he *did* suffer damage and that he suffered it from the individual in question. If the lawyer of the accused finds the proof insufficient, then that occasions a lawsuit against the accuser. The victim has no right to offer any resistance to the criminal if the fact hasn't been established by the court that he is indeed the victim. The accused

* Quarter litre.

has the right to choose his own judges and people's assessors from two or three candidates for each. If the judge is blackballed three times by the accused, he is disqualified.

Other suggestions. Prisoners to have the right of self-government in their place of punishment. The number of guards to be reduced. There should be no more guards or barbed-wire fences because they are an insult to the dignity of the prisoner. The prisoners' families to be allowed to go into imprisonment with them. The prisoners to have freedom of movement and freedom to do what they want during twelve hours out of the twenty-four. Such was the way in which the minds and spirits of the Partygrad liberal thinkers were working.

Another curious event was the co-operative of independent lawyers. Its purpose was to defend criminals. From then on criminals could do their robberies, swindles and theft of public property in close collaboration with their lawyers.

PERESTROIKA IN THE LUNATIC ASYLUM

It was a long time before they told the inmates of the psychiatric hospital that perestroika had begun in the Russian lands. But, as the saying goes, you won't hide an awl in a sack. A new kind of madman had begun to turn up in the hospital: a madman of a specifically perestroikist type. These were the Gorbachevs, the Yeltsins, the Sakharovs, the Solzhenitsyns, the Trotskys, the Bukharins, the Tukhachevskys, the Vlassovs, the Nikolais, the Anastasias, the Stolypins and the imitators of various personalities who were previously considered to be exploiters, reactionaries, enemies of the people and traitors. However, these have now been elevated to the rank of innocent victims of Stalin's terror, of ideological fighters against Stalinism and of geniuses who anticipated Gorbachev's perestroika. In the beginning the authorities didn't dare to put these people into the asylum because they differed from normal people only in that they had a rather higher excitability. But, alas, they didn't stay put on this generalized level of craziness; they started asking for the conversion of all the means of production into private property, for the liquidation of the KGB, for the opening of frontiers, the disbandment of the army, the splitting up of the country into a multitude of independent states and a lot of other things that even the most inveterate perestroikist and Westerners didn't want.

Partygrad was threatened with the complete disorganization of its own life, for it was hard to distinguish the madmen from the healthy perestroikists, so that the population accepted the ravings of the madmen as the latest development of Gorbachev's ideas. It was only when the loonies had accused Gorbachev of being not the original Gorbachev, but a plant by the KGB, that the oblast leaders went into extraordinary executive session.

After a stormy debate in which almost half of the attendance was on the side of the madmen, the authorities took the decision to isolate them temporarily from society. The motivation was this: the perestroikist loonies had run on ahead with their regeneration of society as the dissidents had done before them when they criticized Stalin and Brezhnev. So as soon as perestroika finished, these new loonies, who were also in advance of their time, could be set at liberty.

So they quietly began collecting the crazy perestroikists into the psychiatric hospital. By mistake they rounded up a band of healthy citizens who believed sincerely in Gorbachev's promises and appeals. At first the authorities wanted to let these out. But common sense prevailed and it was decided they were more dangerous than those who were mentally ill. So they isolated them in a part of the hospital that was reserved for especially dangerous criminals. It was the perestroikist loonies and enthusiasts who told the inmates of the hospital about perestroika. Then the latter began to get up to tricks the like of which, as Krutov himself put it, one wouldn't come across even in a madhouse. The new-model loonies demanded self-government, the non-intervention of doctors in the healing process and the conversion of the hospital to self-healing (analogous to self-financing). Moreover, they demanded the right to go off one's head as a fundamental human right.

The old-style loonies declared all this to be counter-revolution and demanded martial law in the hospital. This lot was then set at liberty. So the streets of the town filled up with Napoleons, Lenins, Stalins, Robespierres, Khomeinis, Mao Tse-tungs, Dzhershinskys,

Hitlers, Mussolinis and other notables from the epoch that was vanishing into the past. The old loonies opened their bowels wherever they happened to be, seized everything they could lay their hands on and behaved in such a way that many citizens began to ask to be allowed to go to the hospital where, so it was said, genuine democracy reigned.

THE WORKERS' MOVEMENT

The perestroika fermentation of minds began in Moscow and then spread from the capital into the provinces. In the provinces it began by capturing the brainy summit, that is the government and the intellectuals next to it, and after that it spread to other strata of the population. In this way it went, here too, from the strong-willed and intellectual centre to other parts of the social organism. This road brought it to the oblast's factories. Strikes began, the workers advanced demands, the essence of which was to support Gorbachev's economic reforms; to remove 'conservatives' from all posts and replace them with Gorbachevites. So it happened that not only was the West content with the strike which it evaluated as a sign of communism's imminent breakdown but also Moscow, which regarded the strike as a sign of the victory of the ideas of perestroika.

Other demands were put forward, for instance to improve the food supply and working conditions. The oblast government recognized these demands as just and promised to take the appropriate measures. They asked for patience over soap only until the soap and washing-powder factory was built. The Americans were going to build this factory as an example of the co-operation between capitalism and communism.

The oblast's population was 90 per cent ethnic Russian. Ten per cent of the non-Russians were immigrants from other places: teachers in institutes, musicians, engineers, Party workers and representatives of other non-productive professions. They were people who had joined the oblast priviligentsia and never gave a thought to any kind of special national rights.

All the same the awakening of nationalism in the Baltic States and Transcaucasus did not go unnoticed in Partygrad. In one district there were villages of Bordyan who had lived there throughout the centuries. They considered themselves to be Russian and knew no other language than Russian. Several emigrants from these villages worked in the university.

One day they discovered in some archive or other that the inhabitants of these villages had been forcibly converted to Orthodoxy and also Russified by force. Having heard that the Balts were rebelling against Russian hegemony and beginning to get independence, the Bordyan intellectuals decided to awaken the national consciousness of their own fellow-countrymen. These descendants of the Bordyans drank some gorbachukha and demanded that the oblast government should grant them autonomy and their own constitution, the right to speak in their own native language, to mint their own money (which, moreover, should be convertible).

Representatives of Soviet power arrived from the town and explained that nobody in the whole world now spoke Bordyanskan. And as for studying the Bordyanskan script, one would have to graduate from the university and then pore over papers in a special room for ten years. Bordyanskan money, they continued, wouldn't be of any use because foreigners wouldn't be able to buy anything with it. The Bordyans couldn't secede from the oblast, as their villages lay in the middle of it. If they wanted to go and settle elsewhere, there would be no official opposition. But where would they go? Nobody knew where their historic homeland was. The United States wouldn't let them in. They were already choking with Soviet émigrés. Siberia? By all means!

Having heard these official speeches, the descendants of the Bordyans took another pull at the gorbachukha and punched each other on the jaw, the native intellectuals coming first. What happened afterwards nobody knows.

MASS MADNESS

Having started rolling in one direction the country, which had been deprived of both external obstacles and internal brakes, was bound to end up at the very bottom of a precipice. For a long time Partygrad put up a stiff resistance to this reeling progress by means of its provincial inertia. But once it started rolling, Partygrad quickly made up the ground it had lost and began to roll along with Moscow. In Partygrad, people stopped using the concepts and assertions of Marxism/Leninism. Marx they more or less forgot about completely, while even of Lenin the talk began to be not so much in contrast to Stalin as hints to the effect that it was he, Lenin, who started up all this. University lecturers in Marxism/Leninism and the history of the Communist Party of the Soviet Union, the propagandists and most ideological workers became ashamed of their profession and tried to hide it, sinking with the rest of the population into ideological chaos and cynicism.

The ideological dislocation of society completed itself with a general crisis which affected the people's moral and psychological condition. A state of mind set in which amounted to mass madness. It's hard to call it anything else. Every sort of charlatan swam to the top and became popular. The authorities showed these people respect, offering them the freedom of the press, television and lecture hall. Huge cohorts of prophets, fortune-tellers and healers appeared in Partygrad.

The culmination of the mass madness was the appearance on TV of a man called Ivan Laptev, who had been discharged from a lunatic asylum. In his time Laptev had been famous in the town as a healer and a preacher who intended to create his own personal religion, Laptism.

The Partygraders who remembered Laptev had some difficulty in recognizing him. He had gone grey and shaved off his beard and moustache. He had grown stouter, or rather he had swollen up, because, as everyone knows, it's hard to put on weight on the grub you get in an asylum. Laptev was presented to the population as a legendary personality gifted with an unusual healing capability: a man who had unjustly suffered during Brezhnev's stagnant years. It was explained that Mr Laptev received his healing energy directly from far-off stars, probably Sirius, and that he could transmit this energy to other people and even to inanimate objects. Moreover, this could happen even over the television.

Laptev began a regular series of television seances. At that time the Partygraders were television addicts. In order to acquire a store of healing energy, they put stewing-pots and pitchers with water in front of the television, as well as jars with ointment in them.

Laptev would concentrate his mind on Sirius and, stretching out his long fingers, begin to pour out his healing energy into the televiewers, into the water beside their legs and into their ointment. In this way he was curing thousands of Partygraders within a single hour of their serious ailments and charging many tons of water and kilograms of ointment with healing energy. Afterwards the Partygraders drank the healing water and smeared themselves with the healing ointments. They got well, not in days but in hours.

The miracles of Christ, the Evangelist, paled into insignificance in face of such a miracle of mass healing. The priests, however, did not surrender. 'If there had been television in Christ's time,' they said, 'Christ would have come up with something a bit snappier than Laptev's stuff.'

Party and State functionaries began to avail themselves of the services of Laptev. They charged even their vodka and snacks with healing Laptevian energy. Right round the clock their mothers, wives and daughters anointed themselves with the ointment charged with energy straight from Sirius, assuring their friends that they were becoming healthier, more beautiful and younger every day. The newspapers wrote that, owing to Laptev's fabulous gifts, Soviet medicine had already risen to the highest Western level and that our hospital queues had been halved.

The town was full of rumours. It was said that Laptev, against payment in dollars, would soon be charging Americans with his healing energy via satellite. Also he was about to feed the Partygraders by television. During the seances many people had begun to put empty plates, with forks and spoons, in front of their TVs and these people passionately declared that they would experience the sensation of being full; imagining fillet, beefsteak, chickens, caviare, crabs and other delicious things which they knew about only from books.

The wits called Laptev's TV seances the oblast Laptevization of the population. And indeed only those were healed who were not ill. The others shouted about miraculous healings and extolled Laptev on account of the mass madness that had taken control of the town.

'If this charlatan promises to get the whole town drunk through the TV,' said Gorban, drinking a Laptev-charged gorbachukha, 'then we can say that the Soviet period of Russian history is over. Remember Rasputin!'

Gorban proved to be prophetic about Rasputin. Favourable articles about him appeared in the newspapers soon afterwards. And when the sensation broke about the discovery of the Tsar's family's remains, somebody promptly made a long serial film about Rasputin in Partygrad.

'Force a fool to pray to God and he'll be glad to bash in his forehead doing it.' This was Gorban's summary of the ideological psychological condition of Partygrad society.

'Whom have you in mind?' asked Krutov.

'Everyone without exception. You and me, to begin with.'

'What can we do?'

'Nothing, just wait until this obsession passes.'

THE MULTI-PARTY SYSTEM

The democrats quarrelled with each other and split up into many groups (as a matter of fact, more than fifty), each declaring that it was an independent party. They were: the Democrats, the Liberals, the Socials, the Democratic-Liberals, the Democratic-Socials, the Liberal-Democrats, the Liberal-Socials, the Social-Democrats, the Democrat-Liberals, the Liberal-Socials, the Social-Liberals and others. (The full list was published in *Partgradskaya Pravda*.) The patriots also quarrelled with each other and split up into a multitude of groups (more than a hundred), each calling itself an independent party. These were: the Russia-lovers, the Russophiles, the Anti-Semites, the Anti-Jews, the Anti-Zionists, the Patriotic-Anti-Jews, the Nationals, the National-Democrats, the National-Liberals, the National-Socials, the National Russia-lovers, the National Anti-Jews, the Monarchists, the Monarcho-Liberals, the Monarcho-Democrats, the Monarcho-Socials, the Monarcho-Anti-Jews and others. (The full list is to be found in the same place.)

The inhabitants of Partygrad, who were quite indifferent to the ideological-political distinctions between the parties, did what was done at the time of the great French revolution: they called them by the names of the places where they got drunk and where the sobering-up stations that returned them to consciousness were located. Thus in Partygrad they were the Rubbishdumpers who got drunk near the rubbish dump, the Manurials, who sobered up in Manure Street, the Shitters, who got drunk by the Saransky Market, the Funerials, who got drunk in the cemetery, the Militarists, who sobered up not far from the military factory, and many others. As the newspapers said, nobody could even dream about this kind of multi-party system in the West.

Maotsedunka said on this subject that, given a couple of years more of democracy, every idler in Partygrad, every parasite and even drunkard would have his own political party. Gorban said that it was all fine provided that this rabble didn't ever get together. Gorban's fears proved to be prophetic. The reverse process of party-unification duly began. What then happened could be ascertained only by a computer. The expression 'You won't make it out without a computer' succeeded the expression 'You won't make it out without a half-litre' (which was current during the years of stagnation).

PARLIAMENTARISM

After Gorbachev had become President of the Soviet Union and Yeltsin President of the RSFSR, they began to make all the managers and chairmen president in Partygrad and gave them all special powers. So workshop presidents made their appearance and office presidents and presidents of stalls in the market, and of kiosks, shops and even public lavatories.

Maotsedunka became President of the oblast. Her first act was to decide to pay a visit to the President of the United States, to the Queen of England, to the Pope of Rome and to other important Western personages, in order to promise them to introduce a market economy into the oblast, the multi-party system and parliamentarism and to ask for a hundred billion dollars in exchange for all this.

When she became President, Maotsedunka left the Communist Party of the Soviet Union, joined the Party of the Shitters and was baptized. They baptized her in the town pond because there wasn't a barrel or a tub big enough to accommodate Maotsedunka's behind in the whole town. The christening turned into a mass demonstration. Crowds of Partygraders, who had taken a pull at the gorbachukha, paraded with portraits of Nicholas II, Rasputin, Hitler, Stalin, Mao Tse-tung, Mrs Thatcher, the Pope, President Bush, Chancellor Kohl, Herr Genscher, President Mitterand and everyone else. They marched on the offices of obkom and broke all the windows.

THE CESSPIT OPPOSITION

An old drunken singer nicknamed 'Bard', whom we mentioned earlier, came home to Partygrad from exile. He sang political songs in the open space alongside the market to drunken gatherings. KGB informers wrote them down accurately and, as in the days of stagnation, served up their reports to their chiefs. The chiefs took them to Gorban himself, who was known to be a protector of the arts. And there was good reason for this. What, for instance, Gorban asked himself, was one to make of a thing like this?

THE COMMUNIST CRISIS

All the inhabitants of Partygrad, beginning with the First Secretary of the Party's obkom and ending with the lowest debauchee sleeping it off on the rubbish dump, were convinced that in Partygrad no crises were possible. Right from the school bench they knew the ABC of Marxism which stated that crises happen in the West because too many goods are produced and Westerners simply haven't got the money to buy them. But in Partygrad through the centuries there were either too few goods or no goods at all. When Moscow says that the country is in a state of crisis, Partygraders are dumbfounded. How so? Does that mean that there are too many goods somewhere? But where?

The Partygraders poured out into the streets and moved towards Lenin Square, demanding to take part in the crisis or to be allowed to go somewhere where there *was* a crisis. Maotsedunka, now President of the oblast, explained to the workers that a communist crisis differed from a capitalist one in that under communism there are few goods and that absolutely none are anticipated. The workers were relieved by this, dispersed and went off home, dreaming of the time when they would have the capitalist market economy promised by Gorbachev and a real capitalist crisis would break out.

The whole world cries Hurrah! Hurrah!
Free peoples, all, are most delighted.
The CC of the CPSU's the source of good,
While the KGB's the sanctuary of freedom.

That's sort of all right. But one does feel the hidden sneer.

I don't sing in that choir.
I stand on my own and for my own.
Sometimes the executioners, tired of vice,
Will hide their knout for a time and hand out white loaves.
But time will come, and you'll know it soon
When they'll reach for the whip, having tired of being good.

But this is a hint that there'll be a return to the old severe methods. To be quite honest such a return is indispensable, otherwise we'll end up in total catastrophe. But this is something that we have to decide for ourselves and not via some rubbishy poet. And what is the message of THIS song?

Having stuffed our brains with tempting ideas
Our grandfathers lit a flame from that spark,
And for the sake of the dubious brotherhood of all peoples
They clanked with their chains in prison.
But grandfather's ideas make us yawn with boredom
And we don't believe one little bit
That any of them can be implemented.

Our fathers, who didn't ask for rank and medals,
Rotted in camps and burned in the fires of war.
They knew full well what hell was
When they erected their paradisal building.

We who have discovered a new era
Do not respect our grandfathers' knowledge.
In us their historical exploits
Provoke anger and ennui.

Their sons went not that way or thither.
They never knew the fear of the past GULAG.
They bravely now demand freedom from work
And claim the right to receive free Western goods.

But if father and grandfather were either blind or scoundrels,
From what, if it comes to it, are we?

We are rubbish unworthy of our fathers.

That's the conservatives' mood. Of course in some ways they're right. The people have got out of hand. They don't value our communist ideals. Or our past and our achievements. This 'Bard' sort of wants to say that. But how? These people who assemble on the empty ground aren't our allies. They are just about our future enemies. One can talk to the perestroikists all right. If the directives change, they will all change too in a minute. But those who collect on the rubbish dump will always be our enemies. Better to start rounding them up right away!

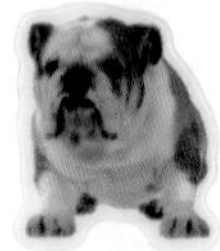

THE NEO-STALINISTS

Of course the neo-Stalinists turned up too. These were by no means unrepentant old Stalinists but young people no older than twenty, basically students. They composed an appeal 'to the citizens of Partygrad', made many copies of it and distributed it in places where a lot of people gathered and put it into post-boxes. Krutov suspected that this was the work of Gorban's agents. But Gorban swore that he had absolutely nothing to do with it, that his own agents were wearing out their legs trying to discover the structure of the organization, who its leaders were and where its secret press and arms depot was. These milksops have, said Gorban, 'proved themselves worthy pupils of Stalin. One has to give them that'.

In their appeal the neo-Stalinists asked whether everything that our nation had lived through was simply one of history's black failures? Did our great-grandfathers go to the scaffold, to prison, to penal servitude in vain? Was the gunfire from the Aurora all a mistake? Was it for nothing that our grandfathers fell at the front in the civil war and froze and starved and sacrificed the dearest things in life – and indeed their lives themselves? Was it in vain that millions of our fathers, mothers, brothers and sisters died on the fronts of the Patriotic War? Was it for nothing that they burned in aeroplanes and threw themselves with handfuls of grenades under the enemy tanks? What about the collapse of fascism: was that nothing either? And the conquest of space? And what about the fact that other nations are afraid to attack us? We've lived through a terrible but grand history. And any other people would be proud of it. But we? What do we do? We blacken and deride our great history with its plenitude of suffering. And the people who have started this blackening of the past are the people ruling us up top: cynical and vain adventurers and careerists who are ready, in exchange for the miserable approval of the West, to betray everything for which our great-grandfathers sacrificed their lives, and our grandfathers and fathers too. Down with these turncoats. We, their sons and grandsons protest! We shall defend the work of Lenin and Stalin against the traitors!

In the flea market people began to sell surviving busts, portraits and books of Stalin. And, what was more, Stalin's books went for far more than the books of émigré writers now permitted and praised by the authorities. The only book that went for still more was the work of Nostradamus, who was said to have predicted perestroika but somehow or other forgot to tell us how it would end.

TIME OF TROUBLES

Gradually and unobtrusively Partygrad somehow slipped into the turmoil that had taken hold of the entire country. Such a masochistic self-unmasking and self-flagellation began that even the most virulent anti-communists and Sovietophobes lost their bearings in it. (Against the background of sedition they came to look like tiny minor complainants and at times even like defenders of communism itself.) Everyone triea to surpass everyone else in his derision of the past and in the denigration of everything done in the post-revolutionary years. Only the priests saved the town from religious obscurantism, only the neo-Stalinists from a democratic debauch, and only the mafia from rule by private traders.

Repeatedly, the writer we mentioned above declared in an interview printed in *Partygrad News*: 'Now we can breathe more easily.' And he trundled off to the West with lectures about perestroika. In Paris he ate and drank his fill at the expense of Soviet émigrés and then let go a burst of sincerity, saying: 'The rubbish that has blown up now in Russia is something that has never happened in the whole of Russian history.' The émigrés drew the conclusion from this that Russia had really set out on the Western democratic road. But nobody wanted to go back to the homeland he had left.

The authorities swiftly lost control of the life of the oblast. The political demagogues held the initiative along with a number of artful dodgers, ultra-cynical careerists, gangsters, hooligans, idlers and other social rejects. Extraordinary measures were needed to stop a process that was leading straight to catastrophe. There were rumours of military detachments being brought in. But they quickly died down. The population understood quite well that, if there were repressions, the West wouldn't provide computers, bread or soap. There seemed to be no issue from the situation. Krutov had to all intents and purposes detached himself from government and let everything drift. He spent days and nights at his dacha or out fishing. Or he sat locked in his office downing bottle after bottle of vodka. And then one day the telephone rang. It was Suslikov himself on the line.

SIGNAL FROM MOSCOW

After that historic meeting with Gorbachev, which we related earlier, Suslikov got in touch with Krutov, it will be remembered, and told him about the forthcoming conversion of Partygrad into a lighthouse of perestroika and about the Special Commission under Corytov which was about to visit the city. When he heard this news, Krutov went in his trousers, guessing what this course of events was laying in store for him. Things smelt bad. If the plan was to exhibit Partygrad to the world with its dirty, grey streets, its empty shops, its endless queues, its irremovable drunkards and all the other attributes of the Soviet way of life, that meant the threat of a world-wide scandal and the transformation of him, Krutov, into a scapegoat. But there was no way out of it. Krutov assured Suslikov that he warranted the Party's utmost confidence. He would have liked to say 'not for the first time', but he remembered just in time that all this was going to happen for the first time in Partygrad and for the first time in his, Krutov's, career as a Party leader at oblast level.

Immediately after his conversation with Suslikov, Krutov had urgently ordered a meeting of the whole leadership apparatus of oblast and town. Obkom and gorkom attended and the divisional heads, the chiefs of the KGB and the MVD (militia), the chairmen of the oblast and town, the trade-union leaders and Komsomol chiefs of oblast and town, the secretaries of the Party's raikom and the chairmen of the district soviets and many other people who played an important role in the life of the oblast and the town. The conference ended long after midnight. 'The commanders of the oblast' (this was Krutov's name for the leading oblast personalities) dispersed to their own departments in order to hold their similar lower level conferences. This happened right down to individual enterprises and institutions, in which there would later be sessions of the Party and Komsomol bureaux and of the trade-union committees as well as general assemblies of everybody and God knows what else.

At the top obkom meeting they set up a commission to help the Special Commission that was expected from Moscow. Similar commissions were established at town and district level and also in the basic Party organizations. Meetings were called and special commissions set up in every institution in the oblast that was affected in any way by Moscow's decision. In short, one telephone call from a Secretary of the Central Committee, Comrade Suslikov, set in motion a gigantic power mechanism in Partygrad oblast and compelled thousands of people to fan themselves into feverish activity.

Moreover, this activity's purpose was not to accelerate the oblast's development or to raise its productivity in the production of all sorts of useful things. Its purpose was to give the appearance that this 'acceleration' and this 'amplification' were really happening. One thing we may say: when it comes to this kind of activity, namely the *imitation* of genuine activity, communist society attains a higher level of efficacy than Western society. For in this field there is no need to compel communists to function in the appropriate spirit. They've been trained to do it from their teens and can fulfil their task to perfection.

THE ARRIVAL OF THE COMMISSION FROM MOSCOW

They used to say that the town started at the railway station. In our epoch of dynamic progress we can say that the town begins at the airport. Partygrad airport, like Partygrad itself, is a fantastic mixture of modernity and antediluvian squalor. The 'concertinas' (imported from the Federal German Republic) to which, in principle, aeroplanes on arrival should be attached, were not working. The planes themselves had more or less to be pulled up to the airport building by oxen. The passengers were then unloaded and led to their 'concertinas', up to which they climbed on a primitive flight of steps. When they had passed through them, their road was blocked by the improbable spectacle of unkempt charwomen with dirty mops and pails, which made passengers with weak nerves sick. And on top of that other charwomen were to be seen dragging cleaning machines, also bought in Federal Germany, which weren't working either.

The airport building was decorated with portraits of the members of the Politburo. Gorbachev's portrait was twice as big as the rest. Even in the time of the now ridiculed Brezhnev it wasn't like this. *His* portrait was only one and a half times as big as the others. Slogans and placards about perestroika were hung everywhere, castigating drunkards, conservatives and bureaucrats. A transparent but bullet-prooí partition divided the main hall into two parts. One part, which was for the passage and meeting of important personages, was usually empty. The other, for ordinary mortals, was filled with the sort of public one sees in railway stations.

The Moscow Commission went, of course, through the VIP section. The transparent wall had been built when Corytov lived in Partygrad. He explained to the members of the Commission why it had been made transparent. The idea had been that the workers would be able to see their revered leaders but at the same time would have no opportunity to play some kind of dirty trick on them. Our Brother Ivan is quite capable, he said, without suspecting it, or any premeditation, of chucking a brick at an important face, or launching an avalanche of swear-words at it if that face happened to pass close by. So it was always better to remove the temptation from him

All the airport's loudspeakers were giving vent to the heartrending wails of a popular female singer who had won first prize in a festival of rock music.

'For the life of me I can't accept these hysterical wails as music,' said one of the Commission.

'It's in fashion just now,' said another. 'Tens of thousands of young people used to come to her concerts at Luzhniki Stadium.'

'That's no indication of the progress of art. Billions of people listened to the priests' gibberish. And today the number of so-called believers is on the up and up. Is that cultural progress?'

'If you don't like it, don't listen to it. Shut your ears.'

'Better to shut the trap of one hysteric with no voice and no sense of pitch than shut the ears of millions of people who are sold on everything from the West.'

Every notable from oblast and town was there to meet the Muscovites. Corytov took his place in Krutov's car. During the journey Corytov told Krutov the substance of his conversation with Suslikov before the flight from Moscow.

'Well, the switch is coming,' said Krutov in triumph when he'd heard Corytov out. 'And high time too!'

'Yes, it's time,' said Corytov. 'We have, as it were, to go underground and let all these shits chatter away on the surface. But we of the Party apparatus deep down must lean on the very best that has been preserved in our people. It was not for nothing that we devoted our efforts to their education for seventy years. What is at stake is the achievements of the revolution and of the whole of our history.'

Corytov's grandiloquent words didn't inspire Krutov. He was the type who spat on everything in the world except himself. If somebody had guaranteed him the position of governor-general in a royalist Tsargrad, he would have betrayed communism's every ideal, plus implementation in Partygrad. But he knew very well that in a democratic or monarchic Russia nobody would even make him a door-keeper. And so he expressed his whole-hearted readiness to go underground while remaining the oblast's first personality and to prepare the Party apparatus for the role of saving the Fatherland.

'We are in favour of perestroika,' concluded Corytov, 'but of a perestroika that does not weaken but rather strengthens the foundations of our social order. How to do that, you know as well as I do.'

Krutov nodded his head as a sign of agreement. Inwardly he was thinking of only one thing: how to come out of the water dry and how to save his own skin. Corytov himself was quite aware of Krutov's feelings. But he also knew that in the actual conjuncture the saving of Krutov's skin coincided with the saving of the system that people like Krutov served. It's a good thing there are Krutovs. If they were to disappear, one could put a cross on the grave of communism.

'We must pay special attention to one thing,' continued Corytov. 'We must do the unmasking of the evils of the past and the short-comings of our society ourselves. It's one thing when the dissidents do it illegally, it's another when it comes from the Party quite openly and legally. We can guide the unmasking in such a way that it's useful to us and wins the public to our side. By the same means we'll reduce the influence of the illegal opposition to nil. Our role must be to take all the ideas of the regime's illegal critics, changing them slightly. We must restate them all again as our own ideas but at the same time put in our "buts". This so that ideas will belong to us, but there won't be anything significant left in them. As regards concrete facts, we should go further than the dissidents. This will make a big impression on simple people, and the illegal criticism will lose all its sense. And then. . . . Well, you yourself know what will happen afterwards.'

'Everything is quite clear, Ivan Timofeyevich! Once the country has gone off in an undesirable direction, it is up to us to dash forward in front so as to stop the ruinous movement gradually. If a herd of horses panic and rush forward towards a precipice, we have to get in front of them and turn them in another direction.'

A FESTIVE DINNER

The Muscovites were lodged in a special house for honoured guests. It was in the district where the highest personalities of the city had their dachas. Andropov stayed there more than once when he was receiving treatment at a spa in the oblast. So did Portyankin and Suslikov, on business and sometimes even for holidays.

In the evening there was a festive dinner in honour of the guests. It went off as such dinners went off in Brezhnev's time, with the best wines and the best hors-d'oeuvres. There was a lot of joking.

They told each other the latest perestroika anecdotes.

'Mikhail Sergeyevich decided to see for himself how the workmen were working in a condition of sobriety. He went to a factory. He went up to a workman who was working more or less diligently. He asked him if a workman could work if he drank a small glass of vodka. The workman answered, rather doubtfully, well, yes, he could. But if he drank two decanters, what then? Would he be able to work? The worker answered more confidently that he could. But if he drank half a litre, could he do his work after that? Gorbachev persisted. "Well, here I am, you see, working away," replied the worker.'

'Shevardnadze and Raisa Maximovna were in bed together. Suddenly there was a knock at the door. Mikhail Sergeyevich had returned earlier than was expected. Raisa Maximovna was frightened. Shevardnadze consoled her: "It's all right, we aren't drinking vodka."'

'Jokes are all very well, but sex is a serious matter! Here we fall behind the West even more than we do in economics.'

'I don't agree. We've got quite enough fucking already.'

'Fucking isn't sex, it's debauchery. Sex is culture.'

'True, we'd better revise our politics in that department.'

'We should open proper brothels. With restaurants. With medical aid. With shows, and rock music. Stripteases and so on.'

'The State will get large revenues from enterprises like that.'

'No, it's best to hand over that trade to the private sector. Otherwise you'll get hackwork there too. Do you remember the story of how a brothel collapsed in Stalin's time? They did everything just like the West, only the whores were old Party veterans.'

'In the years of terror and stagnation no bold new initiatives like that were possible. Now times are different.'

'That's right. No going back. Progress is irreversible.'

In short, the dinner was a howling success. The members of the Commission got seriously drunk, as used to happen in the years of stagnation.

Corytov went off in search of a woman. He tried to break into the housekeeper's room. But the KGB officer had got in before him. Fortunately an elderly washerwoman came to the rescue and carried off Corytov, who by then was falling asleep on his feet, to her own bed.

THE FRESHENING OF THE ATMOSPHERE

At the Commission's first meeting three general questions were on the agenda: the freshening of the atmosphere, the activization of the population and the normalization of supplies.

In Partygrad as in every other Russian town there was a 'freshening of the atmosphere' before each important event. It consisted of the following. From the courtyards of the houses situated near the centre of the town they threw out the rubbish which was heaped around the rubbish bins. They put into lunatic asylums all those people who were patients in psychiatric hospitals and who had some sort of connection with politics. They put in not only the ones who went in for criticism but those who were apologists of the regime. Indeed, they shoved the latter in first because of their habit of unmasking defects with a view to their elimination. The first kind of critic, although he goes in for unmasking, doesn't ask for improvements because he doesn't believe in improvements.

At the same time the authorities put all the duplicating machines under lock and key. The institutions were put on a round-the-clock duty roster. They tested the fire-extinguishers. They increased the number of vigilantes to help the militia. The militiamen were given white cuffs and white belts. The crooks who had been amnestied were sent back to the camps. All potential dissidents were exiled from the town.

In Partygrad, on top of all that the militia, the vigilantes and the military patrols cut off all roads which led from the surrounding camps and industrial factories. The purpose of this was to see to it that no former or actual criminals or 'honest' drunkards from these places fouled up the morally sound Soviet society by their appearance or their behaviour.

On these days there was a larger sale of alcoholic drinks in certain places, and at lower prices. They lowered the prices because the alcoholic drinks were being sold under another name. Under the new name the beverage should cost less than the brand name which they'd sold it under on ordinary days. Besides this they threw foods into the local shops, restaurants and stalls which you wouldn't find in the town at any other time. For instance, the cheap sausage called 'dog's delight'; or the dried roach from the Caspian known as 'God's snack'. These foodstuffs were sold more cheaply; at cost – that is, without the added on costs for transport, etc. As a result of these various cane-and-candy measures, only single persons belonging to the 'suburban rabble' (as the militia called it) percolated into the town. Some did so out of a spirit of contradiction; others from curiosity; others still with the intention to profit by it somehow or other.

In the old days they used to make a list of all those people who should be physically removed from the town as parasites and ill-intentioned destroyers of public order. They would take them out of town on some pretext or other, put them into an asylum or in prison, for a short term. They paid special attention to the 'internal émigrés' – that is, those people who had fallen under the corrupting influence of the West: the sort of people who listened to foreign radios, read forbidden books and liked to associate with foreigners. If they couldn't manage to remove these elements from the town, they had them shadowed by the KGB and its auxiliary volunteers. These were given full powers to resort to extreme measures in case of necessity. Usually they engineered some provocation or other as a consequence of which the 'internal emigrants' found themselves in prison for fifteen days on a charge of hooliganism or in the psychiatric hospital where they would be put under observation.

The 'freshening of the atmosphere' usually began one week, or sometimes two weeks before the event that had prompted it and finished immediately the event was over. Then the status quo was re-established. The present situation was special because the atmosphere had to be freshened not just for a short time but for ever.

Of course perestroika wouldn't go on for ever. But who knew when it would end? It could drag on for a year, or for two years. What was more, this particular freshening-up had to be accomplished within the framework of the fight against drunkenness (which would not be so serious) and also in the context of liberalization and glasnost which were already actual disasters.

'The task of freshening up the atmosphere in the oblast in the conditions of perestroika seems at first to have been simplified or even to cease to exist altogether,' said Corytov, 'but only at the first glance. In fact it has been made more complicated and become even more important than it was. For some irresponsible elements have begun to use the freedom granted to them at a given stage of development of our country. We must bring it home to them that we shall not tolerate the undermining of the roots of our social order, of our power organs or of our ideology. Perestroika does *not* mean the rejection of what we've been doing for the last seventy years. Perestroika is a transition to new methods of building communism.'

The members of the Partygrad commission heard Corytov's nebulous stretch of double-talk with great satisfaction. They understood its hidden meaning.

THE ACTIVIZATION OF THE POPULATION

Until now the operation of activating the Partygrad population had taken the coarsest and most primitive forms. For this reason Corytov thought it would be useful to explain the essence of adapting our activization to the new conditions.

'I want you to look more carefully at what and who can be seen on a weekday in the streets – in the shops, in cafés, restaurants and public places in general. Do the people there fully represent the population of the town and the oblast? Do they represent the most important and active section of the population? Of course they don't. The most valuable people, the ones who determine the character of our society, are working in factories and institutions or are resting after or before their work shift. Nevertheless the "casuals" are probably those among our citizens whom the foreigners will meet.

'I would put a further question to you: where does one best find the essence of our Soviet man, in casual meetings in the street or in public places? Or does one find him in his place of work and where he takes part in the life of the collective, namely at Party, Komsomol and general meetings? I think there can be no two opinions about that. The essence of our people appears most fully and accurately in their working collectives and in their social organizations. Outside these collectives and organizations people's sense of responsibility naturally weakens and the level of their consciousness somehow falls. Life's tensions tire them. And the level of consciousness of the people who frequent the streets and public places in working hours is usually pretty low.

'What conclusion should we draw from what I have said? Should we leave to chance the business of foreigners getting to know our people? Should we limit the relationship to random contacts in chance circumstances, or should we see to it that the foreigners are able to see the essence of our Soviet people in the form that we are used to seeing them, in our work collectives, at work itself and in our social activities? I hope there will be no differences of opinion on this subject either. But a problem does arise which we have in the past really ignored.

'In order to understand our people correctly one needs not hours or days, not weeks or months, but years. And yet the foreigners come to us only for a few days. This means that during a few days we must help them to understand something it takes years to understand. How can we get out of that? The solution lies in our making a selection of people and deploying them at the points where foreigners contact our society, in such a way that these would be, as the sociologists say, sufficiently representative of the population of the town, the oblast and the country. It is that operation which we call 'the activization of the people'. We have to choose people fitted to this task and prepare them in an appropriate manner. Moreover, there must be enough of them so that they can take turns on duty. In that way we shall prepare an army of reliable communists and Komsomol to act as a basis for us when we need them.

'It is these most representative citizens of our society who will influence the rest of the population in its masses, so that, in the conditions of the current directive "Say what you want", the people will feel responsible for what they say and will say what they should say. In the West they talk about the collapse of communism and the start of a post-communist era. We must show the world that it is burying us too soon.'

THE NORMALIZATION OF SUPPLIES

The normalization of supplies in Partygrad used to mean filling up the shops with food that was in short supply or 'objects of common use'. Of course the shops were on the route which the important personages would be likely to take. These personages themselves knew in advance that the shops they would be looking at would have been involved in the normalization operation. At various stages of their own careers they themselves would have conducted normalization operations. But naturally the personages pretended to know nothing about the normalization of supplies and made as if to choose the shops they would visit personally. It was all an unwritten ritual in which they had to play the role prescribed for them.

The goods and the things that were in the selected, that is 'normalized', shops would be on sale only at the exact moment of the personages' inspection. The purchasers were chosen from especially trustworthy citizens who got something in reward for being trustworthy. Usually they were the relatives and friends of the shop workers. These people would have to return especially rare goods if it happened that even Komsomolstsy of proved worth and similar members of the Party failed to return these goods. It also happened that rogues and speculators would manage to infiltrate into the circle of proved worth.

Part of the 'normalization' was the delivery of foods in short supply to the canteens, cafés and restaurants which the important people would visit. Because of that, proved and trustworthy citizens were also chosen as their fellow-customers. The 'dummy customers' were served at exactly the moment when the personages arrived and the service immediately ceased after their departure. It could happen that the 'customers' would sit there hungry for a whole day. But after the visit was over they were given some reward for their hours of dutiful waiting.

Sometimes curious and amusing things happened. Once Portyankin visited Partygrad to launch a routine campaign against drunkenness. They took him to a 'normalized' café. A number of young people were sitting in it whose role was to exhibit their sobriety by drinking mineral water instead of vodka. The youths were indeed drinking mineral water but, out of habit, they were clinking glasses and grimacing as if they were drinking vodka. Portyankin suspected something fishy. He tested the contents of all the glasses in the café. When he discovered they contained no vodka, he called the behaviour of the young people an act of provocation. They were punished for it: they were not given the vodka they had been promised for not drinking vodka.

Another amusing incident happened at a clothing shop. One communist shock-worker asked to be allowed to try on three suits at the exact moment when Portyankin and his suite entered the shop. Having put on all three suits, he left the shop by the back door, as it was stated later in the militia's memorandum. After inquiries it was discovered there was no such shock-worker in the town. The militia and the KGB made titanic efforts to find him. But the man had simply disappeared into the ground.

The normalization operation was used in Partygrad for short-term events in normal non-perestroikist conditions and at a time when there were still some goods somewhere in warehouses and secret distribution points which could be used for window dressing. But now the show had to be a permanent one; and this at a time when even obkom's secret store was completely empty. Foreigners could of course, as usual, be fed separately from the citizens' supplies. But the task remained of giving the impression that the workers' living conditions had been improved, thanks to perestroika.

The Commission considered three alternatives. The first was to admit publicly that we live on the edge of hunger and destitution. One could even exaggerate that a bit. The West would be deeply impressed by our open talk about our difficulties and because we did not hide them from foreigners as we used to do. And then aid would flow into Russia from the West free of charge like a river in a flood. It would be possible to make a system of this. The second variant was to hand over the food supplies to the private sector. Then the private traders would fleece the foreigners of their hard currency. And for that sort of currency they would sell their grandmother.

The third alternative was to hand over the job of supplying the town to Western firms on concession; for instance, to McDonald's.

Each of these schemes had its pluses, but also its palpable minuses. The West would soon stop rejoicing over glasnost and begin to harp on about our destitution. They would produce aid for us but at the same time dictate their own conditions. The private traders would take three skins off their own fellow-citizens and lead the town into a state of affairs in which nobody would be able to buy a sliver of black bread without offering hard currency for it. In addition, everyone from the neighbouring oblasts would try to get into Partygrad. And we've nothing with which to pay our debts to foreign firms.

The discussion reached a dead end. Then somebody remembered the existence of Grobyka. *There* was a man who could find a simple and brilliant solution to the problem! What was he doing now? There seemed to be no news of him nowadays. Somebody said that Grobyka had gone under at the hands of the private traders and the mafia, was hitting the bottle hard and was out of business. Krutov said: 'It would be a crime to throw away such a valuable type of man. We must find him, bring him up to scratch and include him in our operation, giving him unlimited powers. I'm sure he will quickly restore the situation. And there's a special task for the organs of state security – to protect Grobyka from the mafia.'

FOREIGNERS' ITINERARY

Having decided these problems of high policy, the Commission planned the itinerary for the foreign tourists and delegations, taking in the basic aspects of the life of the town. Then the Commission decided to follow the route itself and see what had been selected to show to foreigners. They began with the hotel Ilya Muromets, which had been earmarked for foreigners.

They built a hotel for foreign tourists in Partygrad even in Brezhnev's time. Its construction was a brilliant example of the Party's political far-sightedness. Although the town was then closed to foreigners and nobody had thought of perestroika even in Moscow, they built the biggest hotel for foreigners in the whole of the republic. The hotel was one of the beloved children of Pyotr Stepanovich Suslikov, who was one of the oblast's rulers in those years and later became First Secretary of the Party's obkom. He was already dreaming then of the time when a flood of foreigners would be flowing into a Partygrad ruled by himself.

In front of the hotel's main entrance they erected a monument to the legendary Russian hero, Ilya Muromets, after whom the hotel was named. The Partygrad historians started the hare that the legendary (that is, never-existent) Ilya was a native not of Murom but of Partygrad (formerly Knyazev). It was in Murom, they held, that the first defeat on the Tartar/Mongol yoke was inflicted. Obkom supported the historians' initiative and the hypothesis turned into a theory.

They built the hotel calculating that all the beauties of the town and its surroundings could be seen from the windows. But here they made a mistake. From the windows one could see not only the beauties but secret things such as the military factory, the factory for making artificial limbs, the chemical factory, the atomic electric power-station, the watch-towers of the concentration camps and the psychiatric hospital. Of course the builders were punished for this. But it was too late to put the matter right. While the town was closed to foreigners, they simply forgot about the blunder. After all, these secret objects were perfectly well known even to ten-year-olds.

Now when the town had been opened to foreigners they remembered the mistake. But they decided there was nothing disastrous about the situation; and that it was even a good thing that the foreigners should see it all. Let them see our industrial and military might and draw the conclusions we want them to draw! The psychiatric hospital looks from a distance like an ordinary hospital. And as for the corrective labour camps, the watch-towers could be refashioned to look like towers of the old town or perhaps of a monastery.

They built the hotel with the last word in, no *not* building technology, but in the technology of supervision of foreigners. And of their own people too. They put in bugging devices in every conceivable place so that the hotel guests literally couldn't sneeze without being heard by the KGB's listening-post. The entire staff of the hotel were obliged to spy for the KGB, having first learned tricks like opening and inspecting suitcases and secretly photographing the guests at any time of the day or night and in any position.

Because foreign spies, politicians, journalists and tourists never came to Partygrad, the hotel was taken over by traffickers from the southern fruit-growing republics. The bugging system fell into disuse. Inquisitive speculators rooted out the listening devices. The hotel workers converted the places where the listening should have been done into an additional source of illegal income. The expensive equipment itself (which by the way had been acquired in the USA and transported to the Soviet Union via Federal Germany) was chucked into a cellar and stolen bit by bit.

When the Commission had seen the hotel it decided to remove all the people living there and replace them with selected people from the districts of the oblast and from the town itself. The latter should consist of the intelligentsia from the villages and collective farm workers who were on holiday or visiting relatives. The hotel staff should be strengthened by students from the universities and the institutes once they had learned the not very difficult profession of hotel service.

The Commission decided to refurbish the hotel. They sent a whole battalion of soldiers to help the painters. The soldiers and the painters together drank away the wallpaper and the paint that had been given them. They had to be given more. The authorities then had to employ a battalion of special troops to keep watch over the painters and the other soldiers who were helping the painters. A whole division of these special troops was stationed around Partygrad. They were parachutists armed with the latest weapons and were expert in all forms of warfare, including karate. The special troops forced the painters and soldiers to fix the building in two days, by which time they had drunk only half of the materials with which they had been furnished. The explanation of this type of economics is simple: the speculators were afraid of the special troops and so they sold them spirits at half price.

One member of the Commission considered it likely that foreigners would try to make contact with other guests in the hotel. To overcome this problem another member of the Commission proposed that live eavesdroppers should be hidden in the other rooms. Somebody else doubted whether this measure would be necessary. Why double up on the KGB informers if the guests in the other rooms would be KGB informers anyway? One really must trust one's own people! The KGB representative said: 'Yes, one must trust, but one must also verify the trust.'

FIRST ITINERARY

The main entrance of ILYA gives on to Gorky Street, which leads to an old and dirty part of the town with squalid houses and ends up in a *terrain vague* turned into a rubbish heap. Even before the Commission arrived, Krutov had issued the timely instruction to block traffic in that direction by erecting a gigantic display board. On the board was the design of a building in the Western style of architecture which would apparently be built in that place. According to the project (or promise), the building would contain spacious and comfortable flats for workers and civil servants. Besides there would be swimming-pools, canteens, restaurants, games-rooms, a cinema, a discothèque and other blessings of civilization.

The display board had hardly been erected when a hooligan wrote on it: 'And will there be brothels and drying-out stations in this modern building?' They had to paint over the writing. But then new hooliganistic inscriptions appeared, and pornographic drawings too. Then they had to mount a twenty-four hour guard on the board taken from the militia and the people's volunteers.

The Commission came out into the square and couldn't help admiring the largest statue of Lenin in Russia. Corytov suggested that foreigners should begin their acquaintanceship with the town by placing wreaths at the foot of the monument. This would stimulate the development of horticulture in the oblast. 'Look,' said the chairman of the town commission, pointing to Lenin's monument, 'yesterday there was a whole group of wreaths. And now where are they? Not one left. The swine have stolen them. With us it's always like that. If you take your eyes off them for a moment they either muck everything up or steal it. Mikhail Sergeyevich is absolutely right. We must make a serious drive for order and discipline.'

'But how do they manage to do that?' said the chairman of the oblast commission, not without a certain amount of admiration in his voice.

'We Russians are capable of anything,' answered the chairman of the KGB. 'It's just Russian native wits at work.'

The town inspection included, besides Lenin's statue, the remains of the Partygrad Kremlin, the souvenir shops, museum, and the tomb of the unknown soldier. As in Moscow, newly-weds visit the tomb of the unknown soldier after the registration of their marriage, as well as groups of young soldiers after they've sworn their oaths, and pioneers. All of them laid wreaths. This tradition created two branches of local industry: first the making of wreaths, second the theft of them and their resale. The KGB and the militia are of the opinion that the second industry is actually the daughter of the first. But they haven't been able to catch the thieves yet despite a permanent guard on the tomb by the militia, the people's vigilantes and even by soldiers.

At the souvenir shop the Commission studied the problem of the sale of icons to tourists. Probably currency speculators will appear, offering the tourists 'ancient' icons. In reality the icons are made by local nonconformist artists. The paint hasn't had time to dry on them. But they're better made than the old ones. And they look older than the old ones. For a pair of old jeans the tourist can get a couple of icons; for new ones, only one. Why, you will ask, are old jeans more valuable than new jeans? I shall reply with another question: Why are old icons more valuable than new ones although they're worse than new ones?

Corytov proposed that a private atelier should be set up for making icons. It would be offered the right to sell its products in the souvenir shop. That would deliver a blow against the speculators. The head of the Partygrad commission proposed a factory for the manufacture of icons which would be sold in the West and in the countries of the third world. The KGB representative said it would be better to hand over the business to the priests. The trade-union rep thought that this branch of industry should go to the West on concession.

They decided to include a visit to the town soviet in the first itinerary. The idea was to show foreigners the democratization of the Soviet system of power and government. They decided to fit out a special box in the town soviet from which foreigners could watch the sessions of the soviet. The box would be furnished with facilities for simultaneous translation of speeches into foreign languages.

Corytov advised that, during foreigners' visits, the soviet should arrange discussions such as would permit a pluralism of the Western type. For instance, the question of the repairing of the drains in the new residential district. A heated debate would ensue. The leader of the opposition would pronounce a flaming speech in which he would denounce Stalinism, Brezhnevism and the contemporary conservatives. He needn't speak about the drains. Why batter the heads of the guests with such stinking details? When they'd heard the speech the foreigners would go home and print a load of rubbish about the evolution of our society towards parliamentarism. True, the drains are working badly, as they always have. But that's the fault of Stalin and Brezhnev.

SECOND ITINERARY

The purpose of the second itinerary was to show foreigners the heroic work of Partygraders over perestroika.

When the Commission reached Lenin Prospect, which in one direction ran towards the industrial region of the town, the coach suddenly braked. Two drunkards were crossing the Prospect in an unauthorized place. They were swaying about, falling down, getting up again, helping each other and bawling out songs. Corytov looked scornfully at the representative of the militia. The latter whispered something about 'negligence' and promised to skin the hide off whoever was responsible. The drunks shouted insults at the bus and zigzagged on their way. If they'd only known whom they were insulting!

The coach went past the shop for blind people called Dawn, and the shop for artificial legs called Sprinter. People had become so used to these titles that they didn't notice their black humour. The members of the Commission didn't notice it either: the chairman of the oblast commission said they ought to show these shops to foreigners. For nowhere in the world would you find such concern for blind and legless people as in our country. It wouldn't be a bad idea at all to include a blind man in the foreign delegation. Let them see with their own eyes how we take care of our workmen who have lost their sight!

The coach rushed past buildings bearing the signboards of innumerable offices. Somebody said their number should be reduced. But the representative of the KGB said he'd been in Paris lately and there were ten times as many signboards there. Probably the foreigners wouldn't pay them the slightest attention. In general, people pay more attention to things that do not fit into their usual experience.

The Commission was deeply depressed by what it saw in the industrial district. Everywhere rubbish was around: empty, warped barrels, broken boxes, remains of machinery of an unimaginable squalor. At the aeroplane instruments factory they had built an entrance lodge hardly less large than the factory building itself. But nobody passed through it. And the gates through which, in principle, machines should pass, were closed by a giant padlock; the sort of lock that had probably fastened the gates of the Partygrad Kremlin at the time of the legendary Prince Igor.

The picture the Commission saw at the engineering works was even gloomier. In one of the sections which could be seen from a long way off, part of the wall had simply collapsed. They had hung a plywood shield over the hole. On it there was a drawing of Lenin with a red bow-tie and a cunning smile, his hand slightly out in advance. Underneath were the words *You're on the right path, comrades!* But rain and wind had wreaked such havoc on the placard that even the ideologically pure members of the Commission couldn't restrain their laughter.

'What are we to do?', asked Comrade Corytov, and there was a threat in his voice. 'You won't put *that* in order in a week.'

'Nothing disastrous,' said the chairman of the town trade-union committee optimistically, 'We'll close the Prospect short of Brezhnev Street. It's high time to repair the asphalt surface there. We'll send the traffic round by Brezhnev Street, then by Karl Liebknecht and Rosa Luxemburg Street, and finally by Maurice Thorez Street. So we'll go straight to the electric bulb factory and the textile factory. They block out the whole of the rest of the district. And things are more or less tidy down there. And in a week we can make things really shine down there. So that . . .'

'Only see you don't overdo it,' said Corytov quietly, 'otherwise they'll think we're putting up Potyomkin villages for them. By the way, Brezhnev Street should be renamed.'

'We should call it Bukharin Street,' suggested the representative of the cultural institutions. 'You know that Partygrad used to be called Bukharinsk?'

'Trotsky,' someone corrected.

'What difference does it make?' said the KGB representative. It's time to rehabilitate him too.'

'Better to call the street after Bukharin,' said the Komsomol representative, 'for Bukharin was in favour of perestroika.'

'But isn't it time to call the whole of Partygrad Trotsko-Bukharinsko-Zinovievsk?' cried the trade-union representative enthusiastically. 'Better make it Gorbachevsk.'

'No, it's Stavropol that will be Gorbachevsk. Partygrad will take the name of Pyotr Stepanovich.'

'True. That will be right and proper.'

'In the last resort we could change the whole work itinerary so that there would be no need to rearrange anything,' said Corytov. 'A Soviet-American joint venture has been formed to produce washing-powder. Pyotr Stepanovich thinks we should build the factory here in Partygrad. We must choose such beautiful surroundings for it that people would go there as into a park. We should build a café and restaurants and cinemas. The foreigners would enjoy unwinding there.'

'For the building of that, time would be needed. Not just one year,' said somebody.

'The Germans and the Americans will be doing the building. They will build it quickly – in six months.'

'Remarkable!' exclaimed the KGB rep. We'll be able to show foreigners their own factories. That will make an indelible impression on them.'

'It will be nice to get Western workers into the bargain,' said the trade-union rep dreamily. 'Otherwise our Brother Ivan will let loose his native swinery on to the Western technology.'

'In Moscow we've already thought about that,' Corytov assured him. 'The engineers, technicians and highly qualified workmen will be from the USA and Federal Germany. Our people will imitate their experience.'

'I'm afraid it may happen the other way round,' said the representative of the militia. 'What if the Western specialists are taught drunkenness, hackwork and eyewash by our labourers?'

'That would also be a plus,' said Corytov, by way of humour. 'The worse it is for the West, the better it is for us.'

When the Commission was making its way back to base, the coach had to brake in front of Lenin Square because the two drunks whom they'd seen in the morning had lain down to sleep in the middle of the street. Militiamen on motor cycles with special carts for collecting drunks went up to them. They shoved the disturbers of the public order into the carts and took them away. The road was clear.

'Scoundrels like that should be put in prison,' said the Komsomol representative.

'We should educate them,' Corytov corrected the over-ardent Komsomol leader.

'True,' said the KGB rep in support. 'First educate them, then put them in prison.'

After dinner Corytov remembered that the director of one of the Partygrad factories used to come to Suslikov's office on business. He was an enthusiast of perestroika. Corytov wondered what had happened to him.

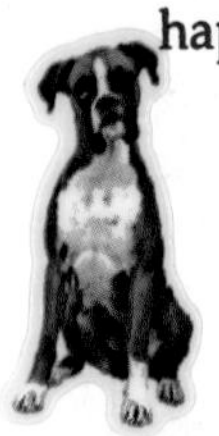

PARABLE OF A FACTORY DIRECTOR

Not all Partygraders took perestroika for a routine governmental spectacle. People could be found who viewed it with sincere enthusiasm. One of them was a man who went in the town by the nickname 'Perestroikist'.

In the years of stagnation Perestroikist was an ordinary engineer without any particular merit. He differed from the others only in his tendency to make exposures. And there was certainly something to expose. Technology was obsolete. Accidents and stoppages happened all the time. The workers were drunk at work, they botched their work and stole everything they could lay their hands on. The plan was fulfilled by cooking the figures. The factory's production was almost completely defective. Meanwhile the manager and his cronies lived it up, helping themselves to flats, dachas, motor cars and to all the rejects they wanted as ordinary articles of use. Without giving bribes the ordinary workmen in the factory couldn't even get what they were entitled to by law. In short, the situation in the factory was as it was in all the factories in the town and had become the normal way of life.

From time to time fighters-for-truth appeared in the factory who tried to make the life of the collective a bit more wholesome. But their efforts ended in failure. What was most striking was that the mass of their co-workers in the factory didn't support the fighters-for-truth. These people knew perfectly well what was going on in their collective. But they themselves participated in that sort of life and adapted themselves to it as best they could. By various means, including theft, hackwork, deceit, conspiracy, back-scratching and illegal practices, they had been clever enough to wrest some share of life's goods. They used means that corresponded with the general style of the life they lived. They were, that is, accomplices in everything that the fighters-for-truth exposed as crimes.

Then came the epoch of glasnost. The high leadership appealed to all citizens to become fighters-for-truth. The factories were afforded unheard-of freedom of action. They were turned over to self-financing; they discussed autonomy and other things that nobody had dared think of before. Our Perestroikist became the mouthpiece of perestroika: he began a frenetic unmasking of the factory manager and 'all his mafia', accusing them of corruption, bureaucratism and conservatism. He wrote a newspaper article. He appeared on television. All levels of the party supported him. The manager of the factory together with a number of other managers were removed from their posts and younger and more energetic specialists were put in their place. They made Perestroikist himself factory manager. 'There, you've got the power, you're free to take your own decisions. Now show us what you're worth!'

For a time it seemed that things were beginning to get better and that the factory would climb to the level of world standards. They imposed a strong work discipline. They reduced drunkenness at work. But the consequences of this progress were discouraging.

Working in the new way the workmen did their daily norm in a couple of hours. Then crazy things started to happen. Mounds of unfinished products piled up near some machine, which couldn't be shifted any further. Other machines had to stop working because of the absence of material to work on. After four hours the factory ground to a halt. And for another four hours they tried to get some order into the chaos.

Perestroikist rushed through the workshop cursing conservatives, hackworkers, drunkards and other enemies of perestroika. The old workmen tried to explain to him that people had become these things not through personal depravity but because of the system of life under which they lived. It simply couldn't be otherwise. They advised him not to be in a tearing hurry and to bring in the new ways gradually. Without destroying the whole status quo. It would be even better, they said, to leave everything unchanged in the factory and to introduce the new methods of work in parallel by creating new factories with new technology and a new organization of work. One shouldn't build the new at the cost of destroying and rearranging the old, but alongside the old system which the new would gradually replace. However, Perestroikist would hear none of this and tried to force both men and machines to work in a manner contrary to their nature.

But it was reality that won. After a short time the old rhythm of work established itself. In the report it looked as if the factory was working in the new way. But this was only a new kind of faking.

To be independent of the State plan and to be free to take initiatives that had seemed so alluring on paper turned out to be something quite different from what Perestroikist had imagined. The law of mutual connections or mutual limitation made itself felt. Enterprises that took advantage of freedom collided with other enterprises they were doing business with, which had also begun to use freedom in their own interests. The intervention of State organs had to be requested to regulate these conflicts and, in effect, to restore the original position. Freedom of enterprise proved to be useful only in a few cases and within very narrow limits.

Perestroikist's factory came in conflict with the suppliers of raw materials and with the consumers of the factory's products. The suppliers discovered more profitable contracts with other factories. Perestroikist rushed to obkom and asked for its help. Obkom replied that it didn't interfere in these matters nowadays. He rushed to the ministry. They told him he wasn't the only one in this awkward position and that he must find his own way out of it. Perestroikist travelled the whole country with his advisers, seeking an optimal solution. He went abroad too. But he got no sense out of anybody and simply exhausted his bank facilities. The workers had to be paid, but the bank wouldn't give any money for that.

Perestroikist rushed off to Moscow. Suslikov agreed to see him. The latter then read him a lecture composed of slogans and abstract phrases. Perestroikist left the Central Committee's building, bought a bottle of gorbachukha from some speculators with the money he had left, drank all of it and threw himself under a train in the Underground. Nobody shed a tear over him in Partygrad.

ITINERARY NUMBER THREE

They decided to dedicate the third itinerary to the 'living conditions of the workers'. For this they chose the newest and most comfortable small district in the town: New Limes. The district was called 'New Limes' in imitation of Moscow's 'New Cherry Trees'. Just as there had never been a cherry tree in New Cherry Trees, so there had never been a single lime tree in New Limes. And the Partygraders interpreted the title as just another piece of trickery.

The mini-district was already built in Khrushchev's time in accordance with certain principles: to combine the kitchen and the dining-room with the lavatory and the bathroom; the bedroom with the hall and the ceiling with the floor. This sort of house was dubbed *khrushchoba*.* Moreover, these houses were built in such a way that they had to be repaired from the moment when they were handed over to the occupier.

But all the same it was a colossal step forward. All the families in the mini-district no longer lived in the communal flats of Stalin's time but in flats of their own. Maybe they were mini-flats, maybe

* Sarcastic name for bad flats built by N.S. Khrushchev. A play on the word *truschoba* = slum.

they were khrushchobas, but they were separate. When the propaganda machine began to emphasize this fact, the intellectuals raised, as a counter-argument, another evident fact: that in the cemetery too every man has his own separate dwelling-place.

The road to New Limes runs through *terrains vagues* and rubbish heaps.

Already in Khrushchev's time they were planning to lay out a park in their place. When they chucked Khrushchev they also chucked Partygrad's highest rulers (who were considered supporters of Khrushchev). They accused them not only of building bad houses but of having failed to honour the promise they'd made to lay out a park.

But throughout the whole of the Brezhnev period they didn't repair the houses.

'There's an example for you of how people lived and worked during the period of stagnation,' said Corytov, forgetting that it was none other than Suslikov who was at the head of the oblast during those years; and that he, Corytov, had then been his assistant.

Somebody suggested they should arrange some voluntary unpaid work and get people to plant trees; along the highway at least. Someone else said that unpaid working days were now looked at askance.

'That's definitely an exaggeration,' remarked Corytov. 'Unpaid working days are and will remain the school of communist work relations. Lenin taught us that.'

When they arrived at New Limes the members of the Commission saw a bronze bust of the late Portyankin. On the forehead of the former member of the Politburo, now demoted as a conservative and a bureaucrat, was painted a famous Russian swear-word of three letters. Noticing this, Corytov proposed that the monument should be removed to another place where foreigners wouldn't be able to see it. And the hooligans would lose the incentive to get up to mischief. Russians played the fool when their antics were visible to everybody. Besides, Portyankin had disgraced himself by getting involved in corruption, so the bust had better be taken away altogether. Soon Suslikov would be getting his second gold star and then the space would be needed for his bust.

The coach stopped in the centre of the mini-district in front of the building of the district council. It was decorated with slogans and portraits of Lenin and Gorbachev. The Commission hardly had time to stretch its legs after sitting for so long when a group of inhabitants approached and handed over a complaint about disorders and defects in the region. They asked that their complaint should be handed to Gorbachev personally. The complaint said that their homes had been conveyed to them in such a defective state that they needed fundamental repairs right now. Holes had appeared in the walls, through which water percolated on rainy days. The flats were crawling with cockroaches from the rubbish chute and the ventilation system. The heating worked badly. The laundry didn't function. In the whole district there were two cafés and one canteen in which there was nothing to eat. There were queues everywhere. Transport was dreadful. Sometimes one had to wait for buses for hours. There was a waiting-list of more than a year to get children into the children's garden.

Corytov reckoned that the complaints were justified. Only the sentences about our backwardness *vis-à-vis* the West caused him to make an angry remark or two. And wasn't it only quite recently that we were glad about our new houses, our hospitals and schools? Didn't we go into raptures about our refrigerators and our television sets? We compared these things with our own past. And now we've begun to look at the West. But then not everyone in the West lived in clover. And Western comfort wasn't given for nothing. People had to work for it. And how!

'You can't make our people work like that. We've forgotten to value what we ourselves achieved. And in the West we see only luxury shops and grand hotels.'

The Commission was depressed by what it had seen in the town's best residential district, despite Corytov's speech.

'It's nothing to boast about, as you see,' said the chairman of the regional council who was accompanying the Commission. 'Consequences of the years of stagnation!'

'True,' said Corytov. 'We shall present it all as the result of the period of stagnation. And we'll screen off the empty ground and the rubbish dump with hoardings depicting the residential district that will be built, thanks to perestroika. It will be the last word in architecture and building technique, of course. And it will take account of all the citizens' needs in the way of comfort and convenience.'

As they left New Limes the Commission members saw this scene. Around Portyankin's monument there was a group of drunks with drinks and eats. One of them opened his bowels into the bushes; the other wee-weed directly on to the pedestal, the third was throwing up the filth he'd been drinking, and the fourth was asleep with his arms wide apart. Stray dogs dashed about among the drunkards. A dirty crow sat on the head of Portyankin which the pigeons had long since fouled. Cheeky sparrows pecked at the breadcrumbs on newspapers. Not far from the thoroughfare stood a torn and ragged old man. He was holding out a piece of paper as torn and ragged as himself towards the coach and the Commission. The coach made an abrupt swerve round the old man and spattered him with mud.

'Who's that scarecrow?' asked Corytov.

'It's Lavatory-pan,' answered one of the Partygraders. 'A well-known madman of the town whom they let out of prison not long ago.'

PARABLE OF LAVATORY-PAN

We were speaking earlier, apropos of the influence of Moscow on Partygrad, of the man who chained himself to the defective lavatory. He was the same ragged old man who stood in the way of the Commission's coach. After the story about the lavatory he received the nickname 'Lavatory-pan'. But his heroic battle against society's evils and for justice began considerably earlier. If somebody were to interest himself in his life and narrate it in detail, a picture might emerge which in its sheer tragedy would surpass all the denunciatory books on Soviet communism put together. Strictly speaking it wouldn't be necessary to write about his personal life; in fact he hardly had one. It would be enough to collect all the letters, statements, complaints and petitions written by him, alone or with others, to the different organs of power and to different official personages, together with their answers.

But in brief the story was this. In 1939 a young Komsomolets, later known as Lavatory-pan, was living in a communal flat with several other families. Finally the lavatory broke down. It had broken down before, but after the combined efforts of all the lodgers who knew something about water-pipes and drains, it was more or less mended. But this time it had broken down altogether. The lodgers addressed themselves to the house management. It didn't help them. They then complained to the district housing authority. It didn't help them. They wrote a letter to *Partgradskaya Pravda*. It didn't help. They wrote a letter to *Pravda* in Moscow, to deputies of the Supreme Soviet, to Voroshilov and Budjonny. No result, just the same.

In the flat the stink was such that life became impossible. The flat-dwellers rushed off to relieve themselves in the neighbouring courtyards, thereby incurring the hatred of their neighbours. At this critical moment Komsomolets Lavatory-pan advanced the idea that a letter should be written to Stalin himself. There was no hope elsewhere; and so the lodgers agreed. Lavatory-pan wrote a heart-rending letter about heartless bureaucrats who were causing damage to our society and to the construction of socialism in one country that was separate from the others (that was how school-children were taught to refer to Stalin's work at that time). The lodgers signed the letter and sent it off. Next day Lavatory-pan was arrested for anti-Soviet propaganda and for the organization of a collective crime. Although he was a minor, they sentenced him to ten years in a corrective labour camp.

The war with Finland began. Lavatory-pan volunteered for the front. His request was granted. He was very brave and he was wounded. Having wiped away his guilt with his own blood, he received a decoration. When he had been demobilized, Lavatory-pan renewed his struggle for the repair of the lavatory. Again letters, petitions, complaints and resolutions went off. One doesn't know how all the red tape would have ended if the war with Germany hadn't begun. Lavatory-pan again went off to the front as a volunteer.

After the war he returned home with a veritable iconostasis of medals and decorations, with three wounds and the rank of lieutenant. There then began years of study and of course struggle for the repair of the perpetually broken lavatory. This time he deepened the struggle by denouncing the ulcers of Stalinism; and they gave him another ten-year sentence. After Khrushchev's 'unmasking' speech he was freed and rehabilitated. He graduated from the institute, became an engineer, married and had children. His old house with the defective lavatory was pulled down. Lavatory-pan was given a room in another house which was also old but not yet scheduled for demolition. He was happy at last. But not for long: the lavatory broke down. Because all the lavatories in the house were unmendable Lavatory-pan headed a struggle of all the lodgers for the repair of the whole drainage system. This was a higher level of social movement and Lavatory-pan fulfilled his social obligations with great enthusiasm, which was made easier by Khrushchev's 'thaw'.

Finally, that house too was demolished. Lavatory-pan and his family got a separate two-roomed flat in the new house. It is impossible to describe how happy the family was. But after only a week in the new flat the lavatory broke down. The next period of Lavatory-pan's struggle ended with the episode we've described earlier when he attached himself with a chain to the broken lavatory.

After his term of imprisonment Lavatory-pan dedicated his life wholly to the struggle against the defects in the district's living conditions. He was divorced from his wife and gave up her share of the family living space. He got a little room of six square metres and by an irony of fate it was in a communal flat with a damaged lavatory.

This was the end of him. He went to the psychiatric hospital. They let him out when perestroika began. They were used to him in the district and made fun of him. And he went on sending complaints to the Central Committee of the CPSU about the lavatory that wasn't working, as well as to the United Nations, the American President, the Pope, Mrs Thatcher, Solzhenitsyn and Sakharov. But, as had been the case in all the previous years, nobody paid any attention to him.

The prospect that Partygrad would be thrown open to foreigners poured oil on the fire of the cultural renaissance. The culture people became unusually alert when the rumour spread around the town. Innumerable devisers of impracticable schemes, supplicants and complainants besieged the Commission. With their help the Commission very quickly worked out a programme of measures, the implementation of which would raise Partygrad and make it one of the country's leading cultural centres.

The Commission decided to allow artists full freedom of creation. Let independent theatres open, of whatever type and as many as anyone wanted. Let every actor have his theatre! Let them show naked males and females on the stage! The more bedroom scenes, the merrier! The less the talent and the more the dirt, the better the foreigners will like it!

The Commission recommended that the local authorities should hold a competition for people who had no voice, no ear and no artistic talent whatever; choose the worst of them, make them into a sort of Western ensemble and stage them wherever foreigners would be. Let them wail their rubbish with their cracked voices, let them twist and turn like monkeys. The foreigners will see that we've got everything they have in Paris, in New York, in London and in Rome; and they will rest content. Ah well, they'll say Russia's launched on the road to democracy. Well, we must help the dear Russians see where that road leads.

The Commission also advised the rulers of Partygrad to create a lot of associations of independent artists and put exhibition halls at their disposal and buy up the daubs of the Partygrad 'Picassiat' or 'Picassery' (as Corytov called them). In the West all this would look like a beacon of 'cultural renaissance'.

'The main thing', Corytov concluded, 'is that the foreigners should see that, although we haven't yet got the results of creative freedom, on the other hand there is something more important than the results of creative freedom, namely creative freedom itself, even if it has bad results or no results at all. So let them paint naked women and erotic scenes. Let them be daring and unafraid of homosexual themes. As Marx himself once said, nothing which is human is foreign to us. And, as Lenin said, we Bolsheviks are not ascetics. Let them open new museums. To each artist his own museum!'

The Commission advised the writers to start up as many magazines as they wanted. To each writer his magazine! At his own expense, of course. Let each man get hold of his own paper, do the printing himself and sell his own books. The profit? Halves with the State. Literary works must be printed without censorship of any kind, without editing and even without correcting the grammatical mistakes. Let the individuality of the author come through! No need to be afraid of writing about murder, robbery and rape. Now that we've begun to live in a new way, we must write about life in a new way.

Corytov promised to help the writers publish a magazine called *The Partygrad Quagmire*. But he advised them to change the title to *Russia's Bum*. He gave the following reason. In ordinary life we can't take a single step without indecent words and obscene language. But if anybody happens to use an innocent word like 'bum' in print or in a public speech, there's an upsurge of moral indignation. In order to avoid the accusation of immorality, we must use accurate and expressive words which are now considered indecent instead of their terribly grey, boring and nebulous synonyms. Instead of the word 'bum', for instance, we use expressions such as the 'hind part of body' or 'what we sit in a chair on', or 'the part of the body which is opposite to the head'. When we do this we accompany these pearls of fine speech with a low sort of laugh. Thus the thoughtful clarity of speech is lost. And at times it is absolutely right to grunt something unintelligible, because expressions like 'As for you, Pyotr Ivanovich, you're a typical bum', 'Our section has buggered itself up' or 'You can all take a running jump at yourself' do not have adequate equivalents in generally approved speech. In this connection the word 'bum' merits special attention. In non-official language it has achieved a degree of generality and universality that permits it to be placed in the same series as philosophical categories such as 'matter', 'consciousness', 'space', 'time' and 'movement'. Now that we've begun to think and live in a new way, we must implement perestroika in language too. You writers should take a lead in the linguistic revolution.

Once we've rehabilitated the word 'bum', we'll be able to tackle the most famous four-letter swear-word of three letters. I'm convinced that it will take its place in all the world's languages alongside 'sputnik', 'perestroika' and 'glasnost'.

THE BLOODY WHEEL

In the evening the Commission visited the Independent Theatre for the première of *The Bloody Wheel*, staged after the novel of the writer we mentioned before. It was an ultra-modern play. As the newspapers were to say, in comparison with it the avant-garde theatre of the twenties seemed like old-fashioned classics. The actors walked about the auditorium asking the audience provocative questions such as: 'What were YOU doing in the years of stagnation?' And they dragged old people suspected of Stalinism and Brezhnevism on to the stage and subjected them to general mockery. The actors wore dirty, smelly costumes to symbolize the past epoch. The stink made many of the audience want to vomit. These were led out of the theatre to the hunting-cries of the actors. And one of the actors wailed: 'And what was it like for your victims?' for general edification.

The play dealt with all the main epochs of Soviet history, beginning with the October revolution and ending with perestroika. First came the scene at the Smolny Institute. Lenin was running about the corridors with his advisers. Stalin came to meet him. Lenin stopped for a moment and, pointing at Stalin, asked Trotsky who that bandit-face was. Trotsky said: 'You get all sorts wandering in here.'

Stalin's yellow eyes flashed, he pulled at his pipe and muttered: 'You wait! I'll show you where you get off!'*

The next scene was a conference of Party leaders. Lenin was half lying in his coffin surrounded by his disciples and his advisers. Milling around were Khrushchev, Sakharov, Gorbachev, and Yeltsin. They were planning measures for the perestroika of every-

* In Russian, 'where the pike spend the winter'.

thing that they hadn't yet begun to build. Rykov proposed that all power should go to the soviets and that elections should be from two candidates. Kamenev suggested that several parties should be allowed. Zinoviev proposed that the functions of the Party should be limited by the ideological education of the workers. Tukhachevsky proposed the destruction of atomic weapons and also short-range, middle-range and long-range rockets.

Bukharin wanted to abolish the collective farms and switch to individual farmers, as in the United States. He assured the meeting that one farmer with his family would produce more than a collective farm with three hundred people in it. Asked what should be done with all the people who would be released from the land, Bukharin advised that they should be sent to school.

Suddenly Stalin ran on to the stage with his colleagues. Besides all the well-known ones, Brezhnev, Chernenko, Gromyko and Grishin could be seen, and also Robespierre, Marat, Cromwell, Mao Tse-tung, Khomeini and even Hitler. Stalin pushed Lenin into his coffin and then hammered down the lid with enormous nails. For a long time Lenin kept shouting from his coffin that Stalin was a brute, that he had seized too much power over the Party and that he must be stopped from being *Gensek*. But Stalin sat quietly on the coffin smoking his pipe. Robespierre and Beria then wheeled a guillotine on to the stage and began to cut off the heads of Lenin's Old Guard. The heads fell from the stage into the auditorium.

As the newspapers said, although everybody knew that the heads were not real heads, the audience derived pleasure from the striking verisimilitude of the portrayals of the spirit of the times. At the same time the stinking artists were wandering along the aisles collecting signatures for a petition for the printing of *Gulag Archipelago*.

Then the play portrayed collectivization and industrialization. Corpses littered the stage. From time to time people took them away and then filled up the stage with new corpses. The collective farmers had three of their skins removed: three times, to fit in with the proverb. The piles of corpses were all over the machines and factories. Workers were shot every five minutes. All this was done by Stalin and his henchmen.

The next act was about the years before the war and the war itself. Stalin was embracing Hitler and fixing the sharing-out of Europe. To show Hitler that he was his friend Stalin ordered the arrest and execution of all the generals and marshals of the Red Army except the stupidest ones. The war began. There was Stalin in a cellar, weeping and trembling with terror and crying: 'Brothers and sisters, save me!' The army was in a state of panic. One general called Vlassov wanted to save Russia. He asked Hitler to allow him to rescue Russia from the Bolsheviks. But Hitler didn't trust the patriotic Vlassov and suffered defeat. When he heard that Hitler had been defeated, Stalin came up above ground and seized the fruits of victory for himself. Then he resumed his old ways, arresting and shooting everyone all the time.

No one can say how all this would have ended if Khrushchev and Gorbachev hadn't come on the scene. They began to make unmasking speeches. Stalin went into a convulsion and fell senseless to the ground. Universal rejoicing. On the stage and in the hall Khrushchevites began to run around with bunches of maize. But the unreconstructed Stalinists headed by Brezhnev stopped all the festive rejoicing. Everything stood still. The stage and the auditorium were sunk in darkness. This lasted for half an hour. The newspapers wrote that this was the strongest episode not only of the play but in the whole of Soviet dramatic literature. There was such a silence in the hall that not even the buzzing of a fly could be heard. (The reason was of course that all the flies had died of boredom in the previous acts.) Finally there was a blinding light. Perestroika had begun. Gorbachev appeared looking like Peter the Great and began to open the window through into Europe.

The members of the Commission managed with great difficulty to sit through the performance. All the same they recommended that the play should be shown to foreigners. In this they were guided by the directive made by Corytov. 'The play of course is controversial, to put it mildly,' he said. 'But for us what is the most important thing at this stage? It is to carry through a specific political line with respect to a concrete historical situation. The play isn't for our people. It's for foreigners. Our people won't be willing to look at much like that. Certainly not if they have to pay.

'Don't give the foreigners bread to eat, let them root about in our rubbish bins. If we show this play to foreigners, we shall be killing three hares with one bullet. We'll be earning hard currency, we'll be showing a critical attitude to the evils of the past, and we'll be allowing an unheard-of freedom of creation. Foreigners least of all are interested in real truth or real artistic creation. Both genius and time are needed to create anything genuine. Just now we haven't either. Well, geniuses we could find. But then geniuses always do the opposite to what we tell them to do.'

BUGGER OFF!

The members of the Commission had hardly been able to come to themselves after *The Bloody Wheel* when it was time to go to see a new film created in conditions of full creative freedom. The film was called *Bugger Off!* The very title produced a sensation in the world of art and its adherents. Even before they saw the film the critics declared it to be the outstanding masterpiece in the history of Soviet cinema. When they did see it the critics didn't know how to react. It was indeed a masterpiece but a masterpiece of mediocrity, baseness, obscenity, caddishness, debauchery and pretentiousness.

'I've never had to drink such filthy slops in all my life, and I've seen hundreds of bad films,' whispered the culture representative to Corytov. 'They've taken the very worst from obsolete Western traditions. They've mixed everything up and turned it into chaos. Add to that pornography, idiocy, intellectual poverty. In short, not simply bad but a cesspit.'

'It's superb,' whispered Corytov. 'It doesn't matter if it's rubbish, as long as it isn't a real masterpiece. Tell the comrades that the film is rubbish, but absolutely in the spirit of perestroika. We will give it our praise.'

When they heard Corytov's instructions the members of the Commission calmed down and merged their reactions with those of the audience. The latter greeted everything that was base, stupid or obscene with wild applause, especially the naked women and the bed scenes. The film ended with the hero shouting 'Bugger off!' at the Party Secretary of obkom. At that, pandemonium broke out and there was a standing ovation. Flowers were thrown at director and cast. After the viewing they sized up the film. They asked Corytov to say a few words. He said that the film could be sent off to the Cannes Film Festival.

'Are you being serious?' asked the culture rep when the Commission had left the studio.

'Perfectly serious,' answered Corytov. 'In the West they regard us as barbarians. If we begin to do things as they do they'll begin to clap us on the shoulder and give our backward shit first prize. But if we're to produce shit, then we can surpass the West in a jiffy. In other words, in culture we'll catch up with the West's shit and outshit it. That's our directive just now.'

'With such an instruction we'll be equal to the task. As you say, the creation of real works of art takes time. And in any case, how does one define a work of art? And besides, our epoch is the epoch in which mediocrity and ugliness have triumphed. All the same, this is rather depressing. After all, we used to make films that shook the world.'

'Yes, but when was that? It was during the time of the cult of personality. The people still believed in ideals. They didn't hanker after the West. In general. . . .'

Corytov didn't finish his train of thought. But it was clear to all of them without his saying anything what he was going through. They all met in his room at the hotel, did some serious drinking and chatted away almost until morning.

THE FIFTH ITINERARY

The next itinerary took in the Old People's Home, the Funeral Complex, the monastery and the functioning church. When they combined these institutions they had in mind not only their territorial but their vital connections. The old people were getting ready for the next world and were thinking about their souls and their life in the grave. Cemetery and church had been indivisible throughout the centuries.

The Commission was extremely gratified at the way in which the priests had transformed the monastery in a very short time. The Prior gave a luxurious dinner in honour of the Commission. He delivered a speech in which he spoke of the growing number of young people who wished to take their vows and to learn in the seminary; of the attraction of Komsomoltsy and even members of the Party towards religion on the one hand and, on the other, the interest shown by serving priests in Marxism-Leninism; about perestroika in the Church; of the readiness of professors from the seminary to give lectures gratis on the history of religion in the anti-religious museum. In his reply Corytov appealed to the clergy to begin a battle of their own against the corrupting influence of the negative sides of Western life on the Soviet people, who borrowed them uncritically along with the positive aspects. 'These chaps won't let us down,' said Corytov to his colleagues as they departed from the hospitable symbiosis of faith and disbelief.

In the functioning church a crowd of well-upholstered priests met the Commission. Their sated, shining physiognomies exuded self-satisfaction and confidence in the morrow. They were dressed as if they were all metropolitans and patriarchs.

'Look at all this masquerade,' whispered the trade-union representative to the KGB representative. 'Any one of them could pass for the Patriarch. Before the revolution priests weren't decked out like this.'

'They've got a tiny little church, but there are more priests in it than in the Vatican,' whispered the KGB rep. 'And here are we struggling against the bureaucracy.'

'That hasn't anything to do with the priests,' said Corytov. 'In our country the Church is separated from the State.'

'Thank God for that,' said the trade-union representative. 'If the Church was joined to the State, we'd never get any peace from the priests. But do you think that God exists, all the same?'

'If he did exist, then he wouldn't allow all this nonsense to go on.'

The Commission advised the priests when the foreigners came to visit the church to lay on a model demonstration of the baptism of infants, weddings and funerals and other ceremonies. The parents of the babies could be members of the Party; the newly married could be Komsomoltsy: the deceased could be former Party workers. In these cases freedom of religion would look more convincing. And in general the church could now work hand in glove with ideology and propaganda.

Corytov promised to help the priests publish material about the persecution of the Church in Stalin's time. The priests for their part requested the strongest measures against ecclesiastical dissidents who criticized perestroika in the Church and set up heretical groups within the Orthodox Church. Freedom *of* religion did not mean freedom *within* religion.

In the Old People's Home they put on an amateur concert for the Commission. The old men sang the current top of the pops and jumped and twisted about as if they were twenty years old. The director of the Home explained that they were, it seemed, by their very nature suited to new-wave influences: for they shook, twisted and whined from old age. If somebody made them up, gave them a new suit of clothes and some stimulants, one could turn them into a rock youth group wilder than any of the ones now in Moscow.

After the concert a group of old Bolsheviks made a proposal to Corytov with the request that he should forward it personally to Mikhail Sergeyevich. The proposal was to take Lenin's sarcophagus on a foreign tour and show him to the public for large sums of money. In that way the country would get hard currency which was needed so much for perestroika. The old men referred to the fact that the mummies of Egyptian pharaohs are carried all over the world and pull in a whole heap of cash. And, after all, Vladimir Ilyich did a bit more for the liberation of humanity than some old Rameses or Amenhotep.

In the Funeral Complex the members of the Commission were at once invited to take refreshments. Although they had already filled their stomachs in the monastery, they could not bring themselves to forgo the funeral meal, so absolutely delicious did it look. The manager of the Complex assured Corytov that the Complex's new management had corrected its predecessors' mistakes. Now the workers in the 'world beyond the grave' would most certainly implement the directives of the Party and the government, would accelerate development without the slightest dishonesty and using the Complex's hidden reserves. In particular the Complex had concluded an agreement with the Old People's Home. Now the inhabitants of the Home would deliver their own bodies for burial in the Complex, and not to village cemeteries.

Similar negotiations were in progress with the psychiatric hospital and with Atom. There were of course difficulties. The productivity of the Complex was held back by the bureaucrats of the various institutions concerned, which supplied the Complex with its raw material. It was the dearest hope of the workers in the funeral world to develop business contacts with Western computer firms. The Complex intended to regulate the construction of coffins by computers which would assure a constant temperature and a constant humidity in the coffin-hall, so that the deceased would be kept fresh in appearance for at least a hundred years. Rumours of the new technology were already about the town. Thousands of citizens had ordered computerized graves.

There was yet another attractive side to this: if such graves could be sold at a discount or even offered free, then millions of citizens might agree to shorten their period as a pensioner to a minimum. In that way we would halt the ageing of the population and we would save the State billions of roubles in pensions and make the housing problem easier.

That evening the Commission was invited to a Court of History which was organized on the initiative of the Old People's Home and the obkom of the Komsomol.

THE COURT OF HISTORY

In Partygrad they interpreted Moscow's directive to 'establish truth' as the profound wish of the Muscovite soul to lie in a new way. People remembered that once upon a time the place was called Trotsky. They petitioned Moscow to give that name back to the town. But Moscow advised them to wait. First Moscow had to exploit the rehabilitation of Kamenev, Zinoviev and Bukharin. When the sensation about that had passed off in the West, Moscow could chuck in a new titbit for the West to make a fuss about. For the time being stick to Bukharin, ordered Moscow. So in Partygrad there was a wave of conferences on Bukharin. An informal Bukharin society even came into being. It put out a brochure which made it clear that Gorbachev had simply borrowed his perestroika ideas from Bukharin. So the management of the Bukharin society was invited to the Party's obkom, which asked them to moderate their ardour.

'What are you on about, comrades?' they said. 'So in 1921 they were talking about perestroika, were they, even before they'd built anything? Wasn't that a bit early? And as to Comrade Gorbachev, mightn't he have something new to say compared with Bukharin?'

The Bukharinists then promised to make the appropriate corrections to historical truth. An anecdote arose in connection with this episode. Khrushchev and Brezhnev met in the next world. They asked each other whether they had built anything. When each said 'no', they were filled with amazement: what on earth were the Gorbachevites *re*building, then?

In Partygrad they began to establish their own local truth as distinct from the truth of the State. They started looking for suitable candidates. It became clear at once that every single oblast leader right up to Suslikov and Krutov had been out-and-out scoundrels. Hundreds of thousands of innocent victims had been obliterated on their orders before they themselves became victims of the terror. In addition, almost all of them had been non-Russians. Finally they alighted on some fellow called Ivanov who was shot as a Bukharinist even though he had never met Bukharin and in any case had nothing to do with politics, as he himself demonstrated at his trial. As a punishment for that, the present authorities ascribed to him membership of a Trotskyist-Bukharinist block. Thus they made this Ivanov the innocent victim and ideological opponent of Stalinism. The authorities called a street of the town Ivanov after him, published his biography and erected a memorial to him. Then it was explained that Ivanov had been head of the Cheka (then the GPU and the NKVD) in the oblast and was shot for his excessive zeal in destroying 'enemies of the people'. But they decided against writing about that.

In the Old People's Home they hunted down one unrepentant Stalinist. The old man was deaf and blind and his mind was utterly confused. All the same they subjected him to a show trial in the Court of History. As judges they chose young people with university education who had become theorists and apologists of perestroika. They held the trial on the premises of the dramatic theatre, where they illustrated the historical excursions of the judges with stage representations of the relevant events.

The hall was chock-full. The trial was shown on television. The judges seated themselves to endless applause. Then in a manly way they proceeded to revile the stick-in-the-mud 'cultist' – that is, the old man, because of his foul crimes during Stalin's time. They accused him, in particular, of the cruel murder of Comrade Ivanov, whom we mentioned earlier.

The old man nodded his head at each question and at each accusation and muttered something incomprehensible. Some elderly woman blathered something to the effect that this court reminded her of Stalin's trials in the thirties, only in reverse. The whole hall fell on her like a ton of bricks and the militia turned her out for making a disturbance. The Chairman of the Historical Tribunal declared that the trial of this one unrepentant Stalinist was a trial of the whole Stalinist epoch. Next day it was explained that they had brought the *wrong* old man to trial before the Court of History. In fact the accused was himself a victim of Stalinism who'd spent more than twenty years in the camps. But this fact was not publicized in order that historical truth should not suffer. And nobody insisted on its being known. Partygrad was longing to free itself from its past sins and to move forward into the future with a clear conscience.

ITINERARY NUMBER SIX

In order to demonstrate the liberalized regime to foreigners, the authorities planned a visit to a strict-regime corrective labour camp, one whose name was known to the whole world, thanks to the surviving victims of Stalinism and to the dissidents. In the Stalin years the camp was one of the biggest in the country. Under Khrushchev it emptied and was almost completely destroyed. Under Brezhnev they partly restored it. Mostly they kept political prisoners there. In the camp there were also the most hardened criminals whose job was to terrorize the politicals. When perestroika began, they let out some of the politicals and distributed the others throughout the ordinary camps. And so the Partygrad camp again emptied.

The KGB representative proposed that they should install a museum of the Stalinist and Brezhnevite terror in the abandoned camp on the lines of Dachau and Buchenwald. The concept of a museum like that would evoke a resonance throughout the whole world. Donations would come in thick and fast. Former prisoners and the families of those who had perished there would shower the museum with materials and exhibits. In the middle of the camp they should erect a monument to the victims of the terror.

'An excellent idea,' said Corytov. 'Only we mustn't lay it on *too* thick. Our past doesn't consist only of failures and crimes. We did become the greatest power in the world. And what a war we won! We saved humanity from fascism. We were first into space. Not everyone was put in a camp. There was such a thing as heroism of the workers. There *was* real enthusiasm. There were repressions and mistakes. But do not let us bring down the whole of our great history to their level.'

The Chairman of the Partygrad Commission grasped Corytov's thought and developed it further. He suggested that they should set up in the camp a branch of the folklore museum, in which a number of stands would be devoted to the Stalinist and Brezhnevite repressions.

After a long discussion the Commission decided that it would be more useful to make a single 'repression hall' in a museum which already existed in the town itself. It would be more convenient for foreigners, and much cheaper.

Having decided the camp problem in the best possible way, the Commission moved on to the other purpose of the itinerary: the psychiatric hospital. The Partygrad *psychushka* also had a very bad world reputation. The very fact that the authorities had decided to let foreigners visit it should make a powerful impression on the West. The hospital was about half an hour's drive from the centre of the town. From the outside it looked quite respectable and no worse than Western institutions of the same type. Inside, there were no longer any dissidents undergoing compulsory treatment for political reasons. They had let them all out or transferred them to other hospitals. The patients who were left were evidently one hundred per cent clinical madmen, as any Western expert could testify.

But the happiness of the members of the Commission didn't last long. They saw that the hospital was bung-full of patients who'd gone off their heads because of perestroika. If foreigners had the chance to talk to the inmates of the hospital, they could come away with a wrong impression: that the patients, that is the madmen, were all sincere supporters of perestroika. Rumours would circulate that the conservatives had seized power in Partygrad and were preparing a counter-revolution from below as a counter to the Gorbachevite revolution from above.

The Commission found this way out of its difficulty. It decided to clear out one section of the hospital of patients altogether and to make it into a club for the former victims of compulsory medicine who had now been set at liberty. In conversation with these victims, foreigners would become convinced that they were normal madmen and spread it abroad that the old stories about compulsory Soviet medicine had been greatly exaggerated.

In the sixth itinerary the Commission included meetings of foreigners with greens, patriots and democrats. The greens had just begun their struggle to save the Partygrad quagmire. They held that the drying-out of the quagmire would mean the disappearance from the oblast of all house-flies, mosquitoes and gadflies. Then the birds would have nothing to feed on and would either die out or emigrate to the West. And then the house-flies, mosquitoes and gadflies would start breeding but in such quantities that all human life would come to an end and everyone would either die or emigrate to the West. In their discussions with the greens, foreigners would have the unrepeatable opportunity to express their humanism and feeling of responsibility for the fate of the insects.

The patriots soon took the hint from the Muscovites and agreed with them about everything except one point: relations with the Jews. The Commission asked the patriots not to show their anti-Semitism openly. But the patriots declared that without open anti-Semitism Russian nationalism wasn't Russian nationalism at all.

A curious thing happened with the democrats, which deserves to be narrated separately.

THE POST-COMMUNIST ERA

Rumours to the effect that people in the West had decided to evaluate the present new Soviet era as the collapse of communism and the beginning of a post-communist era had even reached Partygrad. Ordinary Partygraders were quite indifferent. It made not the slightest difference to them what name was given to the swinery in which they had lived for centuries and in which they were condemned to live until the end of time; whether it was called 'serfdom', 'war communism', 'developed socialism' or 'post-communism'. With ever more speed, but ever less efficiency, the Partygraders scoured the town and its environs in search of something to eat, gulped down gorbachukha and bashed in the faces of perestroikists, conservatives and each other. The West's intention to free them from the yoke of communism was as foreign to them as the intentions of the perestroikists to improve communism.

At the same time the intellectuals were totally absorbed in their discussions on this subject. What on earth remained for *them* to do? All the political anecdotes had been told. All the anecdotes about perestroika made one yawn. All the evils of communism had been unmasked. The whole of Soviet history had been spat upon and smeared to such an extent that there was now nowhere left to spit. Gorbachukha had lost its original power. They'd become used to it and drank it with revulsion.

Then, at this ideologically critical moment, the West threw an earth-shaking theme at the Partygrad thinking élite: how should life be organized in the oblast after communism had entirely disappeared?

The democrats were the leaders of the intellectual movement. Just before the arrival of the Muscovite Commission they addressed a demand to the local soviet, now supposed to be the supreme authority (not a request, mark you, but a demand!), to supply them with premises where the democrats could hold conferences on this very theme. At this conference the democrats were ready to declare to everyone within earshot: 'Yes, there is such a party.'*

In the soviet they went into a panic. After meeting they contacted the Party's obkom. The obkom began by telling them to bugger off. 'Now *you're* the highest power,' it said. 'Make your own decisions!' It was only after that that the chairman of the soviet had been taken to hospital with a massive heart attack. Krutov and Gorban agreed to do what the 'future parliament' asked them to do. Maotsedunka welcomed the idea of a conference, stating that it would inaugurate a new epoch of Soviet history and bring the future parliament into being.

Gorban proposed that an empty barracks in the former camp for

* A famous remark by Lenin about the Communist Party in 1917.

political prisoners should be used for conferences, or the corresponding hall in the psychiatric hospital. Krutov said that the West might well interpret such a move in the wrong way and proposed to put the conference in the circus arena, which happened to be empty during the circus troupe's tour in the West.

Krutov's proposal was accepted amid paroxysms of laughter. The only regret the Commission had was that the clowns, Vaniushka and Petiushka, were also away in the West. Otherwise, during the post-communist conference they could have had them doing numbers alternating with the speeches of the orators. Let us say that a democrat is demanding the privatization of the means of production. After his speech Vaniushka comes into the arena in tears, dragging an inflated rubber elephant on a cart. Petiushka asks him what he's doing. Vaniushka says that the circus is being privatized and they've given him the elephant as his share. But what is he going to feed it on if he has to live on bread and water? And where is he going to keep it? In his little flat the elephant's legs would stick out of the door and that would never do. Petiushka consoles Vaniushka and advises him to put the elephant in store. Vaniushka pulls the stopper out of the elephant and all the air goes out. Vaniushka stores the elephant by hiding it in his pocket. After a show like that the town would be in stitches for a whole week.

A full complement of the Commission attended the conference. Applause greeted its entry. Corytov was invited to sit on the presidium alongside the chairman. There was only one question on the day's agenda: the prospects of communism during the present epoch. The chief democrat opened the conference, and said that the West was strongly of the opinion that communism was about to collapse and that a post-communist era was beginning. The task of the conference was to judge to what extent this opinion corresponded with reality.

The speeches began. And then the Partygrad intellectuals showed that not in vain had they been pupils in Soviet schools, universities and institutes; not in vain had they passed examinations in Marxism-Leninism; not in vain had they experienced life's own school in the Soviet collective. With one voice they said that the very fact that a conference on this theme was permitted was an eloquent testimony to the strength and stability of communism and of its capacity to develop in the direction of democracy. The orators condemned the mistakes and crimes of the Stalinist period boldly and unequivocally, came down on Brezhnev and his 'mafia', paraphrased Gorbachev's speeches and those of other enthusiasts of perestroika, and paraphrased the articles in newspapers and magazines written by the blatherers in the capital.

As regards the economics and the social-political order of the post-communist era, the orators supported the 'platform' of the democrats and of the 'parliamentary opposition'.

After the conference Corytov met Krutov and Gorban. He said that with the 'post-communists' the Party had to be on its guard. They were educated people. One could fill every propaganda post in the oblast with them. But they were capable of every kind of dirty trick. They would start to fawn on foreigners. For the sake of fame in the West they would sell their fathers and mothers as well as all the ideals of communism. We shall have to do educational work with them individually, said Corytov. They must be taught that after dinner comes the reckoning. We can live without them. At the same time we must pay special attention to the informal associations and movements which are much more important for the strengthening of the moral and political unity of our society: associations such as the society of veterans of the Patriotic War, the union of veterans of the Afghan War, the society of the Komsomoltsy of the thirties, the society of activists of the collective farm movements, the society of shock-workers of the five-year plans, the people's vigilantes. In short, there are huge possibilities there and we must make use of them.

As he spoke, Corytov felt himself really to be the emissary of the revolution; not of the demagogic 'revolution from above' that was being stirred up by the Western mass media, and partly by ourselves, but of the one which began in October 1917, whose conquests were now being threatened by the present newspaper 'revolution'.

ITINERARY NUMBER SEVEN

Before the revolution the oblast produced a great deal of meat, butter, vegetables, fruit and bread; that is, it was a backward place.

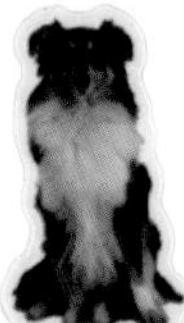

After the revolution all that food disappeared and so the oblast began to regard itself as industrially advanced. Although the oblast's agriculture was in a wretched state throughout the whole of Soviet history, Portyankin, Suslikov and Maotsedunka became heroes of socialist labour for their successes in developing it. Maotsedunka rose from being an ordinary collective farm worker to the rank of head of the agricultural division of the Party's obkom, thanks entirely to the fact that the sections of agriculture that she managed, and finally all of it, gradually went out of production. In the historical moment we are describing the sector reached the very limit of degradation. And Maotsedunka herself expressed decisive opposition to showing the countryside to foreigners. She thought of her aunt who bred rabbits and did a good trade with them on the peasants' market. 'She has sackfuls of money,' said Maotsedunka, describing her aunt as an out-and-out speculator. 'If she'd been able to rent a large piece of land and been allowed to employ assistants, she would have covered the whole oblast with rabbits. Rabbits breed quickly – like rabbits. In a couple of months life would have become completely impossible, as in Australia some years back. On the basis of her rabbits Auntie would have built a poultry farm and a piggery, and then she would have gone in for cattle. All she needs is to be left alone. In two years she would raise stock-rearing in the oblast to the highest world levels. And the town would be choking with meat.'

'An excellent thought, Yevdokia Timofeyevna. All right, let your aunt boost agriculture. All right, she'll be the first Soviet farmer of the American type. All right, she'll get rich, provided the meat gets to the shops. Rabbits OK, even cats OK, so long as it's meat. We'll open a special shop for your aunt. And we'll take the foreigners there and to her farm. We'll do the road up for it.'

They spent some time in the evening in Maotsedunka's dacha. After dinner they reminisced about Khrushchev's perestroika. They remembered the tragic death of a collective farm chairman who had been sent down by Moscow in those hectic years.

PARABLE OF THE COLLECTIVE FARM

It all happened in the first years of Khrushchev's government. The high leadership took the decision to rearrange the work of the collective farms so as to increase their productivity and to improve the collective farmers' lives. From the towns they sent volunteers to become chairmen of collective farms. They gave them bank loans and greater powers. Most of these new men quickly adapted to the real-life circumstances and got out of them what advantage they could. However, there were some idealists among them who believed in the advent of a new era. One such idealist, Envoy, appeared in Partygrad oblast.

Before the war Envoy finished at the institute. Then he went as a volunteer to the front, served until he became a battalion commander, was three times wounded and given many decorations. After the war he worked as an engineer in Siberia. He was given awards for exploits in the course of his work. Finally, he was appointed to an important post in the ministry and lived the life of a functionary with a fat job in the capital. Papers, sessions, lectures, reports. His hair began to go grey and he developed a paunch. And boredom and melancholy started to creep into his soul. What am I fighting for? he asked himself.

At this moment of psychological crisis the Party made an appeal: office workers, go out into the country! He was the first to respond. His wife refused to go with him and they were divorced. He asked to be sent to the poorest collective farm in the back of beyond. They sent him to the Partygrad oblast. He refused all privileges, making a vow that he would improve his personal living conditions only when the collective farmers improved theirs.

Then real life began. The bank credits were next to nothing and the manager's powers illusory. All Envoy's efforts to raise the productivity of labour in the collective farm were shattered by the total indifference of the collective farmers and the hidden opposition of the administration. The collective farm personnel made fun of him, taking advantage of his indulgence to cut their work and work their own plots and to go to town to the market. The administration, while supporting initiative verbally, in reality reduced his to nil. Envoy began to drink; and he got married when he was blind drunk. His wife was a resourceful woman and soon their house was full to overflowing. His wife pulled the strings in all the collective farm's backstage dealings.

The reaction in the collective farm was such that anonymous letters and open complaints began to reach the power organs and the newspapers. One day the papers wrote that the collective farm workers had not given Envoy their confidence and so hadn't elected him as chairman. Envoy went home after the session, put on his best suit with all his decorations, tore up his Party card and hanged himself.

The authorities decided to turn Envoy into a victim of the antediluvian Stalinists. Corytov advised that his memory should be perpetuated by calling the collective farm after him and erecting a monument to him in it. They also remembered Perestroikist. They thought that it might be worthwhile to make him a martyr at the hands of the conservatives. But Corytov advised them to wait. Maotsedunka hinted that it was dangerous to wait, for they could make perestroika into a victim of the reformers. Corytov said that that was exactly why they had to wait. Maotsedunka sobered up in a moment and froze with her mouth wide open.

THE LAST ITINERARY

Finally the Commission dealt with privatization. At first it got into confusion. Private enterprises appeared and disappeared in the course of a few days. It was simply impossible to choose any of them for privatization with the hope of achieving any kind of stability. In most cases the private traders disappeared behind prison bars. Only a few of them escaped this fate and they were those who had cut off their operations in time and vanished from the town with a trunkful of money. Only the private lavatory prospered. And they decided to turn it into an exhibition model of private enterprise.

In the Lavatory Complex the members of the Commission were greeted in the most sumptuous manner. They were offered a seat on the modern Western lavatories. All quite free. Corytov, having spent a full half-hour in the cabin reserved for especially honoured visitors, said that never in his life had he had the good fortune to experience such pleasure sitting down. Not only the defecation system but also his brain had functioned with startling perfection.

When they came out of their cabins the members of the Commission all received gifts: a piece of German soap and a roll of scented toilet-paper. Then the administrator of the lavatory, wearing a tailcoat, suggested to the guests that they should acquaint themselves with certain foreign novelties connected with 'intimate toilet'. One by one the visitors went with the administrator into the depths of the building through a door masked by a mirror. After a certain time they reappeared. Their eyes swivelled lecherously. The men were doing up their trousers with a guilty look, while the women adjusted their skirts and bodices.

'If everybody worked like that in our country,' said Corytov, we would not only catch up the West in economics but also surpass it.'

'We'd better not surpass it,' said the KGB representative.

'Why?'

'Because then everybody would see our naked bottoms.'

Something rather funny happened as the Commission left the toilet. A group of elderly people who thought that the members of the Commission were Americans, handed them a letter for President Reagan. In the letter they asked the President to help them repair the drains and put some windows into their porch. They had been broken, the letter said, by drunken hooligans.

THE HEART OF PARTYGRAD

After leaving the toilet the Commission members made their way to the collective farm market. On the way they disputed the question why the market was called after the collective farm when mostly private traders were doing business in it. They decided to rename the market a co-operative and to give it the name of Bukharin. The sight of the market reminded the Commission of the crush in the darkest years of Soviet history. Dirty, unshaven persons wandered around the place looking for something to steal somewhere. Drunks weaved about. Old women who looked like the witches in fairy-tales were doing deals with sundry debauchees who wanted to change old clothes for hooch. On the counters lay thin bunches of dill and parsley, crooked carrots, blueing potatoes, pieces of violet meat and stinking bones. Behind the counter creatures with red faces – impossible to tell whether they were men or women – sat on sacks. One could smell the hooch in them a mile off.

'Well, yes, this isn't exactly the heart of Paris,' said Corytov, squeezing his nostrils in disgust. 'But all the same we mustn't reject anything that livens up the economy.'

They investigated the prices. Corytov gave a whistle when he discovered how much a wretched-looking piece of meat cost that his own dog wouldn't eat. 'Oho!' he said. 'There was a time when one could buy a whole ox for money like that.'

'Yes, that's right,' muttered a 'kolkhoznitsa'. 'It was like that in the time of the Tsar. During the cult of personality. In the period of stagnation. And now, sweetheart, we've got perestroika. One must thank God that there's something left.'

The members of the Commission cheered up somewhat at the stall where they were selling Russian kvass. The place was emitting fumes of the kind that used to come out of beer booths. There was a long queue. When they'd drunk their kvass the citizens cleared their throats and wiped their mouths with their sleeves. Their eyes swivelled round and round and their foreheads sweated. Tottering and belching, they made their way to the *terrain vague* where their predecessors had lurched about before them. There, some of the drinkers collapsed on the ground. The sturdier ones joined the queue again because the kvass was sold according to the notice 'only one jug per mug'.

The members of the Commission also decided to try the Russian kvass, a beverage which had completely disappeared during the period of stagnation but had recently been resurrected, thanks to perestroika. A thick-jowled old woman bellowed wheezily that the distinguished guests could jump the queue and ordered her assistant, who could hardly stand up, to give them a drink of the special brand. The guests drank a jug and got quite merry. After the second jug they felt their full solidarity with the people and began to make water by the stall. On the way back to the hotel they burst out laughing for no reason, embraced each other, swore eternal love and friendship and bawled old songs in the new rock manner.

A FINAL DREAM

That night Corytov had a beautiful dream. He saw the gigantic shape of the hotel Ilya Muromets rebuilt in accordance with Partygrad's new status. Now it had two hundred storeys. Each storey was half a metre high. And half a metre broad. The rooms looked like drawers. In them the foreign tourists were crawling about on all fours. The whole hotel had one lavatory with two points, one for sitting and the other for standing. Both were attached to the ceiling. There was a huge queue for the lavatory, stretching as far as New Limes. The people in it were telling perestroikist anecdotes.

'Why is there such a queue?' asked Corytov, jumping about on his bare feet with impatience.

'All the State toilets are out of order,' they told him. 'And the private traders have cornered the toilet business. And economically it's more profitable for them to have one toilet for the whole of Partygrad.'

Feeling he couldn't wait any longer, Corytov decided to do his business by the Portyankin memorial. He looked round and made sure that the pensioners weren't looking at him and went ahead. And he wet his bed. For a moment he woke up in horror at what he'd done. Then he turned over on his other side and went to sleep again.

This time he dreamed of the Funeral Complex. There was a queue for the body-compressing section as long as that for the lavatory. And in the queue they were telling perestroikist anecdotes. Corytov asked who was last in the queue. They told him that the living stood in one queue on the other side, but the Gorbachevites were buried 'with acceleration'. Corytov darted off there. On the way he looked into the compressing section, where they were reducing the corpses to matchbox size. Nearby there was a private shop which sold miniature coffins with American computers. Corytov shuddered at the price: the coffin cost a whole year's salary of a medium-rank Central Committee official! 'But where can one get hold of money like that?' he cried.

'If you've got no money, don't die,' they answered.

Russian kvass was being sold there too. Corytov drank a jug, for which he paid his overcoat, his suit, his spectacles and his still quite new underpants. Once more feeling the approach of an actual need, he rushed off to the Portyankin memorial. All the same one mustn't behave like a nihilist towards old Party cadres! But this time the pensioners caught him and took him off to prison. There, perestroika was going at an accelerated pace. The prisoners refused to have expensive guards and had gone over to a self-guarding system. They handed over the empty camps to Western firms, which started up the production of narcotics, prostitutes, abstract painters, democrats, People's Deputies and other attributes of perestroika. Corytov was immediately elected chairman. Once more he wet the bed with joy and slept the peaceful sleep of an emissary of the revolution.

THE LAST CONVERSATION

Before he left Partygrad Corytov had a meeting with Gorban.

'In you, Sidor Yegorovich, a special trust is being placed. You are not to breathe a word of what I am about to say to you to anybody else. Not even a hint of it. You will answer for that with your head. Is that clear?'

'Quite clear, Ivan Timofeyevich! You can rely on me entirely. I shan't let you down.'

'We've got to get rid of Krutov. We need a man of iron who will be capable of taking the lead in the forthcoming coup. Have you got your eye on anybody?'

'Tupitsyn, Second Secretary of gorkom.'

'I know him. He'll do. We'll start promoting him gradually. But we must help Krutov get entangled in some personal fiddles. The time will come when we'll put him on trial for corruption, moral decomposition and adventurism. Meanwhile preserve him as the apple of your eye. Don't do anything premature.'

'All this can be done easily.'

'You will start preparations for an overall purge of the oblast. In all the institutions and all the enterprises you are to form secret cadres of reliable people. Get them to sign an undertaking of non-disclosure on pain of imprisonment for life. If they blow the gaff, punish them without mercy. If the journalists and investigators shove their noses in, no kid gloves with them either. Remember what would happen if anything leaked to the West . . .'

'I understand completely.'

'We'll do the purge like lightning. In one single night. Drawing up in advance a list of the people who are to be removed. Tell everybody what they must do. Select the forms and places of isolation. Be ready to begin the operation at any moment. We'll give you the signal at the right moment.'

'But what about Gorbachev?'

'We want to make him begin the policy switch himself. When he's compromised himself enough in the eyes of public opinion, we'll remove him. But if he doesn't do that . . .'

'Everything's clear, Ivan Timofeyevich. I'll do my duty as a communist and a patriot, at whatever the cost to me! Thank you for showing confidence in me!'

OUR GREAT HISTORY

While the united Commission was grappling with problems of what one may call strategic range in Partygrad, all the town's and the oblast's enterprises and institutions were dealing with problems of lesser importance. This was happening in all Party, trade-union and Komsomol organizations and at all levels of the system of power and government. Policy was being formed at the personal level over such matters as windows, doors, tables, placards, portraits, clothes, words, smiles and handshakes. If all the intellectual and creative energy that was spent by hundreds and thousands of people in doing all these things had been directed towards improving the work of the oblast's enterprises and institutions, then the bound forward could be something really grandiose and impressive.

But communist society is so organized and functions in such a way that it is far better at coping with the *imitation* of doing work than with the *problems* of work itself. Moreover, all the formalities and fuss that surround real work are considered more important than the work with respect to which the fuss arises.

Fuss about work is a familiar affair and easily executed. It involves no sustained effort, no risk and no loss. It looks excellent in reports. It brings satisfaction and definite advantage to far more people than does the work itself. Moreover, its results are immediate, not in the far future. But the main thing about fuss and formality is that they conceal and compensate for the practical impossibility of implementing anything whatever in the form in which it is conceived by the high organs of power.

And so it was that all those who took part in the grandiose formalities and fuss about the conversion of Partygrad into the lighthouse of perestroika did their work with a clear conscience. As the result of the work of many tens of thousands of people, hundreds of thousands of smallish measures were taken which in aggregate were bound to lead millions of people into delusion, a necessary delusion. Tons of documents were composed. They moved upwards, being duly processed, reduced in size and generalized at the innumerable stages of the social hierarchy. Finally, they reached the operative level, that of the Commission of the Party's obkom. Here scores of functionaries from Partygrad's power apparatus prepared the resultant document. This document was delivered to the head of the Commission of the Central Committee of the CPSU, Comrade Corytov. For four hours he read it to the joint meeting of the Joint Commission and the executive chiefs of the oblast. The assembly's loud cheers served as the document's endorsement.

GOODBYE TO PARTYGRAD

The Moscow Commission had fulfilled its appointed task in brilliant style. On a day of clear sunshine the Muscovites left the hospitable city of Partygrad. In Lenin Square they witnessed something that had never been witnessed before in the course of human history. Leaning against a rubbish bin stood a small but unusually stout man with a physiognomy of which the people would say: 'You wouldn't get round it on a bicycle in a whole day.' The man was wearing the dress uniform of a KGB general. A general's hat lay in front of him on the pavement. He was wailing to the whole square in a mournful voice: 'Give as much as you can to a former Stalinist executioner who has destroyed thousands of innocent victims!!!' The passers-by were throwing handfuls of coins and even banknotes into the well-filled hat.

They passed the collective farm market which had been renamed a co-operative. Even through the closed windows of the air-conditioned coach they scented the stink of kvass. On the rubbish dump behind the market (slightly screened by a hoarding with perestroikist slogans and placards) they saw a group of dealers who had been drinking gorbachukha and singing songs.

> 'We've got only one life.
> Let's drink our gorbachukha to the dregs.'

Someone said that if perestroika did nothing more than invent gorbachukha, that alone would justify it.

> 'After one drink let's down another,
> Then we'll perestroika a new bag of tricks.'

The Muscovites burst out laughing when they heard these words. They themselves had *not* succeeded in building anything properly, but they'd already started rebuilding all the same.

> 'We'll take a third glass, thank you,
> And put everything back as it was before.'

Well, that was really too much. Gorbachev had said that the process of perestroika was irreversible. However,

> 'Let the world see it: our primordial Russian spirit
> Is not extinguished.'

Police spies were standing around the singers and noting down the seditious words on notepads. Corytov remembered the parody of Pushkin's message to the Decembrists in Siberia, which he'd heard from Gorban.

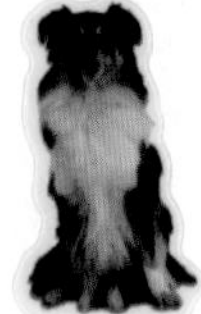

'Comrade, remember, it will pass
This so-called glasnost
And then State Security
Will remember our names.'

He remembered it and broke into a happy smile. Not everything was yet lost! Our healthy Russian spirit hadn't been extinguished! The others in the coach smiled. But at what they didn't know.

A DREAM THAT CAME TRUE

In return for the vast amount of work done to prepare Partygrad for its opening to foreigners and its role as lighthouse of perestroika, Suslikov was for the second time awarded the title of Hero of Socialist Labour. In that way he received the right to have a bronze bust in Partygrad. Corytov and Krutov were given the Order of Lenin. The other members of the Commission were decorated as well as Partygrad's ruling personages.

Suslikov celebrated his decoration with his family and his close friends. Having had a go at the gorbachukha which Corytov had brought him as a present, Suslikov fell asleep at the table. There he dreamed the happiest dream of his life. He saw his native Partygrad which, he knew, had been renamed Suslikovgrad. The town appeared to him in the form of a gigantic rose bottom, glowing with health. On it in golden letters blazed out the fundamental postulate of Suslikovism (which had replaced Marxism as the State ideology): 'Bum first, head second.'

Somewhere above was the bronze bust of Suslikov on its granite pedestal. Suslikov's bald forehead was adorned with the eternally famous Russian word of three letters (this word is recognized as the principal word in *all* languages).

In the centre of the bottom there was a black hole through which all the rubbish accumulated in Partygrad during all the years of

Soviet history was to be pushed out into the West. The shit was pushed out with the same 'acceleration' as the one the initiators of perestroika counted on. And in the West all of it was swallowed up with delectation while everyone praised perestroika and its inspirers to the skies: the Gorbachevs, the Suslikovs, the Krutovs, the Corytovs and the Maotsedunkas.

EPILOGUE

In Intourist they were urgently preparing their guide with the appealing title, VISIT PARTYGRAD! The preface went as follows: 'If you don't want to see sights and attractions but wish to broaden and deepen your knowledge of the ordinary working days of Soviet life and of what is happening in the land of perestroika, then pay a visit to Partygrad. The hospitable citizens of this town will be delighted to receive all Western guests. They will open to you not only their doors but also their souls. The famous spiritual nature of Russia is felt especially strongly in Partygrad.

'By the way, the Russian word "to strangle" is derived from the word "soul"; that is to say, it has the same root as the word "spirituality". (Or, if you like, you can liberate your soul by getting someone to strangle you.)*

'And they will show you the monastery. Otherwise why have they built it? They will show you the little churches in which people are actually worshipping. They have no architectural value but on the other hand they are interesting as examples of conscience (that is, of faith) in Soviet society. Well-fed and well-educated priests will explain to you that you will not find the kind of freedom of religion which obtains in Partygrad even in the Vatican itself.

'And they will feed you with caviare and they will give you vodka to drink . . . you are not Soviet workers but foreign visitors. Compulsory sobriety will *not* be required of you! Drink to everyone's health and as much as you like!

'And they will bring you the painted spoons, the saucers and

* Dusheet = strangle; dusha = soul.

matryoshka dolls from Moscow. And you will be allowed to speak to the people without any limitations whatsoever. And even the agents of the CIA and other Western secret services will not be unmasked or arrested. Quite the contrary, they will be given every help to discover everything that was previously considered to be secret. Make haste to visit free Partygrad, lighthouse of perestroika!'

At the end of 1988 a group of citizens of one Western European country decided to visit the Soviet Union with the intention of seeing with their own eyes the progress of perestroika, of which there had been so much talk throughout the world. These people knew that there were districts in the Soviet Union access to which was forbidden to foreigners. Partygrad was on the forbidden list. In the Soviet consulate they asked members of the group where they would like to go. They named Partygrad, being sure that it would be refused. But to their surprise the visit to Partygrad was permitted. The travellers told the press about it; and that caused a world-wide sensation. Many Soviet émigrés who had had doubts about the seriousness of the Gorbachevite government then suddenly believed in it. They made requests to be allowed to visit the Soviet Union and began to buy dirt-cheap things in the flea market for the delectation of their relatives and friends in their former fatherland.

One famous dissident, who in his time had served five years in a strict-regime camp near Partygrad and had left the Soviet Union with the declared intention of fighting against the Soviet regime to his last drop of blood and his last breath, arranged on the premises of the anti-Soviet magazine that he edited a reception in honour of the members of a routine Soviet delegation. After he had presented them with bouquets of flowers, embraced them three times and kissed them on the mouth, he declared with tears of emotion that Gorbachev's government was incarnating the aspirations of the dissidents, and that the decision to allow Western tourists to visit Partygrad was convincing evidence of that.

The first group of foreigners spent a week in Partygrad. On their return home they published rapturous articles about what they had seen in the Soviet Union. When he looked through the rapturous testimonials by foreigners about perestroika, especially in Partygrad, the head of Partygrad oblast's KGB, Comrade Gorban, said to his assistant: 'We mustn't let these idiots from the West be too sold on perestroika or they will cease to be afraid of us at all.'

Printed in Great Britain
by Amazon.co.uk, Ltd.,
Marston Gate.